"An unmarried woman would never sleep so near a man."

"If you trust me, I don't see why you care. No one will know. Sleep beside me and I'll be between you and any wild beasts that might wonder into our camp," he said.

"You're trying to frighten me," she said.

"Maybe. Maybe not," he said. "But, I'm warm, Miss Chandler. And I'll bet you've never been as warm as I can make you. Besides, it's nice being close. I'm not going to charge you extra, either. Unless you want to pay me more. A warming fee of sorts."

Other AVON ROMANCES

INDIGO *by Beverly Jenkins*
A MAN'S TOUCH *by Rosalyn West*
MINX *by Julia Quinn*
SCANDALOUS SUZANNE *by Glenda Sanders*
SOMEONE LIKE YOU *by Susan Sawyer*
WICKED AT HEART *by Danelle Harmon*
WINTERBURN'S ROSE *by Kate Moore*

Coming Soon

LOVE ME NOT *by Eve Byron*
THE MACKENZIES: FLINT *by Ana Leigh*

And Don't Miss These
ROMANTIC TREASURES
from Avon Books

LADY OF WINTER *by Emma Merritt*
WILD ROSES *by Miriam Minger*
YOU AND NO OTHER *by Cathy Maxwell*

Spring Rain

Susan Weldon

AVON BOOKS ◆ NEW YORK

To Joseph Klein of Altoona, Pennsylvania, a very dear uncle and my most devoted fan. Your support and love have meant the world to me.

SPRING RAIN is an original publication of Avon Books. This work has never before appeared in book form. This work is a novel. Any similarity to actual persons or events is purely coincidental.

AVON BOOKS
A division of
The Hearst Corporation
1350 Avenue of the Americas
New York, New York 10019

Copyright © 1996 by Susan Carey Weldon
Inside cover author photo by Glamour Shots
Published by arrangement with the author
Library of Congress Catalog Card Number: 96-96442
ISBN: 0-380-78068-2

First Avon Books Printing: November 1996

AVON TRADEMARK REG. U.S. PAT. OFF. AND IN OTHER COUNTRIES, MARCA REGISTRADA, HECHO EN U.S.A.

Printed in the U.S.A.

RA 10 9 8 7 6 5 4 3 2 1

Prologue

Colorado, 1872

As Ernest T. Potts brought his mule to an abrupt halt, he gave thanks that, for once, the animal had obeyed him. He called her Charity, though charitable she wasn't. If she wanted, she could cause him enough grief to last a lifetime.

Scraping a hand over the wiry, gray beard hanging past the second button of his dusty shirt, Ernest darted a glance over his shoulder. The sun was about to disappear behind Blue Mountain. He should've started out later in the day and not arrived at dusk. Better yet, he shouldn't have allowed the couple in Denver to talk him into searching for a man he'd never met.

Shadows lurked everywhere.

Ernest felt a shiver crawl down his spine. No amount of money was worth riding through Dead Man's Canyon. The name alone brought frightful images to his mind, but Colorado Springs already lay ten miles behind him.

Dry leaves stirred to his left. Ernest swallowed so hard he nearly lost his tongue down his throat.

The noise came again. Without turning his head, he swung his gaze to the pine forest on a ridge where he thought he'd detected a movement. Ernest inhaled a shaky breath. He decided it hadn't been an unearthly apparition, after all, merely vines swinging from the trees.

"Damn silly fool, 'bout to piss yerself over a lot of weeds." He slapped Charity's rump with the switch he always carried. "Move along, girl. We ain't got all night. We gotta find some dumb city fella who got hisself lost lookin' fer gold."

Though Charity's ears twitched, she refused to budge. Ernest listened intently. A rustle in a thicket somewhere behind him made his hands shake so that he dropped the switch. Charity stepped nervously and snapped the twig into pieces.

"'Taint nothing 'cept yer imagination, girl," he told Charity, but he knew he was lying when a rush of cold air brushed his neck.

His hands still shaking, his breath wheezing from his lungs, Ernest grabbed the rifle slung at the mule's side. The metal felt as cold as the air on his neck. Suddenly his fingers lost their grip and the weapon fell to the ground just as Charity stomped around, bringing Ernest face-to-face with a vision from hell.

The white, transparent form of a bearded man hovered over a bush. Ernest blinked and gasped. Despite the ax embedded in his skull, the man wore a hideous grin. The odor of rotting flesh hung heavy in the air.

A scream stuck in Ernest's throat.

Charity suddenly reared back, moving faster in reverse than she'd ever moved forward.

The apparition bellowed a grotesque laugh and flew at Ernest.

"Sweet Jesus!" Ernest cried.

He pushed backwards, over the mule's rump, and landed with a thud on a large, flat rock. Charity's sides heaved. Within seconds, a hot, foul mass plopped on Ernest's crotch. Suspecting the worst had yet to happen, he swung one leg over the other. He rolled away just as Charity squatted on the rock.

The laughter grew louder as it echoed from the mountain. With repeated desperate brays, Charity trotted away heading the way they'd come.

Ernest wildly swung his gaze around the area. When he spotted the apparition, his eyes bulged.

It advanced slowly. Ernest dug his heels and hands in crumbling soil, and thrust himself away. On his back, he moved inch by tedious inch. But his grotesque tormentor adjusted its motion. It hovered briefly. Within seconds, it seemed to recline. Facedown, it floated a foot over him. The rotten odor, which had been foul before, caused Ernest to retch.

The apparition laughed and disappeared.

Shaken to the core, muttering unintelligible words, Ernest pushed to his knees. As he crawled toward a thicket of scrub oaks, he offered a prayer to the Almighty. If he survived this hellish night, he swore to never set foot in Dead Man's Canyon again.

Quick as a flash, the ghost blocked his path. Ernest lost control of his bladder.

The apparition tossed back its ruined head and bellowed a chilling sound that reverberated throughout the canyon.

Ernest leapt to his feet, his bloodcurdling scream joining that of his ghostly tormentor, and he bolted after his mule.

Chapter 1

Pennsylvania, 1872

Libby Chandler sat straight up in bed and screamed.

The nightmare which had plagued her for six months had, again, awoken her.

Although bright sunlight pierced her eyes, in her mind she still saw the image of a man leave a small cabin in an area of fallen red rock. He then became involved in a struggle with another man, the outcome of which left her trembling with fear. The nightmare always ended the same.

Clarence Trout, her intended, getting stabbed in the chest with a dagger.

Libby blinked and focused on the long, narrow window beside her bed, where white lace curtains gracefully stirred from a slight breeze.

She realized her fingers bunched up the crocheted counterpane and her hands shook uncontrollably. Each nightmare caused terror to grip her heart.

"He's not dead!" she said aloud. "Clarence has

just been preoccupied and has forgotten to write, or he's struck gold and wants to surprise me."

Another voice inside her head, however, told her differently.

She hadn't rested easy since her intended had left Maryville and headed for the California Gulch gold fields in Colorado. Despite the fact that he'd made a decent living as a storekeeper, Clarence had owned little else of value. He'd claimed a burning ambition to better his lot in order to support her in style. It was best, he'd said, if he tried his hand at gold mining *before* they married.

Libby's hands trembled again. She had tried to convince him that they could live well enough on his income, but Clarence hadn't listened. He'd been gone for a year and a half. Her nightmares had begun six months ago, shortly after his letters had stopped arriving. She feared he'd been injured or even killed.

She performed her morning ablutions and dressed quickly. Little Roy Cummings, one of the children to whom she taught piano, was due to arrive at ten o'clock for his lesson. Libby doubted any correspondence from Clarence awaited her at the general store, but she expected news from another source—the man who'd replied to the ad she'd placed in the Denver newspaper seeking someone to search for Clarence.

Upon descending the one flight of stairs, Libby cleared her mind of her dire thoughts of Clarence and walked across the street to Clara Peabody's Boardinghouse. As was her daily custom, she went directly to the kitchen. Her stomach was still churning, so she decided against breakfast. She'd just finished a cup of tea when a slight, gray-haired woman swept through the door.

"Good morning, Clara," Libby greeted her dearest friend.

"You've had the nightmare again, I just know it."

"I know I'm being a dolt to worry so, but I can't help it."

"It's not foolish to worry over someone you love, dear," Clara said, concern showing in her hazel eyes. "When my husband was alive, I imagined the most dastardly fate would befall him every time he left the house. Then, when he came through the door each night, I was ever so grateful for my good fortune."

Seeing moisture fill the kind woman's eyes, Libby's throat grew thick. Mr. Peabody had suffered a dastardly fate, after all. Just two years ago he'd stepped on a nail and died from blood poisoning. But, while Libby felt the utmost remorse over the possible loss of her intended, she didn't feel the same agonizing despair as Clara Peabody suffered. Clarence Trout, though a kind, morally decent, hardworking man, had never inspired in her the devotion she'd once felt for another man.

Libby's thoughts drifted back seven years. At eighteen she'd been madly in love with John McNab, a handsome young man who had swept her off her feet. A pain stabbed her heart. People had always regarded her as plain, yet John had found her desirable. On the day of their wedding, however, he'd fallen from his horse and broken his neck.

Libby shook her head to dispel the sad memory.

She'd survived an overwhelming devastation and made a life for herself teaching piano. Until Clarence had expressed an interest in her, she'd resigned herself that she would most likely remain unmarried, destined never to have a child of her own.

Clara squeezed Libby's shoulders, offering sympathy. Thank goodness the woman had two daughters to help her run the boardinghouse. Libby felt a moment's regret that her own parents had perished seven years ago. She had no one to call her own.

An hour later, Libby stood in front of a polished wood counter in the local mercantile, her fingers wrinkling the telegram in her hand. The man she'd hired had vanished from the face of the earth. And so had the money she'd paid him.

Mr. Culpepper, the current storekeeper, offered her an encouraging smile. "No luck, huh?"

"No one has seen or heard from Otis Leech since he left Denver."

"Most unfortunate," Culpepper commiserated. He paused to accept a dime from a stout woman in a red-and-white-striped dress. Then, turning back to Libby, he offered her a stick of candy. "You're not giving up, are you?"

"Certainly not." Libby acknowledged Mr. Culpepper's gift with an appreciative nod and tucked the peppermint stick into her reticule. Using paper he kept handy on the counter, she scribbled a missive. "I have acquaintances in Denver, friends of my father. Perhaps they can help. Maybe they know of someone more capable of locating Clarence." She slid the paper across the counter's glass top. "Please send the telegram to Mr. and Mrs. Taylor as soon as you can."

While Culpepper saw to the task, Libby occupied herself by idly looking through an assortment of newly arrived ribbons. She hadn't noticed the two women who stood by bolts of cotton domestic, but their whispered conversation carried only too well. Libby closed her eyes. Hearing her name wasn't unusual. The townspeople often spoke about her, though not always unkindly. It was no secret they regarded her as a highly respectable *old maid*. But how could they not? She was twenty-five and still unmarried.

"The poor dear must be ill-fated," Mrs. Kemp said softly. "Why, Mr. Trout is the second man to suffer a calamity after aligning himself with her."

"And she's not liable to find another," the other woman whispered. "If she'd been blessed with a more comely appearance, a man might be more willing to take a gamble."

"More's the pity. She's lovely to the children and would make a good mother."

Libby's cheeks flamed. She touched her tightly knotted hair then tugged the narrow brim of her hat lower over her brow. She moved away from the ribbons. If the women suspected she'd entertained the thought of purchasing one, they'd no doubt pity her even more. A ribbon would do little to improve her looks.

Mr. Culpepper chose that moment to reappear. "You should have an answer later today. I'll run it over myself."

"Thank you, Mr. Culpepper," she responded woodenly.

"Can I do anything else for you today?" he asked.

After a longing glance at the ribbons, Libby shook her head and left.

Libby looked past the small head of her student to watch Mr. Culpepper hurry down the street. A month had passed since she'd wired money to Mr. Taylor to procure the services of one Ernest T. Potts. The down-and-out mule skinner had been the only man Mr. Taylor could bribe to look for Clarence.

Mr. Culpepper's quick pace set Libby's heart racing. Was it bad news he brought? Or had Clarence finally been found?

Unable to bear the suspense a second longer, she dismissed her young student and met the storekeeper halfway down the walk.

"Miss . . . Libby," Culpepper managed as he heaved a breath. "You've news from Denver."

Her heart skipped a beat. "Has Clarence been found?"

Mr. Culpepper handed over the telegram. "Forgive me. I didn't mean to get your hopes up, but I thought you'd want to know right away."

Libby's enthusiasm gave way to dread, so she read the telegram as fast as possible. Afterward she sighed. Ernest T. Potts, upon whom she'd counted to find Clarence, had returned to Denver babbling about having been accosted by a bad-tempered apparition with an ax protruding from its skull.

"Utter nonsense," muttered Mr. Culpepper. "A ghost with an ax in his head."

Libby's shoulders slumped. "Mr. Potts must've seen *something* out of the ordinary. Mr. Taylor says the man became so agitated no one was able to make sense of his rambling."

"Libby, what is it?" Clara Peabody yelled from her doorway. "Has Mr. Trout been located?"

Despite her gloomy mood, Libby thanked the storekeeper before she joined the woman. She waited while Clara read the telegram.

"What will you do now?"

"I'm not sure."

Libby followed the woman into the small, comfortable kitchen which smelled of freshly baked bread. She sat wearily at the table to consider her alternatives. She couldn't continue to dip into the inheritance her father had left her. Though it had been a substantial amount, it was her only security.

But she also couldn't resume her normal life until Clarence had been properly buried. Her nightmares had come every night lately, convincing her the soul of her intended wasn't at rest.

A cup of tea appeared in front of Libby. "Drink this and you'll feel much better," Clara said.

Libby absently sipped from the steaming cup. Thinking how Clarence Trout had professed a deep and abiding love for her, she felt an overwhelming sadness. She loved him but not in the special way she'd loved her first intended.

Could her conscience be responsible for the dreams? Had she inadvertently said or done anything to make Clarence think his lack of wealth mattered?

Whatever the origin of the scenes which played

in her mind at night, she was sure of only one thing. She must do her best to find Clarence, even if it meant going to Denver.

Suddenly, she sat straight. "I'll go to Denver," she mumbled.

"Libby! Have you lost your mind?"

"Perhaps I've found it at last. If I want to see this through, my only recourse is to go to Denver and personally find a man to search for Clarence. Obviously, the men I've hired thus far haven't possessed the necessary qualities."

Clara set pans rattling in a tub of soapy water. "I suppose you must do as your heart tells you." A brief pause followed before she asked, "You aren't thinking of hiring one of those gunmen?"

"Most assuredly not! But there has to be a courageous, proficient man in the area who won't come back babbling about having been frightened silly by a phantom."

Clara glanced over her shoulder. "Do you think there really are ghosts?"

Remembering her very real nightmares, Libby allowed, "Anything's possible, though I can't imagine what Mr. Potts saw. It's easy to jump to conclusions when it's dark. For all we know, he might've seen a bush move."

A week later, Libby left the Cosmopolitan Restaurant, feeling much better for having taken the time to eat a full meal. Her first day in Denver had proved quite pleasant.

After she'd left the Denver Pacific Railroad depot, she'd inquired about directions, then she'd taken a room at the Belvidere House on Larimer Street where she'd found the proprietor, Mr. R. J.

Emmerson, friendly and efficient. She'd also arranged to have her funds transferred to the Colorado National Bank.

The weather, though cooler than back in Pennsylvania, appealed to her, making her long to explore the town. First, however, she should call on the Taylors, whom she hadn't seen in five years. Harry Taylor had been a lifelong friend of her father. She remembered Ema Taylor as a small, plump woman with a sweet nature. Deciding she could accomplish both objectives at the same time, she set out on foot.

Several men waiting on a corner tipped their hats. One gentleman even flashed her an appreciative smile. Unsure how to respond to the unusual attention, she gave them a short nod and continued on. She hadn't taken any special pains with her attire today, had simply worn a green dress she found particularly comfortable. Men rarely showed any outward interest in her, but maybe they tended to pay more attention to women in Colorado.

Libby had crossed a street and passed several businesses before she heard a commotion in an establishment she was nearing. The commotion grew louder as she went closer, piquing her curiosity. The sound of glass breaking caused her to pause. A tremendous bang followed by splintering wood made her stop dead.

"You low-down, dirty snake," someone yelled.

She heard a thump and more glass breaking. Then a gunshot.

"That dadgum mirror come all the way from St. Louis," another man shouted with authority. "You're payin' for my mirror, McCord."

A vulgar response followed before an earsplitting cry made Libby move forward. It was too much. The suspense of not knowing what was happening inside drew her to the double, swinging doors. She'd just peered over the top when a large body slammed against the doors and pitched Libby backwards.

Before she could blink, she found herself prone, pinned to the wood walkway by an oppressive weight. Since her head had struck the walk, and the air had been forced from her lungs, several seconds passed before she regained her senses. She attempted to draw in a much-needed breath.

Mercifully, the weight upon her shifted. Libby abruptly sucked in enough air to clear her mind and gazed into the bluest eyes she'd ever seen.

The man on top of her had dark hair and beard, both of which desperately needed a trim. He looked like a creature who had just materialized out of the deepest woods. The strong smell of whiskey on his breath compounded her distress.

His eyes twinkled with unbridled amusement as he met her gaze. Though he lifted himself slightly to brace himself on his elbows, he made no move to rise.

Jamming her hands on his shoulders, Libby attempted to shove him away.

"Lady, if you want me to get up, all you need do is ask."

Still too stunned to speak, Libby swallowed. His eyes had been his only redeeming feature, until a slow, knowing grin revealed remarkably sound teeth. She shoved at his shoulders again. To Libby's dismay, he continued to grin at her. She pounded his shoulders. "Get off of me this instant, you unmannerly ruffian!"

He shook his head, looking for all the world as if he meant never to let her go. A rise of panic stole Libby's breath. Only a brute would imprison a woman beneath his large body on the walkway in front of a saloon. She glared at him as she searched for a way out of her ridiculous predicament.

"I usually give a woman anything she wants," he whispered, his tone low and seductive, ". . . unless she shrieks orders and calls me names."

Libby's eyes popped open wide. This couldn't be happening! Not to a woman like her. Plain old maids were usually spared the unwelcome attentions of men. When she heard masculine laughter from her right, she groaned. Not only was it the most humiliating moment of her life, her normally quick wits had deserted her.

"Are you going to ask me nice?"

Libby gave an indignant sniff. "I'll die first."

"Lady, it's your choice," he said. "I'm not anxious to get up, you see. There's an irate fellow just itching to blacken my eyes and break my nose."

Libby sniffed again. "A well-deserved fate, if you ask me."

He ran a hand down her side, over her hip. "You feel awfully soft for such a heartless woman."

Instantly furious, Libby cracked her hand across his cheek. She received a low laugh in response, which fueled her temper even more. Not caring what retribution he had in mind for her, she balled her right hand into a fist. In one swift movement, she pounded his ear.

An obscene oath stung her ears. Cheers from onlookers turned into a riotous ovation. When he clapped a hand over his injury, his action allowed enough space for her to wiggle slightly out from under him.

With a grunt of pain, he finally climbed to his feet and caught hold of Libby's hand, unceremoniously yanking her to her feet also and startling a gasp from her.

"My apology, ma'am. It wasn't my intention to exit the saloon so abruptly. I'm not in the habit of throwing women on the walk. The fact of the matter is," he said, pausing to aim her a rakish grin, "the illustrious barkeep ejected me."

The barely detectable thread of laughter she'd noted in his voice unnerved her almost as much as the man himself. Determined not to meet his gaze again, Libby began to dust off her skirt. "Your apology is not accepted."

Without warning, large hands gripped her shoulders and spun her around. He slapped at her skirt, sending particles of dirt flying. Libby's breath lodged in her throat from his sudden move. She whirled back around with the intention of giving him the scolding he so deserved.

But words escaped her.

Although he'd apologized, he still didn't look the slightest bit remorseful. Why, the rascal had actually enjoyed those humiliating minutes when he'd had her pinned beneath him on the walk!

Another thought came to her. He might resemble a creature from the deepest woods, but his body had felt hard and lean, and so very masculine, the way a man *should* feel, she realized. Hot color rushed to her cheeks.

As he stepped closer, he looked her up and down. "Lady, you're a mite too thin, but you're the softest bed I've had in quite a spell." Touching his ear, he remarked, "Shame you're so damn unfriendly."

Libby choked on a gasp. With the pretext of straightening her hat, she turned to leave. Strong fingers wrapped around her wrist, staying her.

"I don't even know your name."

She glanced down at his large, sunbrowned hand before she glared at him.

Deviltry flashed in his eyes.

Libby yanked her wrist free and clutched her reticule tight against her chest. "I'd rather give my name to Satan," she retorted with as much dignity as she could muster.

His mouth lifting on one side, his voice lowered again. "Experience has taught me Western women aren't as prone to hold a man's faults against him, but you sound and look . . ." He raked his eyes from her head to her toes. ". . . Eastern to me. You sure you won't accept my apology?"

Libby squirmed under his bold gaze. He might look like a creature from a swamp, but his impertinent manner suggested a man who had rarely been rejected by a woman. "Quite sure." In response, he flashed a handsome grin.

Libby heard clapping. She glanced to the side and noticed a man sporting a bruised jaw and a swollen eye leaning against a wall. The opponent in the fight in the saloon, she concluded. Quickly, she looked back at the blue-eyed devil in front of her. By God, he *was* a devil. He was still grinning at her.

Feigning good humor, she said, "Perhaps I have been a bit too hasty." She gave him a sweet smile as she moved closer and looped her arm through his. "If you'll walk with me to a more private area of the street, you may ask me again. I'll consider your apology."

He cocked a dark eyebrow at her.

Plainly, she lacked the know-how to lure a man, she thought. But he surprised her. He swept an arm in a wide arc to offer her a choice of a direction. The confidence flickering in his remarkable blue eyes lightened Libby's mood. She steered him to the right, directly in front of his bruised opponent.

"Sir," she said to the man with the swollen eye, "I believe you were having a discussion with this ruffian." Libby wore a triumphant smile as she slipped her arm free. She stepped a safe distance away. "You may continue your brawl with my blessing. Perhaps you might teach him some manners as well."

A burst of familiar masculine laughter made her smile fade. Since the blue-eyed devil had seemed reluctant to resume his fight, she'd thought her maneuver would be just retribution for his rude treatment. She hadn't gotten the best of him, after all.

Her face hot, Libby pushed her way through a crowd of onlookers who seemed overtly disappointed to see her leave. She heard a thump. Against her better judgment, she weakened and peeked over her shoulder. She watched the two

men roll into the street, fighting in earnest. The
crowd cheered in unison as they formed a circle
around the combatants.

Grateful the townspeople had already forgotten
about her, Libby rushed down the street.

Libby spent two hours visiting with Mr. and
Mrs. Taylor, her friends in Denver. Mr. Taylor,
though, knew of no other possible candidate to
search for Clarence because of local speculation
regarding the presence of Henry Harkins in a
place called Dead Man's Canyon.

Not anxious to chance a repeat run-in with the
man with the penetrating blue eyes, she allowed
Mr. Taylor to drive her to the hotel in the fashion-
able buggy he'd purchased for special occasions.
After she'd promised to visit them again, Libby
went directly to her room. Mr. Taylor had been a
bit vague when he'd referred to the fellow named
Henry Harkins. She had sensed Mr. Taylor's wont
to protect her, so she hadn't pressed him for more
information. If Ernest Potts had truly seen an
apparition, it would be common knowledge about
town.

By morning Libby felt ready to brave another
walk through the streets of Denver. She found the
office of the *Rocky Mountain News* on the south
side of Holladay Street without difficulty. William
N. Byers, editor and proprietor, greeted her
warmly and brought out a back copy of the paper
containing the story written about Ernest T. Potts.

As she'd surmised, Mr. Taylor had omitted
important facts. Potts had happened upon a man
who had mentioned that, until his disappearance,
Clarence had taken on a mining partner by the

name of John Cox. Cox, who had last been spotted in Canon City, had sworn he hadn't seen Clarence for two months prior to his disappearance.

"What about Mr. Potts?" Libby asked as she laid the newspaper on the editor's littered desk. "I'd like to question him, myself."

"So would I, young lady. Ernest T. only stayed in town a day before he lit out for the hills. I don't expect we'll see him in these parts anytime soon. He's lost his wits, that's for sure."

"Do you think there's any truth to his story?"

Byers raised a brow. "If you mean about being attacked by a transparent bearded man with an ax in his head, I couldn't say. I can, however, cite many instances where the very same apparition has harassed people along the Cheyenne Mountain road." He opened a drawer in his scarred oak desk and brought out a small notebook from which he read, "One mule skinner, one bull-whacker, and several freighters were pestered for miles. A few also reported having seen phantom horses."

Libby drew in a breath before she asked, "The ghost of Henry Harkins?"

"All have sworn it was him."

"What happened to Harkins?"

"He operated a sawmill. In the spring of '63, he was found dead near his cabin with an ax in his forehead. Some believed a band of Mexican religious fanatics, brothers by the name of Espinosa, killed him, stole his white horse, then robbed his cabin."

Libby gasped at the gruesome image her mind conjured.

"Sorry to distress you, miss."

Libby rose. "You've been very helpful. I have just one more question, if you'd be so gracious. If you were to hire a man to search for someone close to you, and you wanted to make absolutely sure this man was honest, trustworthy, and brave, what would you do?"

"You won't find anyone willing to go to Dead Man's Canyon, if that's what you have on your mind, Miss Chandler. We've a superstitious lot around here."

"No one? Surely there must be *one* man."

The editor briefly scratched his head. "You might check at the city jail."

"The jail?"

"Sheriff Cook knows everyone hereabout."

Relieved by Mr. Byers's clarification, Libby thanked him again and left the newspaper office. She found the city jail on the east side of Front Street. Sheriff Cook had gone to break up a fight, so the jailer welcomed her instead.

Introducing himself as L. E. Thaw, he forced a cup of coffee into her hands. He ushered her to a chair opposite him at the desk in one corner. Behind him posters of wanted men lined the wall. Close by, a well-used cabinet housed one long rifle and two shotguns.

"How can I help you, ma'am?" he asked.

Libby set the chipped cup on the edge of the desk and promptly related the events regarding Clarence's disappearance. "Mr. Byers sent me here. He thought Sheriff Cook might know of someone I might hire."

"That I might, young lady," came a gruff-sounding voice from the doorway.'

The jailer leapt from his seat at the curt inter-

ruption, toppling the chair in his haste. Libby
decided the sheriff must take exception to an
insubordinate sitting at his desk in his absence.
She hid a smile as Thaw repeated her story word
for word, then scooted past his superior.

"You want a tracker, I presume?" Cook asked.

Libby considered the question before she explained, "A person with experience of that sort
would be most helpful, but the man should also
have exceptional courage. The area, you see, is
called Dead Man's Canyon. Also, there's the matter of an apparition seen by Mr. Potts." She stared
at the shiny tin star pinned to the lawman's black
vest. "Thus far I've paid two men and have
nothing to show for it. I need a man who is not
afraid of anything and whom I can trust."

Sheriff Cook sat on the edge of his desk. "I've
heard the rumors of ghosts in Dead Man's Canyon, little lady, but I don't buy any of that
horsepucky. You might as well go on back home."

Libby held her spine rigid. "I've come all this
way, Sheriff, and I have no intention of leaving
until I find out what happened to Clarence. He has
no family to worry about him."

The lawman stared at her for a long moment.
"You won't find anyone willing to work for—"

"A woman?" she finished.

Cook flinched.

"As to the matter of the ghost, none of us can be
certain of its authenticity, can we? However, the
editor of the newspaper has printed a story on
Ernest Potts. It seems to me that if Mr. Byers
thought the story feasible enough to report, he
must believe in the possibility of an apparition."

A hint of red color inched up the lawman's neck.

"I expect you, as sheriff of this town, should—"

Cook held up a beefy hand. "You've come a far distance, little lady. I don't want to be the one to put a cork in your bottle, but—"

Libby came to her feet. "Sheriff Cook, kindly stop addressing me as *little lady.* I am not regarded as small in stature. As for putting *a cork in my bottle,* nothing you can say will change my mind. I mean to find my lost intended. Now, either you know of someone I can hire or not."

The sheriff stood also. "You got sand talking to a man in that sassy tone, missy." Seconds passed before he spoke again. "I know of only one man fearless and foolhardy enough to go where you want. Ex–army scout. Faced danger more times than you can count and came away unscathed. He could find your fiancé. He's even presently unemployed."

Libby's hopes lifted. "If you tell me the man's name, I'm sure I can persuade him to take the job." She gave the sheriff a coaxing smile. "I've been known to be quite persuasive when I put my mind to it."

"Persuasive, hell. McCord, for all the good it'll do you."

The name sounded impressive enough. "Have you a suggestion as to where Mr. McCord might be located?"

Thaw gave a hoot of laughter but ceased when the sheriff sent him a censuring look.

"Having sand and sass will only get you so far, Miss Chandler. He's temporarily detained." Indicating the back room with his thumb, Cook added, "Reno McCord is locked in my jail for disturbing the peace."

Chapter 2

"**W**hat you do mean, he's in jail?"
The sheriff nodded at his over-turned chair and then waited while his deputy set it upright. "A slight altercation, that's all. Trust me, Miss Chandler, I'd never suggest you hire McCord if he lacked moral fortitude."

"If Mr. McCord is so morally gifted, why haven't you allowed him to bail himself out?"

The lawman sat and propped his legs on the edge of his desk. "Moral fortitude he has, miserly he isn't. McCord likes a good time when the situation warrants. Unfortunately, he likes every-one around him to share in the fun."

"In other words, he's a ne'er-do-well," Libby ventured.

"Maybe just a mite too indulgent."

"How much does Mr. McCord owe?"

"Two hundred dollars."

Libby grimaced. "That seems high for a slight altercation."

The lawman's mouth slanted into a wry smile. "I have the bills right here."

Libby tapped her foot on the floor as she

considered the man's motives. "Surely you're not suggesting I pay for your prisoner's misdeeds?"

"That depends."

She sighed. The man's indirect answers were trying her patience. "Depends upon what?"

"Either you want the best, or you want to hire another Ernest T. And that's supposing you can find anyone loco enough to take the job."

When Libby felt her shoulders slump, she made a conscious effort to sit straight. "Sheriff Cook, I'm in desperate need of a man to find my fiancé. If you think Mr. McCord is my only recourse, I'm willing to take a look at him."

The deputy tittered and earned a frown from his superior.

"Is there something else I should know about Mr. McCord?" she asked.

The lawman dropped his feet to the floor, stood and seized a ring of keys from a wooden peg behind him. "If you put a high store on appearances, Miss Chandler, you might be put off."

"I'm concerned only with Mr. McCord's character, Sheriff. I'm not looking for a suitor, you know. If he's trustworthy, brave, and morally upstanding, I don't care about his appearance."

Silently the sheriff led her through a door into a section where sturdy bars served as outer walls and to divide small cubicles from one another. She'd never been inside a jail before. Already, she longed for a breath of fresh air. "McCord's in the one on the end. The rest are empty. Holler if you need me."

Libby watched the lawman depart and close the outer door, sealing her inside. She suffered a moment's uncertainty. But her reaction was silly, she thought. The sheriff was within hearing distance, the prisoner locked behind bars. Confidently, she walked to the end cell.

One glimpse of the incarcerated man shook Libby's poise. Dear Lord, he was the man who had knocked her down!

Tall, broad, and unkempt, with his shoulder-length hair, he looked more disheveled than she remembered. Were someone to hang him from a clothesline and beat him as soundly as they would a rug, she felt certain they'd not have him free of dust.

He was pacing. Restless energy radiated from him, unnerving Libby. Didn't he see her? Surely he'd heard the sheriff open the door and speak to her. "Mr. McCord," she said softly.

He spun around and Libby retreated a step. The startling deep blue of his eyes robbed her of further speech. She'd heard stories of savage animals who could entrance their prey, thus rendering them helpless. But he was a man, not an animal. Why did she feel as if bonds held her in place?

And, dear God, why did his gaze create havoc in her stomach?

Libby shut her eyes. When she opened them she studied the rest of his face instead. She noticed a small, jagged cut above his left brow, several bruises on his cheekbone, another cut at the corner of his mouth. His nose looked slightly swollen. If he sported any other injuries from his altercation in front of the saloon, his dark, bushy beard hid them.

One sudden, long stride put him against the bars.

Libby instinctively stepped backward. When she detected a slight curve to his mouth, she cursed her cowardly maneuver. How could she persuade him to help her if she continued to flinch every time he moved a muscle? Feigning a bravery she didn't feel, she approached the cell.

"We've already met," he said.

The low, smooth timbre of his voice dismayed her. She wanted no reminder of those humiliating minutes when he'd had her pressed to the walk.

"You wouldn't tell me your name." His bold gaze flashed over her. "Yet you've come to visit me?"

Libby swallowed the knot in her throat. She had a suspicion the sheriff had been right. It would take a great deal of persuasion for this man to work for a woman. "My name is Libby Chandler, and I've come all the way here from Pennsylvania."

His mouth moved again.

She had the distinct impression he was laughing at her. Feeling a trifle flushed, she stammered, "I'm in dire need."

"Been in *dire* need, myself. Plenty of times."

She pretended not to have heard his remark and began again. "I need a man—"

He chuckled.

"I do not believe I've said anything to—"

Controlling himself, somewhat, he cleared his throat.

"As I was saying, I want—"

"A man," he cut her off again. He plucked at his soiled shirt and pants, grinning all the while. "I'm not very presentable at the moment. Also, I sincerely doubt our good sheriff will let me out anytime soon."

"*Mister* McCord!" Libby inhaled a harsh breath. "If you allow me to finish a sentence, you might learn how wrong your assumptions are."

"You have mettle, Libby Chandler." He leisurely considered her before he said softly, "You've aroused my curiosity. What could you possibly want badly enough to come to me?"

His change of manner calmed her enough to say, "I wish to hire you to search for a man who's been missing for six months."

"How much?"

Caught off guard by his blunt question, Libby considered her total worth. "How much do you want?"

"My services come high. *Very* high."

She tightened her hold on her reticule. "Sheriff Cook mentioned a bill for damages."

"Yeah," he said, his tone disgusted. "That goddamn mirror from St. Louis."

Reprimanding his choice of language with a pointed look, she offered, "I'm willing to put up your bail and pay the damages to the saloon. Will that suffice?"

"No."

His reply stunned her. He was locked in jail with no apparent means to pay what he owed, and he'd just refused her offer.

"I will, however, work for you for five."

"Five hundred dollars?"

"And you pay my bail and for a . . . darn mirror, one chair, and a bottle of whiskey."

"Whiskey, too?"

McCord shrugged his shoulders. "The whiskey's for me."

"Oh!"

She found his offer so ludicrous, she withheld her refusal. She watched him pace the cell again. He might look like the devil incarnate but she sensed he possessed a stout heart and a will of iron. Instinct told her no one would dare cross Reno McCord, not even a cantankerous ghost sporting an ax in his head. Despite McCord's brash behavior and rash demand for more money, he was her sole recourse.

More importantly, she had purposely omitted facts: that he would have to travel through a deadly canyon and perchance meet up with a ghost. It also seemed premature to mention nightmares drove her to find Clarence.

McCord appeared in desperate circumstances, but he might refuse her anyway. If she led him to believe she was wealthy, he might be induced to commit himself to helping her. Once he'd made a commitment, she suspected he would honor his word. She had no idea how she'd arrived at this conclusion. His appearance didn't inspire confidence.

"One hundred dollars, Mr. McCord. Not one penny more."

He stopped pacing. "No chance, Miss Chandler. I wouldn't go down the street for such a paltry sum. Now, if you see four hundred, I might reconsider."

"Two," she fired back.

"Lady, we can argue the point all day, so save yourself the trouble."

Libby released a sigh. "How much will *you* settle for, Mr. McCord?"

He came to within an inch of the bars. "I'm feeling generous. I'll work for you for three hundred."

"Generous! You're a thief, Mr. McCord."

"What'll it be, Miss Chandler?"

Though it annoyed her to have to surrender, intuition told her it would be futile to bargain any further. Besides, she thought, she wanted him to think she was wealthy. Hoping no outward sign of her exaggeration showed on her face, she said, "Why, three hundred dollars is a mere pittance. But I need to be sure you'll fulfill your end of our bargain."

"A mere pittance," he repeated.

Taking his sarcastic tone for agreement, her confidence soared. "I'll amend my offer somewhat provided you give me your word to hold to our agreement."

He raised a brow. "Amend, how?"

"Half, Mr. McCord. After you've honored our deal, I'll see you get the rest."

"You've a shrewd mind, Miss Chandler. Do you mind my asking who this man is to you?"

"Not at all. Clarence Trout is my fiancé."

McCord gripped the bars with both hands. "What of *your* word, Miss Chandler? How do I know you won't renege?"

Libby stiffened. "As I see it, you aren't in a position to question my honor. Quite frankly, you'd be a fool to turn me down. Perhaps you have another way out of your predicament? Do you?"

"I don't and you damned well know it!"

Encouraged by his frustrated reply, she grew more confident. "I have what you need, Mr. McCord."

"Do you, indeed?"

According his suggestive tone to his disgruntled mood, Libby retorted, "Money to bail you out of jail! Unless you choose to serve out your sentence in this decorous room, I suggest you accept my extremely generous offer."

"Or what?"

"Or I might retract it!"

He scowled. "You have a devious mind, Miss Chandler, but I think you're royally bluffing."

Libby touched her hair as she averted her gaze. "Call my bluff, McCord. There are any number of men I can hire for less money."

She held her breath while she awaited his answer. She'd never been a person to gamble and found the anticipation exciting. Or maybe she found the prospect of winning a private battle of wills with this man exhilarating. She wondered if many people could claim they'd maneuvered Reno McCord into doing their bidding.

Reno tightened his grip on the bars. The lady had bested him, but she was still a godsend. He had been feeling like a caged animal before she'd arrived. God, he hated being confined. Years of living outdoors hadn't prepared him for incarceration in a dark, stuffy cell. Libby Chandler offered freedom; however, he'd already learned not to underestimate her.

Her features were pleasant enough, but her prim attire lured a man's attention from the rest of her. Her severe green dress buttoned to her throat. Her hair had been pulled so tightly back into a knot at her nape that her skin looked strained. Everything about her suggested an unyielding nature. She didn't seem coldhearted, though. She was going to extreme measures to hire him, which proved her devotion to her intended.

She appeared uncomfortable as she patiently allowed him time to consider her offer. He had an inkling there was more to the story than she was telling him. Testing her, he asked, "What haven't you told me, Miss Chandler?" Her startled expression revealed he'd been right to follow his instincts. "Is your man running from something?"

"Heavens, no. He's a kind, law-abiding person, a storekeeper by trade." While she shifted from foot to foot, her long, graceful fingers turned the beaded reticule. "There's one small obstacle to be overcome in searching for Clarence."

"And what might that be?"

"Do you believe in ghosts, Mr. McCord?"

"What kind of a question is that? Ghosts!"

"Apparitions, to be precise." She tilted slightly forward. "Phantoms. The notion of transparent spirits who fly at people and terrify them."

"Hell, no."

She released a long, satisfied sigh. "Good. You're definitely the man for the job."

"Would you think I'm presumptuous if I asked why you feel not believing in spirits is significant?"

"Certainly not. I suppose I should've told you right off, but I—"

"Wanted to surprise me?"

"Well, yes . . . I mean, no. Mr. McCord, the last known whereabouts of my intended was directly beyond an area referred to as Dead Man's Canyon."

"Go on."

"Rumor has it, and I stress it is merely a rumor, that a ghost inhabits the area. But since you don't believe in such beings, I presume you'll think nothing of going there."

She seemed so deadly earnest, he smiled. "You're right."

"I'm pleased to find you're as sensible as I thought. Dare I hope you've decided to take the job?"

"As you've so eloquently stated, I have no other option at the moment. You will, however, have to supply me with more information about your Mr. Trout."

"Of course. I'll settle things with Sheriff Cook, and meet with you later today. When you're free you might speak with Mr. Byers of the *Rocky Mountain News*. He seems well versed on the area I mentioned." She pinched open her reticule and, holding it so he couldn't see inside, slipped out two coins. "A small advance, token of my undying gratitude."

Tempted not to accept, Reno quickly regained his senses. She had hinted she possessed wealth and regarded three hundred dollars a mere pittance. If she seemed reluctant to part with even this small amount, it must be due to a prudent nature.

Their fingers brushed. Hers were as cool and smooth as he'd expected. It was another reason to admire her. Most women would be hesitant to touch him in his shabby state, much less want to hire him. Libby Chandler seemed to have the ability to look past a person's appearance to the man inside. And she was smart, all right. He *was* an expert in scouting out trails and people, and he didn't frighten easily.

"Do you have a room?" he asked. Her delicate eyebrows lifted, so Reno clarified, "Some place where we can meet?"

"I hardly think meeting privately would be fitting." She held her vision lowered. "I'm not very familiar with Denver, though I know where the Express Office is."

"Three o'clock then."

"All right. Thank you, Mr. McCord. I'm indebted to you."

She left, her step brisk, allowing him no opportunity to respond. He attempted to eavesdrop on her conversation with the sheriff, but their voices were too muffled. Five minutes later, when the lawman came, a ring of keys dangled from a finger. He unlocked the door.

"You have me to thank, McCord, else you'd still be rotting away in here."

Reno stepped out of the cell. "Thanks."

"I like her," Cook said. "Shame about her intended. Did she tell you the whole story?"

"I'm meeting her this afternoon. Why?"

"I met Trout's partner once. John Cox is a sneaky bastard."

"I'll keep it in mind." Reno stretched aching muscles. "Am I free to go?"

Sheriff Cook stepped back, extending his arm. "Don't get into any more scrapes. You might not find as charitable a benefactor next time." He followed Reno into the front room. "You locate Trout, you let me know."

Reno snatched his hat from a neat stack of his belongings on the desk. "Sure thing."

The lawman picked up Reno's bedroll and gunbelt and thrust them at him. "Treat the lady right."

Plopping on his hat, Reno grinned. "The lady's virtue is safe, Sheriff. She's not exactly my type, and she's already promised, anyhow."

"Can't see as how such matters would concern *you*." Cook broke into laughter. "Why, Trout's likely dead. Miss Chandler is too good for the likes of you, but maybe you shouldn't dismiss her too quick. Seems to me, a no-nonsense woman like her might be just what you need. She'd make you mind, and see you don't squander your money."

Reno stared long and hard at the lawman. "I'm not the marrying kind. And if I wanted someone giving me orders, I would've stayed with the army."

"Well, they didn't teach you a goddamn thing!"

Reno headed for the door. "They tried, I'll give them that."

At ten past three, Libby arrived at the corner of Front Street. She gazed up at the two-story brick building which housed Wells Fargo & Company's Express Office. She'd meant to be on time but earlier, finding herself with several hours to spare, she'd indulged in a rare shopping expedition. She'd bought a new dress and hat and then decided her extravagance demanded a different coiffure as well. She'd even purchased a bustle petticoat to assure that the fullness at the back of the woolen dress wasn't compromised. After her exasperating meeting with Reno McCord, she'd needed to do something to lift her spirits.

Panic assailed her. What if he didn't show up?

Libby calmed herself. Just because the man was a few minutes late wasn't a reason to panic. He needed funds and she'd agreed to pay him three hundred dollars. No man in his right mind would turn his back on such an offer.

But she'd given him an advance. Maybe she should've walked past the Crooked Creek Saloon to make sure he hadn't stopped there. She wasn't about to bail him out of jail a second time.

"You're late, Miss Chandler."

Libby started at the softly spoken chastisement from behind. Then, recognizing the decidedly masculine voice, she countered, "You are late as well, Mr. McCord."

He stood beside her. "I was here at ten 'til three and waited for fifteen minutes."

"It was commendable of you to arrive early."

"Let's say I was curious."

"About what?"

"About you. I figured you'd arrive at the precise hour."

"I needed to buy a few things and lost track of the time."

After a few minutes, he said, "Time well spent, if you want my opinion. The color of your dress suits you."

Flustered by his words, she touched her hair. "Thank you for your gracious compliment, Mr. McCord."

"Lady, no one calls me mister or gracious." A speeding carriage veered too close to the walk.

Deftly, he seized her arm and pulled her to safety. "Did you bring my money?"

She faced him with the intent of thanking him for saving her from bodily harm, but words suddenly escaped her. He'd shaved off his bushy beard. She knew she was staring stupidly at him, but she would never have guessed that the beard had hidden such an arresting chin and perfectly hollowed cheeks, or that his mouth would be positively seductive.

Dear Lord! The brash barbarian who had knocked her down, and who was now in her employ, was breathtakingly handsome.

She noticed other things about him as well. His hair still hung to his shoulders. He wore a clean blue shirt, dark pants, and he'd bathed. He smelled sinful. The bruises and small cuts he'd incurred during his brawl didn't detract from his good looks.

"My money," he reminded.

"Yes, I have it," she said. Heavens, he must've noticed her ogling him. "You don't want me to dispense it to you here on the street, do you? Why, someone might see and later decide to rob you."

His lopsided grin convinced Libby she'd just suggested an impossible feat. Her realization prompted her to tell him about the decision she'd made last night. First, though, she needed to clarify her previous remarks. "I didn't mean to imply anyone might find you lacking in . . . vigor, Mr. McCord."

"I didn't think you did. You strike me as an intelligent woman."

"However, before I give you what we agreed

upon, I think it's only fair to tell you I've added a condition to our bargain."

He tilted his head. "Our bargain has been sealed. You can't add *conditions* at this late date."

Libby quickly aimed him a bright smile. "When you hear all of my story, you'll see why I've decided to . . . go along."

"The hell you will." He turned on his heel and strode down the street.

Libby dashed after him. She leapt in front of him. "You're behaving rashly, Mr. McCord."

His hands spanned her waist as he lifted her aside. "I'm not traveling with a woman. Either I go alone or you find someone else."

He started to walk off but, desperate to detain him, Libby seized his shirtsleeve. "Wait! Please."

"I've nothing against you, lady. It's just that you'd slow me down, not to mention the hardships. Do you even ride a horse?"

"Of course I can ride," Libby swiftly lied.

His eyes briefly narrowed on her. "You're one hellava lot of trouble."

"And you have no money. How do you propose to repay me for what I've already spent on your behalf?" His intense scrutiny rattled her, yet she still managed to finish her say. "We need one another. You see that, don't you?"

"Lady—" A scowl captured his mouth.

"I wouldn't be any trouble to you, I promise." Seeing two gentlemen leaving a clothing store, Libby lowered her hand and her voice. "Have supper with me, allow me a chance to explain."

He shoved his fingers through his hair, grumbling, "You offering to buy my supper?"

"Yes, Mr. McCord, I am. Are you man enough to accept?"

Bold, blue eyes searched her face. Seconds passed before he offered his arm. "I have a condition of my own. I pick the restaurant."

Libby slipped her arm through his and, elated by his capitulation, allowed him to lead her down the walk. Again, she'd managed to bend Reno McCord to her will.

But for how long would he allow her to manipulate him?

Chapter 3

Reno resisted an overwhelming temptation to take Libby to the most expensive restaurant in town and instead chose one where he liked the food. As he seated her on a roughly hewn bench at an oblong table covered with a red-checkered tablecloth, he watched for any sign to give away her reaction to his choice of eating establishments. She seemed content, so he seated himself across from her.

"They make the best beef stew west of Missouri. And the corn bread melts in your mouth."

Slowly, she peeled off her gloves. "It sounds delicious. Is that what you're having?"

"About three platesful." When her eyes widened, he added, "The food they serve prisoners is godawful."

"I imagine so. It's probably meant to deter a man from breaking the law again."

He watched her lay her gloves atop her reticule and set them close to the edge of the table. Next she slipped a pearl-tipped pin from her hat and placed it with her other belongings. The hat boasted a ribbon which matched her dress. He decided the lack of frills suggested a forthright, prudent nature.

But she wasn't prudent enough. And he wasn't taking her along.

When she turned her head to speak with Violet Graham, the buxom young woman who served meals, Reno noticed his employer wore her brown hair softly rolled at her nape, not pulled into a tight knot. In the dim light of indoors, she had a flawless profile.

"Hello, Reno," Violet said, interrupting his thoughts. "You havin' the stew, also?"

"You know I am. And pile the plate higher than last time." He glanced at his dinner companion. "Libby Chandler, meet Violet Graham."

Libby extended her hand. "I'm pleased to make your acquaintance."

Reno smiled. Violet was a ravishing beauty with red hair and green eyes and a figure to drive a man wild. Women, however, usually spurned Violet's friendly overtures though she possessed a sweet, innocent nature.

Violet shyly glanced at Libby's belongings. "That sure is a pretty hat, ma'am."

"Why, thank you, Violet. You can try it on if you want."

"Oh, no, ma'am."

After the girl had left, Libby whispered, "She has such beautiful hair and eyes, it makes me pea green with envy."

Satisfied he'd detected no hint of guile in her tone, he confided, "The child has had an unfortunate life."

Libby leaned forward. "In case you hadn't noticed, Violet is not a child."

"In my eyes, she is. She's seventeen and lost her family two years ago when outlaws raided their farmhouse in Missouri. They left her for dead."

"Seventeen?" Libby looked toward the kitchen area of the restaurant. "I thought she was much older."

"My detachment found her starved, beaten half to death, and roaming the countryside. We saw her safely put on a wagon train heading west. Somehow she ended up here." Seeing the pity marking Libby's eyes, he tackled another, less depressing subject. "You invited me here in order to explain a few things."

"Yes, I did." She folded her hands on her lap. "A year and a half ago, Clarence went off to find gold at California Gulch."

"And left his intended to pine for him?"

"Clarence wanted to better his lot in life," she said defensively. "He thought it best if he tried his hand at gold mining *before* we married. He wrote to me almost every day for a year. Then, six months ago, his letters stopped arriving."

Several reasons for Trout's negligence popped into Reno's mind. Not wanting to suggest the man might have found someone else, he offered, "The miners I've known have all had one thing in common. They hit on a strike and become obsessed with striking it rich. They forget everyone and everything else."

She shook her head. "Not Clarence. He would've written to me right away." A slight flush stained her cheeks. "He was desperately in love with me . . . and I . . . but . . . I just know he would've wanted to share news of that sort."

"Miss Chandler," Reno said. He also leaned

closer. "Your intended's claim might have proved worthless. A man has his pride. He might've decided he didn't want to return empty-handed."

"Clarence owns the general store and makes a sufficient living. No, I feel certain he's come to harm. And that's why I've traveled all this way to find him. The first man I hired disappeared. The second returned to Denver out of his mind with fright. You, Mr. McCord, are my best chance to find Clarence."

"We agree on something at least." He waited, expecting her to plead with him to take her along. But she said nothing more. "I work alone. I always have. It's one of the reasons why I preferred to act as scout for the army. I'm used to being on my own, and I'm too old to change."

She looked away. "I would be no bother to you, truly."

"Lady, I sincerely doubt that."

"But I—"

"No."

"But, Mr. McCord, you don't understand." Her hazel eyes ablaze with passion, she continued, "I'm driven to find him. I can't go back without knowing for sure what happened. He'd never allow me a moment's peace."

"Whether he's gone, or just never returns, he can't ruin your peace of mind unless you allow it. You'll find someone else in time."

"No one will have me now," she said in a soft, distressed voice. "I'm . . . ill-fated."

He didn't know how to respond. She'd spoken so earnestly he knew her remark hadn't been a ploy to gain his sympathy. "What do you mean?"

"I was betrothed once before, when I was eighteen." Her expression turned sad, as if the news she was relating had happened recently. "On the day of our wedding he . . . he died."

He didn't want to feel compassion for her. Libby Chandler was a job, nothing more. "You shouldn't blame yourself for things you can't control."

"I don't blame myself, Mr. McCord," she said, her voice touched with indignation. "But everyone back in my hometown believes I'm bad luck for any man. I know the dreams I've been having won't cease until Clarence is found or properly laid to rest."

Plagued by a premonition that she'd just bound him to agree to anything, he asked, "What dreams?"

"Of Clarence. Ever since his letters stopped coming, and every night of late, I see him in my dreams."

"You dream of him? I see nothing out of the ordinary in imagining a loved one, especially if he's ceased contacting you."

"They're not those kinds of dreams. I see the same dream each time: of Clarence leaving a cabin and meeting another man. There's red rock all around. I believe this other man is speaking in a hostile manner. Then Clarence struggles with the man and gets stabbed in the chest." Her brows pinched together as her face contorted with pain. "Sometimes I sense it isn't a dream at all, and Clarence is making it happen. It's as if he's attempting to contact me."

"Have you told anyone else of your dreams?"

She gave him a faint smile. "Just a dear friend back home and, now, you."

He wanted to tell her that her imagination had conjured up the visions. She seemed rational in every way, but the lady could also be crazy. Sane people didn't go around claiming they were being contacted from beyond the grave. Neither did they admit to having seen a person's actual death in their mind.

"Clarence is calling out to me. I know he's been dealt with foully. He wants me to find him and see his murderer caught and punished."

Unsure how to respond, Reno said nothing.

"You must take me with you. I must see this through."

She *was* crazy. But he must've been crazier for having committed himself to helping her. No one would blame him if he backed out of their deal now.

When tears started to well up in her eyes, he mumbled an oath. Her hands trembling slightly, she dug in her reticule and pulled out a white handkerchief with dainty crocheted edges. She dabbed daintily at her nose.

He was doomed. If he didn't help her, she wouldn't give up until she'd found someone else. She might end up the victim of a man of more unsavory character than he. Reno groaned. At least *he* had some scruples. He'd never rob or cheat anyone.

"I'm sorry," she said. "I don't usually carry on so. There's no one else I can trust, leastwise no one as capable as you, and I—"

"I haven't changed my mind."

She gave her nose another swipe with the handkerchief and sniffed. "You wouldn't even know I was—"

"You can come along."

"I promise I won't . . . what did you say?"

"I said I haven't changed my mind about working for you. You can come with me, but on *my* terms."

Libby's mouth slid into a broad smile. "Oh, that's wonderful news. How can I ever thank you?"

"Don't thank me yet. You haven't heard my terms."

"I'm sure they'll be acceptable."

"Concerning your dress," he said, noticing the attractive deep rose color again. "You'll have to wear pants, and heavy boots, preferably in a man's small size, and then—"

Libby held up a hand. "Did I hear you correctly? You want me to wear a man's trousers?"

"You'll need a hat as well, but not of the sort women usually wear. It should have a wide brim. And then—"

"Mister McCord! Surely you jest."

Reno folded his arms on the table. "Lady, I'm dead serious. You'll have to keep up with me. I won't have you tripping over your skirt, bruising your feet, falling over rocks, or any number of catastrophes destined to happen if you wear women's clothes."

"Your suggestion is highly inappropriate."

"It's not a suggestion. It's an order."

Her eyes widened. "But—"

"There are no buts, Miss Chandler." He wanted to smile at her shocked expression. Remembering her speech to him at the jail, he repeated, "Quite frankly, you'd be a fool to turn down my offer. Or do you have another way out of your predicament?"

A ghost of a smile crept over her lips. "I don't and you know it."

He grinned. "As memory serves me, I had used a *damned* in my answer."

"So you did. A proper woman dresses appropriately at all times," she said with conviction.

"Horse . . . feathers, lady. Either you abide by my wishes, or I just might retract my very generous offer."

Her mouth fell into a taut line as she regarded him. "You're mocking me. Or are *you* royally bluffing?"

"I never bluff. What'll it be?"

"It appears I have no choice."

He stuck out his hand. "Do we shake, or do you want a written contract?"

"A handshake will do." She slipped her hand atop his. "You have my complete trust."

He doubted she'd give her trust so quickly, but he squeezed her fingers gently. Her hand was smaller than he'd thought, soft and dainty. The thought struck him that she might be more vulnerable than her candid temperament let on. The only women he'd ever known who were as outspoken as Libby Chandler had been beautiful, overly confident their charms alone could render a man weak. But if Libby were ravishing and voluptuous, he'd be in deep trouble. Theirs was a business relationship.

He noticed she was staring at their locked hands. He wondered what fascinated her. Looking down, he discovered he had been unconsciously grazing his thumb over her knuckles. Her skin felt as hot and supple as fine leather under a blazing sun. Judging by her pink cheeks, his familiar gesture distressed her.

Abruptly he relaxed his grip to allow her to draw back first. Her lingering retreat, however, baffled him, a slow, sensuous brush of her fingers over his. Then, suggesting regret on her part, she swiftly tucked her hand beneath the table. He tilted his head and studied her. To his amusement, she refused to look up and meet his gaze. His palm felt warm where she'd touched him, and mixed emotions flooded through him.

His feelings toward her weren't sexual. She loved another man. Why, then, was he considering her mouth and sure in his mind that beneath her straitlaced manner dwelled an untapped passionate nature?

Annoyed his thoughts had drifted off track, he asked, "Do you have it with you?"

Her gaze flew to his.

"The half of the money you promised," he explained.

After she gave a short nod, she dipped her fingers into her reticule and under cover of the table, counted out an amount. Reno smiled. She managed her funds prudently but did she ever allow herself to enjoy any of it? If he had half the wealth she probably had, he'd sure as hell treat himself to a grand time. And when the money ran out, well, that was the way of things. Rich one day, poor the next.

She glanced around the room before she slipped the money to him. "I subtracted the twenty dollars I advanced you yesterday."

Reno hid the money in his pants pocket. "You can give me the bottle of whiskey when we leave tomorrow."

"Tomorrow? But I—"

"Surely you weren't going to say you need more time?" he asked with a challenging smile.

She lifted her chin. "Why . . . no. I prefer to find Clarence as soon as possible. I believe in efficiently making use of time, so I'm happy you're of the same opinion."

Their meal came and they ate in silence. Reno found himself sneaking glimpses of his employer whenever he thought she wasn't looking. She intrigued him. He'd never spent this much time alone with a decent woman and wasn't sure what she expected of him. He just wished he hadn't allowed her to talk him into taking her along. She was sure to slow him down.

He cherished solitude, being alone on the trail with only nature as company. Grudgingly, he admitted to himself that he'd enjoyed the time he'd spent with her so far. That unsettled him. Women didn't usually challenge his mind. Working for a woman would be laced with pitfalls but, strangely, he looked forward to matching wits with her again.

After they'd finished their meal, he escorted her to the door, then outside. "If you tell me where you're staying, I'll see you safely there."

"You needn't bother. I'm used to taking care of myself. Besides, you said you want to leave tomorrow. I should see about purchasing the necessary clothing."

"The morning is soon enough for that. I have things to buy, myself."

"It's kind of you to think of my welfare, but I must see to an errand before I go home."

"I only want to see you to the door. You said you trusted me."

"Oh, I do," she said quickly. "But I . . . there's a chore I want to tend to before I go home."

"I'll go with you." The downward slant of her mouth made it clear that was the last thing she wanted. Curious about her reason for rejecting his company, he taunted her, "You've hired me, yet you're refusing my offer of protection?"

"For pity's sake. You're harder to get free of than a fly hovering over a pot of honey!"

"I'm partial to honey." He watched her cheeks grow pink and bit back a laugh. "You might as well tell me your destination. You'll find I'm as persistent as a fly."

"I sincerely hope this isn't an indication of how your behavior will be once we leave town."

"It might be." He lost the battle not to laugh but managed to get out, "It's my duty to guard you from harm."

She released a heavy sigh. "Wait here, if you will. My errand is inside the restaurant."

She hurried back inside while Reno waited for several minutes before he walked straight up to the smudged window. Cupping his hands on either side of his face, he searched the dim interior until he spotted her. He shook his head. Libby was speaking with Violet.

A ticking sound drew his attention. A matronly woman stopped near him, and he realized she'd just clicked her tongue to reprimand him for looking through the window. "The cook stepped on a frog and dumped a potful of beans over the mayor's head," he said without betraying a trace of amusement.

To Reno's delight, the woman shoved him aside in her haste to peer through the window herself. He saw Libby exit the restaurant. Wearing a broad grin, he strode toward her.

"You look pleased with yourself, Mr. McCord."

"Yes, ma'am, I am." He looped her arm through his. As he steered Libby along the street, they passed the other woman. With an innocent expression on his face, he clicked his tongue loudly until the woman shot him a lethal glare and marched in the opposite direction.

Libby gave him a questioning look. "Should I ask what you've been doing while I was gone?"

Reno didn't respond. Through the glass he'd caught a glimpse of Violet and his employer's mission became clear. Violet was presently taking someone's order, acting for all the world as if nothing had changed during the past few minutes. Perched on her head was Libby's new hat.

Libby didn't sleep well that night. Dreams of Clarence, and excitement over the following day, plagued her until nearly morning. At dawn she tossed back the covers and left her bed. It was no use. It was impossible to rest with so many matters traipsing through her mind.

And that was not counting Reno McCord.

He had wandered in and out of her mind at unexpected moments, sometimes in the midst of other thoughts. Those spellbinding blue eyes of his seemed intent upon haunting her.

She'd lied to him several times. She consoled

herself with the thought that her cause, to find Clarence, or see him properly laid to rest, was a worthy one. She would allow Reno to believe she was wealthy only until they'd reached the end of their arrangement. Then she would confess.

Her other fabrication might very well prove foolhardy a bit sooner. But how hard could it be to sit a horse, she wondered. It had seemed imperative at the time to manufacture a slight prevarication. Otherwise he wouldn't have agreed to take her along. Considering his proclivity for frequenting saloons, and his imprudent tendency to share his funds with anyone near, she'd made a wise decision. Despite her assurance to him, she didn't trust him. Having so much money at once might tempt him to spend it all at once.

She dressed and set out to procure the necessary garments for their travel. When he'd left her at the door to her hotel yesterday, he'd said to meet him at noon at W. L. Wakeman & Brothers' Livery Stable on Cherry Street.

Her stomach churned at the idea of traveling alone with a handsome devil who not only possessed a wit that surpassed hers, but who seemed to take pleasure in taunting her. Yet she had to remember that Reno was merely in her employ, not a suitor, which might explain his manner. He wasn't out to impress her and gain favor; he could afford the luxury of simply being himself.

By nine, Libby was exasperated. She'd visited three clothing stores and managed to buy two pairs of men's trousers which she guessed would fit reasonably well. To preserve her dignity, she'd told the store clerks she was purchasing the garments for a younger brother nearly the same size as she. The boots were another matter. She'd been forced to try on pair after pair, yet none had fit. Finally, the clerk in the last store had referred her to another establishment which carried a variety of children's footwear. The largest boots, however, had turned out to be too small, requiring her to settle for the smallest size made for a man. Though they were slightly too large, she would have to make do.

The hat, at least, had proven an easy purchase. Having an abundance of hair alleviated one problem. She bought a shirt in a shade of blue which reminded her of Reno's eyes, and, on impulse, a drab brown dress a size larger than her own. Her employee had demanded she wear men's attire, leaving her no choice in the matter.

A smile split her face. She'd found a way around his unseemly demand.

Her arms full of bundles, she returned to the hotel and re-dressed in the new clothes. Upon seeing her reflection in the full-length mirror, she grimaced. She looked shapeless and dowdy, pounds heavier. The waist of the pants bunched under the dress and restricted movement. Lifting the hem to her hips, she peered over her shoulder, and frowned. The trousers hugged her legs and backside so tightly they displayed the lines of her body most indecently. There was no way she was traveling with Mr. McCord without benefit of the dress.

The man had an unnerving habit of boldly roaming his eyes over her. Satisfied that, no matter how hard he tried, he wouldn't have a glimpse of her legs, she rolled her hair into a large roll and anchored it high on her head. The wide-brimmed hat fit perfectly atop the mound. She didn't know how long they would be gone, so she crammed clean unmentionables, brush, and everything else which would fit into one small traveling bag.

After she'd left word of her whereabouts with the proprietor for Mr. and Mrs. Taylor, she paid her bill. Walking was difficult in the stiff boots, so she hired a buggy to take her to the livery. Despite her numerous chores, she arrived early. A boy shoveling out the stables directed her to the last stall where she spotted Reno.

Securing a rope around an assortment of supplies, he obviously had not heard her enter. But he surprised her by remarking, "You're on time today."

"Actually, I'm thirty minutes early," she countered.

"That'll give us a few minutes to settle up before we leave."

Suspicious of what *settle up* meant, Libby moved behind him. She held out her bulging bag. "Is there a place left for my belongings?"

Reno snatched the satchel. He looped the rope through the handles, then tied it with the other supplies on the ugliest mule Libby had ever seen.

"Is he the best you could find?"

"He's a she. Her name's Charity. The owner bought her from a mule skinner named Ernest T. Potts who was anxious to leave these parts."

Libby swallowed hard. She considered telling Reno that Potts had been previously in her employ. Not wanting to dwell on the bizarre coincidence of how they'd ended up with the man's mule, she asked instead, "Where is your horse? I don't see it."

"In the next stall." He pointed to her left. "Yours is over there."

When Libby glanced in the direction he'd indicated, her confidence wavered. The dun-colored horse looked so very large.

"Do you like her?"

"Yes, she's very nice."

"She's the best you'll get, unless you want to part with more money."

"She appears sound of limb. So long as she's good-natured, that's more important, isn't it?"

"I suppose so." With a hint of laughter in his voice, he asked, "Do you judge men the same way as you do horses, Miss Chandler?"

Libby stared at his shoulders and noted he wore the same shirt as yesterday. "I beg your pardon?"

"I know you heard me."

Impossible man. "Yes, I do judge men the same, if you must know."

"Not very particular, are you?" He finished tying the bundles, turned, and finally took a good look at her. His mouth pulled into an unpleasant line. "What the hell are you wearing?"

Libby desperately wanted to retreat a step but purposely held her ground. "I'm dressed as you requested. I did, however, take the liberty of disguising my unseemly attire. I'll not have people stare at my . . . I'll not be made to appear loose."

"Where did you get that godawful dress?"

"I purchased it this morning."

"I asked you to wear pants."

"You didn't ask, Mr. McCord. You ordered."

The corners of his mouth lifted in a semblance of a smile. "An order you saw fit to disobey."

Libby heaved a fortifying breath. "I'm wearing the pants."

"Are you, indeed? I can't see them."

"Exactly." She didn't like the look in his eyes, a look hinting at mischief. "You'll have to accept my word."

"Show me."

"I most certainly will not!"

"Lady, either you show me or I'll see for myself."

Libby scooted backward, until she met the resistance of planked boards. She stuck out a hand. "Stay where you are or I'll scream."

He observed her through narrowed eyes. "Be reasonable. You act as if I'm asking to see your drawers."

When he started forward, Libby released a squeak.

He reached her then, a wicked grin playing over his mouth. "Go right ahead and scream, Miss Chandler. With or without your permission, I'm looking under your dress."

Chapter 4

He was too near, and grinning to boot.

Libby flattened her back tighter against the rough boards and felt a sharp edge dig into her spine. Reno McCord was just brash enough to do something scandalous.

He grabbed a fold of her skirt and would've pulled up her hem; but she bent over also and pressed both of her hands over the material, holding it in place.

His face inches from hers, he inclined his head. "Have something to hide, Miss Chandler?"

"If you were any kind of gentleman, you wouldn't think of lifting a woman's dress."

"Who said I was a gentleman?"

Her breath turning shallow from his suggestive tone, she remarked, "Certainly not I."

"I mean to know for sure," he said as he tugged her skirt. "You might as well let me see."

As close as they were, his eyes looked a deeper shade of blue. The most peculiar sensation swept through her. Something about this man made her mind, body, and emotions jolt to life. The thought so disturbed her, she straightened abruptly. And lost control of the moment. Her brash employee jerked her skirt to her knees.

"So . . . you were telling the truth."

"How dare you!" Libby leaned down and snatched the material from his hand, knocking her forehead against his nose in her haste. Pain splintered through her head but his bellow far surpassed her moan.

He spun around in a circle, his fingers clamped over his injury. "Dammit! Lady, my nose was just getting back to normal size."

"I . . . I'm sorry," she stammered before she remembered the fight he was in recently. "A little foresight on your part would have prevented your injury."

Several colorful oaths floated to her.

"You shouldn't have behaved so coarsely, Mr. McCord."

As he touched one finger to his nose, he shot her a wounded glare. "Well, my nose isn't bleeding. I guess you haven't broken it."

"You're fortunate, indeed," she said. "In the future, however, I insist you behave decently."

"We're not going to have a future if you keep giving me orders." His mouth slanted in an unfriendly line. "I knew it was a mistake to bring you along."

Libby heaved a deep breath to calm herself. She shouldn't purposely antagonize him, she thought. An unpredictable man like Reno McCord could change his mind and leave her behind. Unfortunately, she wasn't feeling wise at the moment. "You, Mr. McCord, caused your own injury. You have the manners of a jackass."

His mouth quirked up on one side.

Her throat went dry. Determined not to allow him to intimidate her, she stretched to her full height.

"You aren't paying me to have manners, Miss Chandler. You're paying me to find your intended."

"Nevertheless," she spouted, "you *are* in my employ."

He aimed her a lopsided grin. "And you've put yourself in my care. I'm guarding you against harm no matter what it takes."

Had she made a mistake entrusting her welfare into his hands? He was rash, and forward, and he set her stomach on edge. If he had no compunction about lifting her dress within sight and hearing distance of others, what might she expect when they were alone in the wilderness?

She'd already given him a large amount of money, committing herself. The sheriff had recommended him, though he had admitted McCord overindulged upon occasion. There was no way she could change her mind at this late date. She needed McCord.

But until he fulfilled his end of their bargain, she meant to keep an eye on him and her money!

"You'll trip over that skirt," he grumbled as he fished a piece of paper from his shirt pocket.

Libby raised her chin. "I've been walking in dresses all my life, Mr. McCord."

He raised a dark brow at her. "Lady—" Cutting off the remainder of his remark, he handed the paper to her.

"What's this?"

"The bill for the supplies. I bought the whiskey, too."

A rise of panic clogged Libby's throat. Without looking at the amount, she forced a smile and tucked the bill into her bodice.

He watched her silently, his gaze expectant. After a moment, he said, "I think we should settle up now."

"I haven't any money with me. It's in the bank."

"You want me to wait, is that it?"

Libby steadied her vision on his black belt. "Are there stores where we're going?"

"None we're visiting."

"Did you buy everything we'll need?"

"And then some."

"And you intend to use half of what you bought?"

"What are you getting at?"

"Nothing. I was just speculating."

"Now, listen, lady, you're financing this expedition. You can't expect me to—"

"Well, then," she said as she raised her head. "You might as well wait until we return. The money will be safer in the bank."

He stared at her for a long moment. "You're not trying to trick me, are you?"

"Positively not." She wasn't trying to trick him, merely to gain some time, she thought. When they returned to Denver, she would simply persuade him to share their expenses. If he refused, she'd have no choice but to reimburse him for what he'd spent. Hoping to take his mind from the matter, she asked, "Are your things in order? We should leave soon, before the day's totally gone."

Mischief twinkled in his eyes as he clicked his heels together. Next, he executed a smart salute. "In order and at your service, ma'am."

Though tempted to laugh, she thought it best not to encourage his wont to taunt her. No one had ever teased her before, and if she wasn't careful, she might come to like this man too much. Not only was he brash, he was the most forceful man she'd ever met. He could easily overwhelm her. A man like him probably didn't know how to treat a good woman decently.

She watched him recheck the knots holding the rope secure around the mule's belly. He wore a gunbelt low on his right hip today. Having heard stories of gunmen doing the same, alarm shot through her. He might be dangerous. Sheriff Cook had also said that Reno McCord had been an army scout. Naturally, a soldier would be proficient in the use of firearms.

He led Charity out of the stall, then took the mule and the two horses through open double doors in the rear of the livery. "Come along, Miss Chandler."

Libby blinked and hurried after him. The moment she'd been dreading had arrived. She'd seen men mount horses her entire life. Assuring herself that mounting couldn't be any more difficult than climbing into a carriage, she walked right up to the horse Reno had purchased for her. While the horse had looked large in the livery, its immense size intimidated her outside.

A muttered curse stole her attention. She glanced at Reno and found him standing between his horse and the mule. Charity, having taken exception to the horse's presence, stepped nervously, jostling Reno. In self-defense, Reno braced his back against his horse. Lines of strain wrinkled his forehead as he shoved the mule to no avail.

Libby bit her bottom lip to ward off a grin.

Reno muttered more loudly and slapped Charity's rump. His chastisement, however, had dire results. Charity swung around and nipped his shoulder. The horse neighed loudly and sidestepped also. Squeezed against the jittery mule, Reno cursed loudly.

As much as Libby wanted to see how he handled the situation, she needed those few minutes to mount without him seeing her. She hurried to her horse, grabbed hold of the saddle horn and stuck her boot into the stirrup.

"Damn animal has a mind of her own" came an annoyed voice from behind. "I have an inkling of why she was such a bargain."

Libby's spirits sagged. Reno had mastered the contrary mule far too easily. Thinking quickly, she asked, "Would you kindly lend me a hand?"

He appeared next to her. "Sure thing. But I'm surprised you'd ask."

Feeling silly standing with one boot stuck in the stirrup and her arms stretched up, Libby lowered her foot to the ground. "Women have been known to ask men for their assistance, Mr. McCord."

"Yes, they have. You, however, strike me as a self-reliant woman. I would've bet my last penny you'd prefer to do things for yourself."

Unsettled by his insight, she said, "I've managed on my own for years, but women usually allow a man to assist them in order to pamper the masculine ego."

"Do I look like I need my ego pampered?"

Reno McCord should've been born with a wart on his nose, she thought. "You certainly do not. I imagine your ego's as large as they come."

He aimed a broad smile at her.

His startling blue eyes roamed her face, making Libby extremely uncomfortable. He should have *two* warts on his nose. She stuck her boot back into the stirrup. "As you pointed out, I'm paying you for your services. Help me, please."

Reno moved behind her. "Should I ask why?"

"You should not."

"Lady, you're footing the bills. Anything you want, you just ask."

Libby nearly choked. If she'd sensed an insinuation in his tone, it could only have been her imagination. An imagination which needed scolding. Anticipation flitted a prickly sensation over her skin. In the restaurant, when he'd held her hand and rubbed his thumb over her knuckles, tingles had swept up her arm. She'd never experienced such a disturbing reaction to someone's touch. She hadn't wanted to draw back her hand, to relinquish the pleasant sensation. When his large hands spanned her waist, Libby froze.

"Up you go," he said.

Libby straightened her leg and began to rise. At that exact second, Reno leaned his body against her and to her horror, her knee buckled, causing her backside to slump against his chest. Hearing his chuckle, she attempted to force strength into her leg. Unfortunately, he moved faster. His hands left her waist and cupped her backside! Libby gasped at the familiar move.

"Swing your leg over."

Too shocked to do anything else, she sent her leg over the horse and plopped down on the saddle.

"Lady, any time you want to pamper my ego, I'll be happy to oblige."

Blood rushed to Libby's face. She leaned forward to seize the reins but he grabbed them before giving them over to her. "Mr. McCord! You . . . you put your hands—" Seeing the amusement dancing in his eyes, she faced forward. "You did that on purpose!"

"Did what, Miss Chandler?"

"You know very well what I meant," she shot back.

"You asked for my help, and I obliged."

Furious that he'd make light of her embarrassment, she turned and glared at him.

"Why, Miss Chandler, you're blushing."

Dear Lord, she wanted to strangle him. The heat stinging her cheeks confirmed he'd been right. "You are most certainly deluded. I'm not blushing. I am justifiably outraged because I've had the misfortune to hire an ill-mannered, rude, insulting—"

"Ruffian?"

"It's not the word I had in mind, but it will do. It won't work, you know. Nothing you say or do will change my mind. If you think to frighten me into staying behind, you've sorely underestimated me."

He shook his head. "Lady, you sure don't know how to laugh, do you?"

She had definitely made a mistake in hiring him. If only she could turn back time. She watched him deftly mount and set out at a sedate pace, leading the mule.

A fresh wave of panic assailed her. He was an expert horseman, whereas she had no actual experience. He looked so at home in the saddle, her confidence dipped. She'd thought it would be easy to pretend she knew how to ride. How did one make a horse go?

She'd just decided to forgo her pride and call after Reno when her horse abruptly trotted after him. Libby wrapped her fingers around the pommel in a death grip. Thank goodness he was riding in front of her. At least she needn't worry he'd witness the sorry sight she must have made. Her backside left the saddle with every clop of the horse's hooves, bobbing her up and down. She felt sure her teeth would be loosened before an hour had passed.

Shortly, after they'd passed the outskirts of town, Reno headed for a set of railroad tracks a sight narrower than what she'd assumed were standard. Although she questioned his destination, she kept silent. Soon, she spotted a smaller locomotive, hitched to smaller cars than was customary.

Reno halted alongside a front car and dismounted. After he'd spoken with the portly engineer, he returned to her.

"You might've mentioned we'd be taking a train," she said.

"I made the decision this morning."

"*You* made the decision? May I remind you that I—"

Not allowing her to finish, he said, "I figured it would be easier on you to travel part way by rail. Do you have an objection?"

Unable to dispute his logic, Libby begrudgingly shook her head. When he held his arms out to her, she felt a rush of panic. Each time he touched her, no matter how innocent his motive, her insides twisted.

A slight smile hovered on his mouth. "Pamper my ego. Allow me to help you down."

Hesitantly, she leaned toward him. If he intended to test her in some way, *her* ego craved winning, but her thoughts of winning a battle with him fled her mind. His hands spanned her waist as he lifted her from the saddle. Her breath rushed out as he brought her close against him. Her heart jolted before it settled into an irregular rhythm.

"I'm not dressed for traveling in public," she stammered to hide the distress brought about by his nearness.

"You sure as hell aren't." He stood her on her feet. "There's not much you can do about your . . ." A grim set to his mouth, he looked her over. "Clothes now."

"We agree on one thing, at least," she said softly.

Since, for once, he seemed content not to taunt her, she swept off the wide-brimmed hat and checked to be sure her hair had remained in a neat roll. He was a man. Naturally he wouldn't understand her concern about men gawking at her body, but at least he'd been thinking of her comfort during their ride, if not when he'd helped her to mount and dismount. How could he have guessed he possessed some unholy power over her senses?

A loud neigh stole Reno's attention. "We have dissension within the ranks." He started to walk away. "That damn mule will be the death of me."

"Where are you going?"

He shot her a glance over his shoulder. "I think it's better if I ride in back with the animals. Otherwise, disaster might strike sooner than I expect."

Libby watched him stride away with purpose in his step. The engineer climbed into the front, leaving Libby on her own. She paused at the step to the car in front of her. One peek down the way convinced her Reno had been right to stay with the animals. Charity kicked out with one foot, barely missing the leg of Reno's horse. The horse neighed and backed away. To Libby's amazement, Reno brought his company under control within minutes.

The obstinate mule, however, attempted to nip his shoulder again. He slapped Charity's backside and, finally, managed to restore order.

Libby wore a grin as she boarded the car. Reno McCord deserved every ounce of resistance he received. She would've preferred to see how he managed to herd his charges onto the train, but she wanted to settle herself before the train got rolling.

The only woman among several men, she felt conspicuous in her silly attire, so she took a seat in the rear of the car. She guessed that the other passengers were miners. Gazing out the window, she noticed for the first time that the range of mountains in the distance appeared much closer than she supposed they were.

After an hour had passed, Libby felt weary. The lighter-looking locomotive and small cars certainly didn't ride the same as the larger trains to which she was accustomed. As they passed over obviously uneven joints, the entire train swayed sideways and lurched forward and back, making a clickety-clack sound. Her stomach roiled from the jerky movements. Riding a horse couldn't be any more tiresome than this.

By the time the train squealed to a halt, Libby felt positive the hardy breakfast she'd eaten hours earlier had been jostled up to her throat. Although uncertain whether Mr. McCord meant her to disembark here, she made the decision for him. She'd rather walk than be shaken silly another minute.

Relieved to find he'd left the train also, Libby twisted her upper body to realign her bones. The locomotive belched smoke, startling her and, apparently, McCord's three charges. Dissension erupted within his ranks again. Libby attempted to hide her amusement by holding a hand over her mouth. Reno, his horse, and Charity stomped in a circle. Her horse seemed the only one gifted with manners while the other three released their protests loudly.

Steam spewed from the smokestack, discharging soot and sparks in every direction. The train began to move, slowly at first, then with increased speed.

Reno snatched off his hat and slapped it against his leg. Charity broke free. She kicked out her back feet while her rump shot into the air. Disorder turned into chaos. The mule brayed and went one way, Reno's horse the other. When Reno threw his hat on the ground and cursed vehemently, it took extreme effort for Libby not to laugh aloud.

One short whistle brought Reno's horse trotting obediently back. Charity, however, wasn't so disciplined. Unfazed by a series of threats given by Reno, she headed straight for Libby. Libby didn't move until the mule came close. Then she grabbed the animal's lead rope.

"Careful, Miss Chandler. She's got a pea for a brain."

She petted Charity's head. The mule offered no protest, so Libby grew confident enough to speak softly. After a few minutes of the soothing ministrations, the mule offered no objection to being led, until they arrived beside Reno. Strong resistance on the rope confirmed Libby's suspicions.

"She doesn't like you, Mr. McCord," she whispered.

"Tell me something I don't already know."

Scratching between Charity's ears, Libby continued to whisper. "Perhaps it's your rough handling to which she takes exception. Have you no experience with women, Mr. McCord?"

"I've never had any complaints."

His gruff tone amused Libby. "I find that odd considering—" She saw the scowl tugging at his mouth. "What I mean is, most women appreciate being treated kindly. I suppose a mule is no different."

"Lady, if you think I'm sweet-talking a lousy, stubborn mule, you can just think again."

"Don't raise your voice . . . please. Unless you want this *dissension within your ranks* to continue, I'd advise you to do just that. Besides, I think Charity's former owner probably handled her roughly. See the marks on her sides. Why, I believe he might've beaten her with a stick." Libby heard a muffled response. "Did you just agree with me, Mr. McCord?"

He mumbled something more before he narrowed his eyes on her. "I made a bargain for one contrary female, not two. Do you expect me to sweet-talk you, too? Or do you bite as well?"

Subjected to his bold inspection, hot color flooded Libby's cheeks. No man had ever looked at her quite the same. Disconcerted by the warmth trickling through her veins, words escaped her.

"I've never needed to sweet-talk a woman before, but I'm sure I could have you purring like a kitten this side of ten minutes. Would sweet words sweeten your manner, Miss Chandler?"

Momentarily speechless from his boastful claim, Libby stared at him. He deserved a cluster of warts on his nose! He was intentionally trying to rile her, and doing a good job of it. But at least her ability to form words had returned. "Kittens do have sharp claws, Mr. McCord. Think twice before you make such a foolhardy wager."

With both horses in tow, Reno cautiously approached her. Libby gritted her teeth and looked at the small, desolate-looking train station some distance away.

"You blush beautifully, Miss Chandler."

She swung her gaze back to Reno. Several retorts sprang to her mind but she quickly dismissed them. He wanted her to lose her temper and fight with him. "Shouldn't we be on our way?"

"Yes, we should. Before we do, there's something we should get straight."

The speculation she read in his eyes gave away his thoughts. "The dress remains!"

"You've made your point, lady. We both know you hold the reins. If you knew how dowdy you look with layers of clothing all bunched up around your—"

Libby held up a hand to stop him from saying

more. "You certainly have a way with words, Mr. McCord. I see how easily you must charm women."

After he'd stared at her for a long minute, he grinned. "I'll eventually win this battle. You might as well surrender now."

Libby set her mouth in an obstinate line.

He leaned close, his voice lowering. "Enjoy your little victory, because it's only temporary. But consider this. Push me too far, Miss Chandler, and I just might remove the damn dress, myself."

Her heart lurched. She had no doubt he meant his threat.

Slowly, he took charge of Charity's rope. His eyes trained on Libby, he lowered his voice again, saying to the mule, "Come on, precious."

Relieved he'd turned his attention elsewhere, Libby breathed a sigh of relief. "Charity isn't putting up a fuss now, is she? It's not what you say, rather the tone in which you say it."

He aimed Libby a patient look. "Lady, I know a mule can't understand what I'm saying."

"Did I say otherwise?"

"You implied it." He ran a hand down the mule's nose. "You aren't going to give me any more trouble, now, are you, precious? You've all the beauty of a horned lizard, and the temperament of a hornet, but I need you to tote packs."

"That wasn't very nice. Charity can't help being homely."

"Charity, darlin'," he spouted in a deeply sensuous voice, "you've stolen my heart. Say you'll be mine, and I'll be your slave to eternity."

"Very funny."

Despite Reno's silly words, the mule now allowed him to lead her. Libby had to admit, his low, beguiling tone might have had the same effect on any female, even, to her chagrin, her. Something about this troublesome man stirred her emotions.

Libby frowned as he walked her horse to her side. Either she had to learn how to mount without assistance or suffer his disturbing touch repeatedly. Determined to alleviate the problem once and for all, she grabbed the pommel. She stuck her foot in the stirrup and would've swung up by herself but it seemed Reno was intent on giving her a boost.

"Will you . . . kindly not put your hands on my . . . person."

He grinned. "But my ego."

Was Reno McCord genuinely dense, or just possessed of a peculiar sense of humor? The twinkle in his eyes told her the last at least must be true. But she'd forgotten to include "brash" on her list of faults. Before she could say anything more, they were on their way.

To take her mind from her troubles, Libby studied the scenery. Colorado differed vastly from Pennsylvania. Not only was the soil different, a gray or pale brown color, it appeared sandy, gravelly, and infertile. The grass, what there was of it, wasn't lush and green. Short and dead-looking, it grew in tufts and patches. Behind them, precipitous bluffs broke undulating plains. Ahead, the land was hilly with sharp ridges. They were traveling upward, beyond the hills, toward magnificent mountains which seemed to jut almost to the sky.

Discomfort slowly intruded upon her appreciation of the landscape. Within an hour, the tender insides of her thighs were chafed. Three hours later, Libby was in extreme misery. Wearing two sets of clothes wore a person down, she discovered. And, despite the cool weather, she had grown very warm.

She groaned. Reno's imposing bearing frustrated her. She felt like a wilted flower, while he looked as if he'd just started out!

She wondered if the man ever tired. Or got thirsty. Or hungry. Her throat felt thick, her mouth dry as dust. She found it amazing she could crave a drink so badly with nature's call so insistent. Did the blasted man have hollow legs as well?

She endured another fifteen minutes before she decided to forego her pride. It was ridiculous to suffer unnecessarily. If he refused to allow her time to see to her physical needs, she could always fire him.

"Reno," she called, but her voice came out barely more than a squeak. "Mr. McCord, kindly stop this minute."

Much to her surprise, he obeyed. He quickly came beside her and dismounted. A knowing smile touched his mouth. "Thought you'd never ask."

"You were waiting for me to ask?"

"I can wait all day, but I figured a woman would have to go—"

"Please . . . don't say any more." Her cheeks felt hot under his observant gaze. She hadn't considered the ramifications of traveling with a man. With *him*. It would be difficult to tend to private functions. "How much farther are we going today?"

He examined the surrounding area, which happened to be a moderately forested glen at the base of a hill. After he'd listened intently, he announced, "There's a stream somewhere near. We might as well set up camp. It'll give me a chance to decide which way we should go in the morning."

Unease channeled through her. "Don't you know?"

"I haven't been in this area for a very long time."

"But you were a scout for the army. I presumed you knew where you were going."

"Lady, I was a scout, not the Almighty."

"Did you speak with Mr. Byers, like I suggested?"

"I didn't have time."

Libby rolled her eyes. It was just like a man to head off blindly into territory about which he wasn't familiar. Sheriff Cook had expressed the utmost confidence in Reno's abilities. Thirst, hunger, and nature's call seeming more urgent, she pushed the matter to the back of her mind.

Her fate was in Reno McCord's hands. Lord help her.

Chapter 5

She looked worn out, Reno thought, as he stepped forward to help his employer from her horse. He had assumed she'd ask him to stop long before this.

"I believe I can get down myself," she said quickly.

He crossed his arms on his chest. She was the stubbornest woman he'd ever met. "You'll break your damn fool neck."

Her chin lifted a degree higher.

"Be sensible, Miss Chandler. You're paying me well. You might as well get your money's worth."

"Before our journey's over, I imagine you'll have earned every penny, Mr. McCord."

She was right about that. They'd barely begun their travel. Already he regretted his brief moment of compassion for her. "Have it your way. I'll be here to catch you when you fall."

"I'm entirely able to get down without injuring myself," she returned.

Reno conceded the point and watched her swing her leg over the saddle, then slide wearily to her feet. He caught her a second after her legs buckled. With a supporting arm around her waist, he lifted her upright. "It happens with an inexperienced rider. You'll get used to straddling your saddle in a day or two."

"You knew?"

"Lady, you've been bobbing like an apple in a tub of water." He watched her brows furrow together before he stated, "You lied to me."

Her eyes popped open wide.

"Do you have any more secrets I should know?"

"You wouldn't have taken me along otherwise." She walked several steps, testing her legs. "I need to see to a private matter. Which direction do you suggest I take?"

Reno frowned at the ease with which she'd just maneuvered their conversation. He pointed west. "Go that way and yell if you need me. You might as well take off your dress while you're at it."

With her fists on her hips, her eyes met his. "The dress stays."

"I warned you not to push me too far, Miss Chandler," he threatened.

Suddenly, she wiggled. Her cheeks turning pink, she hurried away as fast as her oversize boots allowed.

Reno grinned. Her movements were awkward in her haste, no doubt caused by layers of clothing. When she reached a cluster of pine trees, her skirt caught on something he could barely make out. Impatiently, she tugged until she freed herself, then disappeared from his sight.

Twenty minutes later she returned. He shook his head as he counted the number of times she stumbled over rocks or uneven ground. He noticed a streak of dirt on her cheek and a rip in her dress. Miss Libby Chandler didn't look anything at all like the fashionably dressed woman he'd met in Denver.

She dashed a hand across her forehead, leaving another smudge of dirt. "I didn't mean to be gone so long."

"Did you hurt yourself when you fell?"

"How did you—? There was this dip in the land, and I lost my footing."

"Did you hurt yourself?"

Her mouth quirked up on one side. "Just my dignity."

He spared a smile. "I told you—"

"I didn't trip on my dress," she fired back before he could finish his sentence.

"Well, you will!" He considered her red cheeks. Hell, she looked hotter than a pancake on a griddle. "You've got on too many clothes. Tonight, when the temperature drops, you'll feel it more."

"You're most likely right. You're used to being out in the elements."

"But?"

She glanced away. "Mr. McCord, surely you know my reasons for dressing this way."

"The name's Reno, and, yes, I guess I do. Lady, I've seen a woman's legs before, if that's what worrying you. If you're afraid I'll stare at your ass, you—"

"Mr. McCord!" Her cheeks flamed bright crimson. "It's unseemly to mention a woman's . . . bodily parts. And it's particularly unseemly to refer to . . . Oh! You are too forward by far."

Reno sighed. It was going to be a damn long

journey if she didn't learn to bend a little. "Hell, it's just the two of us."

Her eyes drifted closed before she caught herself.

"Lady," he said more gently, "I know I don't have many social graces. I've spent most of my life around men." Seeing her eyelids flicker again, he slipped an arm around her waist. He led her to a smooth area under a tree. "You're not listening to me. Sit here while I make you a place to rest."

"I'm not tired. If you want to travel farther, I can keep up."

"Sit," he said more firmly. He nodded when, for once, she obeyed him. He brought her a canteen and waited while she drank her fill. "Want something to eat now?"

She yawned. "I was so hungry. Now, I think I will take your advice and rest awhile."

He unpacked the mule and found blankets, and the coat he'd purchased for her in case the temperature at night dropped too low. When he returned to her, he made a bed out of the blankets. "You should find this more obliging. I put pine needles underneath."

She scooted herself to the makeshift bed. "Thank you, Mr. McCord."

Since they would be spending time alone together, he'd hoped she would relax a bit. If he'd known she could be so hardheaded, he wouldn't have agreed to bring her along. "You don't have to thank me every time I do something for you."

"I know," she said, her voice fading with her weariness. "It's kind of you to see to my comfort this way."

He squatted beside her and tucked the coat

under her head. While he tossed a blanket over her, he said, "Maybe I'm not being kind, just practical. A man would be a fool if he risked his employer's health."

"What are you saying?"

"Only that you said you're wealthy. I can't very well let you take sick now, can I? I might not get the rest of the money you owe me."

She released an unladylike yawn. "You're teasing me, of course."

The laugh he'd been holding back escaped. "You think you know me?"

Libby nodded.

Reno slipped off her hat and set it aside. Several of her pins had worked loose and a thick coil of hair fell onto the blanket above her head. The sun struck the coil, reflecting red. Satisfied she'd drifted to sleep, he weakened to an impulse and ran his fingers through the coil. The strands felt as soft as they looked. He marveled that the hair he'd thought brown was actually a deep, radiant auburn.

He wondered what other surprises awaited him.

She had proven she was frugal, yet she'd given her new hat to Violet. She was rare, he thought; a woman who judged men the same way she did horses. A woman with enough backbone to stand up to him and bravely flout his orders.

She was a challenge in many ways. And obstinate as hell. If he accomplished nothing else on this trip he meant to have her out of the shapeless dress she'd chosen to wear. His concern was foremost for her safety, but partly because she'd turned his order into a contest of sorts.

He loved nothing better than winning a game, either of wills or chance.

His nose still ached. Remembering her outrage when he'd lifted her skirt, he smiled. Fire and determination dwelled within her, and maybe passion, too, though he had no doubt she was a good woman. Sheriff Cook had said she was *too good* for him. It was a truth even *he* couldn't dispute.

Having never given a thought to his future, he lived each day as it came. He cringed at the idea of being tied down. Even if the notion had occurred to him, he had nothing to offer a woman. When a woman got too attached to him, he moved on to another town, and another woman. That was the way he liked it!

Dismayed with the direction of his thoughts, he took care of the animals, paying particular attention to the mule. He spoke softly to her and begrudgingly admitted his employer had been right. The poor creature had been mistreated by her former owner. After he'd gathered sticks to make a fire, he explored the area and found the stream he'd heard earlier. By the time Libby stirred, he'd done all his chores.

It was strange, he thought. He'd always cherished his time alone on the trail. Though he'd never wanted for female company, his relationships with women had been based on sexual needs and just plain having a good time. As he watched Libby slowly sit upright and stretch her limbs, an unsettling thought came to him.

As much as her resistance to his orders annoyed him, he'd thoroughly enjoyed taunting her. Not only did he intend to win their battle of wills, he might actually teach her how to have a little fun as well.

Every muscle in Libby's body hurt.

She crawled to her knees and sat back on her heels. Finding that the boots made an uncomfortable seat, she forced herself to stand. She didn't know how she'd walk even the short distance to the campfire, where Reno sat with his legs crossed and his elbows propped on his knees. The steam rising from the tin cup he held lured her to make the effort.

The insides of her thighs felt so chafed, she dreaded the thought of riding a horse again. Because her injury was located in a private area, she vowed to suffer the discomfort silently or die in the attempt.

Thank goodness he sat sideways, content just staring into the flames. She shuffled to the fire and quickly sat near him.

"Feeling better?" he asked.

"Much." She spotted an iron pot suspended from a roughly hewn pole, a covered skillet set off to one side, and a dented enameled coffeepot half in the fire. "Why, Mr. McCord, you've made supper."

"Did you think I intended to starve you, Miss Chandler?"

Responding to the challenge in his voice, she returned, "Actually, yes. Were I to grow weak from lack of nourishment, you could say or do anything."

"If that's what it takes to make you listen to reason, I might try starving you tomorrow. After the aggravation you've put me through today, though, I'm hungry enough to eat a skunk."

"Most likely a relative," she muttered as she searched for another plate. "I'm hungry, also."

"It's just beans and corn bread, so I hope you aren't too disappointed."

His lack of emotion hinted he'd overheard her uncharitable remark. Surely he wouldn't retaliate.

"And this," he said as he reached for the coffeepot.

She watched him grab the handle. Then, muttering a foul oath, he seized a well-singed hot pad nearby. He filled another tin cup and held it out to her. "It's hot."

"Quite hot, Mr. McCord. Hot enough to burn your fingers if you're careless." Using the hem of her dress to cushion the cup, she sipped the brew. Then, amazed by her discovery, she looked at him. "Tea?"

He rammed a stick into the charred wood he'd used for fuel. "I prefer coffee, myself, but I suspected you'd like tea better." Finished stoking the fire, he stuck two fingers into his mouth and sucked loudly. Afterward, he returned her scrutiny. "Sorry to disappoint you, Miss Chandler. Skunks heal quickly."

Libby choked and nearly dropped her cup.

He filled her a plate of food and sat silently while she devoured every bite. After she'd finished, he put her empty tin plate with his, then he picked up his cup. He gulped down the remainder of his drink.

She felt uncomfortable, at a loss for words. These circumstances were foreign to her. She'd never been alone with a man she barely knew with no one within calling distance. She looked at him again and watched the firelight reflect in his eyes. The gold sparks fascinated her. Like twinkling stars against a midnight blue sky, she thought.

She found his profile handsome. Despite a slight swelling, his nose fell in a straight line. An image of Clarence Trout popped into her mind. He and Reno were direct opposites.

Of medium height with brown hair, Clarence's features were unremarkable. A moment's sadness plagued her. Going off to search for gold had probably been his sole daring deed in a docile, orderly life. Quiet-spoken and extremely mild-mannered, he'd run the general store efficiently. He'd gained the admiration and friendship of everyone in town. Always willing to help anyone in time of trouble, Clarence had even refused to accept payment for goods if he'd thought the person in dire need.

Clarence had held her hand several times when no one had been looking; but he'd never kissed her, except the one time after a dance when he'd given her a peck on her cheek. He was a nice, hardworking, dependable man.

Now, he was most likely dead.

Libby's hand shook the cup and hot tea splashed on her bodice. She sucked in a horrified gasp.

Reno reacted swiftly. He grabbed a rag, the worn pad he'd used for his coffeepot and slapped it over the wet area on her dress. "Did the tea burn your skin?"

It burned the center of her chest, right above her breasts. Still, having him touch her anywhere on her body started Libby's heart racing. He seemed truly concerned, so she said simply, "I don't think so."

"You jerked so suddenly. Did something bite you?"

The lights she'd noticed in his eyes drew her. He shouldn't be so handsome. It was indecent for a man to have so many captivating features that a woman lost her train of thought.

"Did something bite you? Or did you just want me to sit closer?"

Libby abruptly lifted his hand away. "How could you suggest such a thing, Mr. McCord? I had a distressing thought about Clarence. I most certainly have no desire for you to sit closer to me."

He twisted his hand over and caught her fingers. "You should be more careful, Miss Chandler. You might have been seriously burned."

Mortified by the tingles racing up her arm, she pulled back her hand. Minutes before she had been thinking of her lost fiancé. "Mr. McCord!"

"Did you love him?"

The blunt question so surprised her, her mouth fell open. "That, sir, is none of your business."

"I gather you didn't. I've found a woman who thinks she's in love has no qualms about saying so."

"And how, pray tell, could you know such a thing?"

"Because more than a few have fallen in love with me, that's how."

His blue eyes bored into hers, scattering her thoughts. She supposed it could be possible for a woman to fall under his spell. He was so very good-looking. She shouldn't answer his question, she mused. It *wasn't* his affair. Suspecting he'd pursue the subject if she kept silent, she said, "Of course I loved him. Clarence was the nicest, most dependable man I've ever known, except for my father. Why, no woman could have hoped to marry a more generous, steadfast man. He would've been a devoted husband and a wonderful father."

He reached for her hand again.

"Please!" Libby lurched away. "Please . . . don't touch me."

"Sorry. I just wanted to . . . hell . . . comfort you somehow, I guess. We might not find your intended, you know."

Libby regretted her hasty move. He might actually have been offering comfort. She considered telling him the reason she'd pulled back, but she couldn't bring herself to say the words. More likely than not, he was playing with her. It was uncanny that such excitement coursed through her veins when he touched her. Unsure which she believed of him, she said, "Forgive me for giving you the wrong idea."

"You weren't going to thank me again, were you?"

"Yes, I'm afraid I was. For so long I've held firm in my belief that Clarence would be found alive."

"And now?"

"Somehow I know it won't happen."

"I'll find him for you. I promise."

"I believe you will." She offered him a smile. "If I had hired you sooner, this would all be behind me."

"Do you have any family?" he asked.

His change of manner puzzled her. Apparently,

Reno McCord could behave nicely when he wanted. "My parents passed away seven years ago."

"How did they die?"

Libby swallowed against the painful memory. "Mama had a lung ailment. Papa died of a broken heart, I think." After some moments, she asked, "Have you lost someone, too?"

"My parents and little sister live in Kansas."

"Don't you miss them?"

He captured her hand, curling her fingers over his and pressing his lips above her knuckles. "I find it rather touching that you're concerned about me."

As she'd come to expect, a prickly sensation slid up her arm. She found it most disconcerting. Once again, she jerked her hand from his. "It's obvious I shouldn't let down my guard around *you*. Why, I do believe you'd take advantage of any situation if it's to your advantage."

His mouth curved up on one side. "You don't like me touching you. Or is it my imagination?"

"It's definitely not your imagination." When one of his eyebrows lifted, she clarified. "It's difficult to put into words."

"Try."

"You startle me occasionally by acting so forward. I'm not used to being . . . handled familiarly."

He broke into a smile. "Handled?" he repeated with obvious amusement.

"Touched by a . . . a man, Mr. McCord."

His smile turned into a wide grin.

Libby stiffened. "You're laughing at me."

"Not in the way you're thinking." His expression turned serious. "So . . . you feel things when I touch you."

Libby wiggled into a more comfortable position. "The ground is certainly hard, don't you think?"

"I hardly notice anymore. I've slept on it for a good portion of my life. Admit you feel things when I touch you, and that's why you draw back."

"My, you are the most conceited, persistent man I've ever known."

"Pesky as a fly."

He tilted his head forward and searched her eyes. "There can never be anything between us, Miss Chandler. I wouldn't know how to settle down even if I wanted to."

Libby's mouth would've dropped open if she hadn't caught herself in time. "Mr. McCord, you're entirely too presumptuous. Why, I could never have a romantic interest in you. You're in my employ, rash, forward, and I do not find you the least bit attractive."

"A man could take your protest to mean the opposite," he said with a bit too much confidence.

Judging by his spellbinding eyes and captivating smile, plus the conviction she'd heard in his voice, she knew he, at least, was confident in his appearance. She'd always accepted her plainness, but for once she wished for a more comely appearance. To what purpose, she didn't know. Reno McCord wasn't a possible candidate for a husband.

"Was your Mr. Trout handsome?"

"The most handsome man I've ever met," she lied.

"Did he make you feel quivery like when I touch you?"

Libby gasped at the suggestion. "Mr. McCord! It's hardly fitting to speak of him in such a manner. Poor Clarence—. And you most certainly do *not* make me quiver."

He gripped her arm. "Forgive me, then, for mentioning your intended." Amusement flickered in his eyes. "I'm touching you, Miss Chandler. Deny you just quivered."

She glanced down at his hand, then at his face. The sun had sunk behind the mountains. Firelight played over his features and danced in his eyes. How could she feel anything at all for him when the man she'd intended to marry had never sparked the slightest feeling in her?

Mesmerized by Reno's penetrating gaze, she mumbled, "You have a fanciful imagination, Mr. McCord." Gently, she withdrew her arm. Butterflies invaded her stomach. It wasn't just this man's touch that sent her emotions reeling. *He* unsettled her. "Perhaps you suffer from a nervous affliction which misleads you?"

"Touch me and find out."

Libby shook her head adamantly.

He laughed low in his throat. "Coward."

She was no match for him. He turned everything she said around, and she came out the fool. She pushed to her feet. He was in her employ, and behaving rashly. He was not a man a woman could trust with her heart. A handsome man like Reno McCord must've had plenty of experience with women . . . pretty women. What did he hope to gain by playing games with a homely old maid? He would probably flirt with a twig if he thought it would amuse him.

"What's wrong?"

"You honestly don't know, do you?" she asked as she brushed vigorously at the back of her dress.

She heard tin rattling and knew he must be collecting their supper utensils. Reno hadn't answered, which meant she might've gotten the better of him. The idea soothed her rattled emotions. "I'll be happy to help you clean up," she offered.

"Rest," he said, his tone curt. "Tomorrow will come before you know it."

She noticed that the temperature had dropped along with the sun. A shiver shook through her. She shouldn't have been so stubborn, she thought. The two layers of clothing now felt like gossamer in the night air. She started to walk back to the spot he'd prepared for her. By this time tomorrow the inside of her thighs would be thoroughly rubbed raw.

"Miss Chandler!"

Sure some terrible animal had wandered into their camp, Libby spun around.

"Catch!"

Without thinking, she stuck out her hands. A jar smacked against her palms. When she held the container toward the fire, she saw lettering on a faded label of sorts.

"I'm going down to the stream to wash out my pans. You have precisely fifteen minutes to grease up those raw spots on your—"

"Reno McCord! You mind your tongue."

"Yes, ma'am," he returned from a distance away. "Fifteen minutes. Get cracking, lady, unless you want to really pamper my ego. I'd be happy to put the salve on your thighs for you."

Libby froze. Fire licked her cheeks at the intimate image his words conjured. How had he known of her tender skin? Despite her discomfort earlier, she'd managed to walk as normally as possible. His threat looming in her mind, she whipped up her skirt. Unmindful of being in the open, she tugged down her britches.

He'd allowed her fifteen minutes. She vowed to tend her ailment in five.

Chapter 6

When Reno returned, he found Libby sitting by the fire with the jar of salve perched on her knee. He noticed her gaze shy from his, so after stowing his pans, he strolled toward her.

With her legs tucked beneath her, her skirt covering all but the tips of her boots, and her back ramrod straight, she stared at the fire. Without saying a word, he snatched the jar and returned it to his saddlebags.

As he moved Libby's makeshift bed closer to the fire, he felt her gaze, though only when she thought he wasn't aware of her scrutiny. He rolled out a blanket beside the others and stretched out on his back with his arms under his head.

"Surely you don't intend that we sleep so close."

He smiled at the distress in her voice. "I gave you the warmest spot, Miss Chandler."

"That's not what I meant." She fell silent and then said, "It's not decent."

Tempted to smile, Reno pretended to count stars. "What's not decent? Me?"

"Oh, no, I didn't mean you. Why I have every

trust in you. It's just that . . . an unmarried woman would never sleep so near a man."

"If you trust me, I don't see why you care. No one will know. Sleep beside me and I'll be between you and any wild beasts that might wander in too close."

Minutes passed before she spoke. "Wild beasts? What kind of beasts?"

Although it grew harder not to smile, he rambled off, "Bears, coyotes, snakes, maybe even a tiger or two."

She harrumphed. "You're trying to frighten me."

"Maybe." He turned so he could see her. "Maybe not."

She set her spine in a perfect line. "I believe I'll stay here for a while longer. I'm not sleepy now, because of my nap."

"Join me when you're ready."

He wasn't sure how long he waited for her to change her mind. Aware only of the crackling sounds of the fire, he drifted into a light sleep. A rustle in the trees pulled him fully awake. He decided the noise had been either a slight breeze or some small night creature. Libby, however, came to another conclusion. Immediately after she heaved a startled gasp, she scrambled to the bed he'd made her.

By cracking open one eye, he saw her lying on her back, a full two feet away. She was also shaking from the cold. "Come closer before you freeze to death."

"I'm fine, thank you. Please go back to sleep."

"The hell you are. Your teeth are making such a racket, rattling together, neither of us will get any sleep." When he received no response, he sighed. "I'm warm, Miss Chandler. Bet you've never been as warm as I can make you."

He smiled at her sharp intake of breath. Why did she have to be so stubborn about everything? He made no further attempt to persuade her for ten minutes. Afraid he'd find a corpse beside him in the morning if he didn't take matters into his own hands, he rolled onto his side. "I'm used to the cold and don't mind it, whereas you'll likely freeze to death."

"I didn't . . . think . . . you intended anything improper, Mr. McCord."

He shook his head. "You sure do tell a lot of lies, Miss Chandler."

She wiggled a foot closer. "There. I've moved near you. Will you kindly go to sleep and stop worrying about me?"

"Not likely." He flipped the coat out from under her head. When she rose up in protest, he tossed the coat over her, locked an arm over her waist and hauled her against him. "You leave me no choice. Be pigheaded as you want tomorrow. Tonight, I give the orders."

He expected a blistering tirade, or an argument of some sort. He received neither. Instead of considering himself lucky, he grew suspicious. Then, realizing she held herself rigid, he asked, "Who don't you trust? Me? Or yourself?"

She struggled against his hold. "I knew it was a trick! You only wanted me near so you could . . . why, my imagination can't begin to fathom what scandalous deeds you have on your mind."

Reno bit back a laugh. "Give me credit for *some*

intelligence, Miss Chandler." Her words to him about the mule flashed through his mind. He pulled her back down and snuggled close again. "When I have designs on your virtue, I'll let you know. For now, I only want to keep you warm. Now, admit you're warmer."

She nodded.

"You aren't afraid of me, are you?"

She shook her head.

"You feel so good," he whispered, meaning every word. For such an unfriendly woman, she was soft. "It's nice being close. I'm not going to charge you extra, either. Unless you want to pay me more. A warming fee of sorts."

"I'm already paying you too much, Mr. McCord. You'll not get another penny."

Reno smiled in the dark. At least he could count on her to respond with an amusing comeback.

Libby remained awake for a very long time but not from the cold. She was toasty warm. Much too warm. Warm in disturbing places. While she felt comforted being so close to Reno, and safe from harm, his presence brought her senses alive. Slowly, she eased to her side. But her action compounded her problem. He mumbled and came with her, his arm falling across her breasts.

Libby held her breath. She relaxed only after she heard his light snore. Then she slid his arm lower, around her waist. Her movement, however, roused him. With a soft moan, he bound his arm tighter around her.

Suddenly, his hand roamed higher and cupped her breast.

The most stimulating sensations flitted over her

entire body. His breath felt hot against the back of her neck. She didn't want to move ever again. It must be wicked to experience such pleasure when a man touched her, she mused. Sanity returned quickly and she chastised herself for the moment of weakness. She tugged his arm lower. Satisfied that his familiar move must've been an unconscious reflex, she relaxed.

Thank goodness she wore so many clothes she couldn't detect the actual outline of his body. Still feeling wonderfully alive, she listened to the regular sound of his breathing. It was a long time before she fell asleep.

She saw him through a haze, a man of medium height with thinning brown hair. He looked tired, his clothes covered with dust. As he walked from the doorway of a crude cabin, his boots dragged on hard-packed soil, and his shoulders sagged. He carried a torn, floppy hat. Behind him, fallen red rock littered the area. When he put on his hat, he looked up.

Another man with indistinct facial features appeared. She sensed hostility—and danger.

Words were spoken. The man seized a handful of Clarence's shirt, hauled him close, and a struggle began. Sunlight glinted off metal a second before a wicked-looking dagger plunged into Clarence's chest.

A bloodcurdling scream woke Libby. She bolted upright, rolling Reno over onto his back. The coat which had been covering her landed three feet away. It had been her own scream she'd heard.

"What the hell? What happened?"

Libby drew in several calming breaths in an attempt to still her wildly beating heart. When

Reno's arm came around her shoulders, she fell against him. "It . . . was . . . the dream."

She felt the tension leave his body. "God dammit, lady. You just robbed me of ten years of my life."

"I'm sorry."

"It's all right." He patted her arm. "Dreams can't hurt you."

"Well, they sure enough try. This one's so real, I swear I'm there."

He pulled her against his chest. "You're never there. You just have an active imagination. Your Mr. Trout—"

"Please . . . don't tell me he's alive and well, because I don't believe that anymore." She grabbed at his shirt, desperately trying to see his eyes in the dark. "The man in my dreams murdered Clarence. I just wish I could see his face. Why can I imagine Clarence so clearly and not his murderer?"

"Because you know Trout. You can't imagine someone you don't know."

"I suppose you're right." She rested her head on his chest and listened to the steady beat of his heart. He was sturdy and warm. She wouldn't have guessed he knew how to comfort a hysterical woman. "Thank you."

"There you go again, thanking me. What am I going to do with you, Miss Chandler?"

"I can't help being grateful. Normally, when I awake from the dream, I'm alone."

She wondered what he was thinking. Had he ever felt alone?

He bound her in his arms. "Dreams can't hurt you," he repeated gently.

The fire had nearly died out. Only a faint glow allowed her to see his face.

As he lowered his head, his voice sounded much deeper than before. "You're right. It is nice to have someone to hold on to when a nightmare awakens you." He angled his head again, his eyes a deep, rich blue, reminding her of a night sky.

She started to smile at him, but her smile faded with the realization that he was going to kiss her. Panic welled in her heart. She didn't want him to kiss her. He was totally unsuitable, a man who had probably kissed hundreds of women. But before she could react, his lips brushed hers. Her heart fluttered wildly when, a short time ago, she had been shivering with cold. Now, she thought of spring, of snow melting from the branches of a dormant tree under the rays of the sun.

His kiss was over in seconds yet she felt reborn. She felt like that tree, as if she'd been dormant all of her life instead of just for the winter. She felt . . .

Good Lord! She had let *him* kiss her, make her feel things she'd never before felt.

"I guess you want to slap me for taking liberties?"

His voice was low, sensuous, and slightly hesitant.

"No."

"No?"

Not about to admit she'd allowed something as simple as a kiss to rob her of her senses, she said, "You weren't taking liberties."

He chuckled. "Wasn't I?"

"Not you, Mr. McCord. I prefer to think you were just trying to make me feel better."

"Did I succeed?"

"Yes, thank—. Yes, you did." He might have argued with her, she thought. He might have lied, said he'd found her desirable, and had kissed her because he'd wanted to. Stunned by her musings, she pushed away from him. Casting about for a neutral subject, she stammered, "The fire has gone out."

"I hadn't noticed." He drew a finger over her cheek. "You're embarrassed."

"I most certainly am not."

"There's no need, you know." A pause followed. "I liked it, too."

Libby pushed farther away. "I'm sure I don't know what you're talking about."

He chuckled. "You know what I'm talking about," he said. "You liked that kiss as much as I did, though it wasn't my best."

Heat worked its way over her cheeks. "I beg your pardon."

"I can kiss better. I've had plenty of practice."

"Have you, indeed? One can only hope you didn't slap the woman's backside afterward."

His laugh boomed in the quiet night. Eventually, he regained his self-control. "Lady, you're as surprising as hell."

"There's nothing at all surprising about hell, Mr. McCord. It will be quite hot!"

"Now what's got you all fired up?"

"I'm not fired up," she said a bit too abruptly. He'd made her lose her temper, and she'd always managed to master her emotions.

"I only meant that, not only did you mention a body part, you lied, again. I thought it was forbidden to mention a woman's—"

"It just slipped out," she shot back before he could say the word. "And it wasn't a lie."

Although he refrained from laughing, she sensed his smile.

"My mother once told me it wasn't bad to manufacture a small fib in order to spare a person's feelings."

"A lie's a lie. So . . . you did tell an untruth. You liked my kiss."

Libby drew in a breath at his cunning. "I . . . I—"

"Liked it very much," he finished for her.

She refused to answer. The man was impossible. His tendency to tease her could easily have her admitting things better left unsaid.

He cupped her elbows with his hands and stood, bringing her with him.

"If I were to really kiss you, Miss Chandler." He put his arms around her and brought her closer. "I'd hold you like this."

"Please . . . don't."

"Then I'd tilt your chin so you were looking into my eyes."

Libby shoved her hands against his chest and forced a much-needed space between them. Instinct told her he wasn't serious, merely amusing himself. He'd already proven he possessed a peculiar sense of humor.

"A little reluctance on the woman's part adds to the allure. Or so I've been told. Women usually want me to kiss them."

"Do tell? In case you hadn't noticed, I don't want you to kiss me."

"I'd tell her how beautiful she was."

"Now who would be lying?"

"Damn, lady, you sure—"

"Don't want to continue this conversation." She lurched from his arms and whipped around. Choking on her words, she muttered, "You're obviously bored or you wouldn't be acting like this. You told me, yourself, you couldn't settle down. Well, I *am* the marrying kind. I want a husband, and babies. Lots of babies. So, you see, play of this nature is pointless."

Reno mouthed a curse and shoved his fingers through his hair. A ragged sigh tore from him. *Pointless.* About that she'd been right.

"It'll be light soon," he said. "I'll show you where the stream is so you can wash up. Then we better move out. You want your bag?"

"Yes."

He stoked the fire, after which he left her long enough to fetch her things and gather more wood. He ignored her while he set her bag nearby and pitched wood on the embers. He watched the flames, marveling that a few minutes ago the same had happened to him. With all the woman he'd kissed, he'd never once let his emotions get the best of him. There was much to be said for just pure physical gratification.

Libby Chandler scared the living daylights out of him.

This morning he made coffee. Strong coffee. He thought she'd protest, but she disappointed him. Why did she have to be so damn easy to get along with? Each time she sipped from the tin cup, she grimaced. Reno shook his head.

"Rousing coffee," she finally remarked. "I imagine it's good for one's soul." She met his gaze, her mouth briefly curving. "Sort of like a sharp jab of a pitchfork. Two jabs and you're fit as a fiddle and ready to run a mile."

He mastered a smile as he plopped bacon in a skillet. "I hope you're hungry. We won't eat again 'til supper."

"I know how to cook," she offered. "And I only burn my fingers every other time."

So . . . the lady had a sense of humor, after all. Although the discovery pleased him, he didn't feel in the mood for teasing banter. He shouldn't have let his compassion get the better of his common sense. Kissing her had been a mistake.

"The bacon's ready to turn."

Pulled from his musing, he grabbed the skillet's handle, dragged the pan out of the fire, and gave it a mighty jerk. The bacon flipped before it smacked back down, sending grease flying. The fire snapped and leapt higher for several seconds.

"That was impressive," she said. "I wouldn't dare attempt such a maneuver for fear I'd make a mess and send my house up in flames."

Naturally, she owned a house. She was wealthy. He owned nothing but his horse, gun, and a meager assortment of clothing. The only money he had was what she was paying him. And he couldn't wait to spend it.

Libby ate her meal in silence. Reno seemed withdrawn, determined not to converse with her. But it was just as well, she thought. She didn't want to chance a repeat of last night.

Making sure he was looking in the other direction, she ran her tongue over her mouth. She still felt his kiss. She wondered what would have happened if she hadn't stopped him. Would he have actually kissed her in the manner which he'd been describing? She'd never even dreamed a man would ever hold her in his arms in such a manner. Or call her beautiful. She wasn't beautiful and never would be. She was an old maid.

"How old are you?" she asked without preamble. She noted the swift turn of his head. "If you don't mind my asking."

"How old are you?"

Libby groaned and hoped that, for once, her complexion remained pale. "I'm twenty-five."

"I have you by three years."

She released the breath she'd been holding. When he lifted a dark eyebrow at her, she could've bitten her tongue. Sensing he must have realized the reason for her rude inquiry, she busied herself by collecting their eating utensils.

"You look younger than twenty-five," he said. "Not as long in the tooth as you should."

A tin plate slipped from her hand. She refused to look at him. If she saw a smile on his face, she might be tempted to rap the plate over his head. "I'm not paying you to spout nonsense, Mr. McCord."

"Lady, if you'd loosen your corset, you might learn to laugh a little."

She shot him a glare. "Did you or did you not just call me long in the tooth?"

He sighed. "I was teasing you, Miss Chandler."

"Oh." Embarrassed, Libby watched his mouth twitch at the corners. He hadn't shaved today, and a dark growth of whiskers covered his lower face. "I guess I don't know how to have a good time, do I?"

He shook his head. "But, for a price, I'd be happy to teach you."

"I imagine you would," she retorted as she reached for the plate she'd dropped.

"I'll do that, Miss Chandler."

"Allow me to be useful."

"I didn't think people of wealth did for themselves. The ones I've seen have all had servants do their menial labor."

Libby sat back with a frown. "Not all."

"You're paying me. Let me do my job."

"I hired you as a guide, Mr. McCord, not as a cook and parlor maid."

He groaned.

"I shouldn't have used the word *maid,* should I?" she asked with a wry smile.

"I've been called a lot worse. In the future, however, I'd appreciate it if you at least referred to me as a butler, or even a stableboy. One favor, though, okay?"

"I have to know what it is before I agree."

"Stop calling me *mister.*"

"I'll try."

His eyes were so blue, they held her. She found the color mesmerizing. Never had she seen eyes so vivid, so captivating, or . . . Darn. She pushed to her feet, dusting off her skirt with her free hand. It was much safer to address him formally, to maintain some distance from him. She piled the utensils together.

"I'll wash them after you've bathed," he said.

"The sun has risen. If you'll show me the way to the stream, I'll manage."

"I'll take you. It's best to secure the area before engaging in any maneuvers."

Against her will, she smiled. "Yes, Captain."

He rose and picked up her satchel. "I made captain once."

"And?"

He shrugged and strode off, obviously expecting her to follow close behind him. "Another town, another saloon."

"And another mirror?"

"Close enough."

While she rushed to keep up with his long-legged stride, she asked, "Who paid the damages?"

He sent her a look over his shoulder. "My commanding officer. He wasn't nearly as amicable as you."

Clearly, he held no remorse over his loss of rank. His lack of ambition puzzled her. He appeared quite educated, a capable and intelligent man who she felt positive could handle any situation in which he found himself. She'd seen other unmotivated individuals with much less to offer. Shiftless drunks. Lawless men who stole for a living rather than earn their way. Men with no education who lived off others.

Reno McCord definitely was an enigma she meant to figure out.

Chapter 7

❧ ⌒⌒◯◯⌒⌒

The incline was steeper than Libby expected, but she saw the stream below. Morning sunlight glinted off the swiftly moving water, reminding her of sparkling silver. Catkins grew on both banks and in several places a well-placed tree afforded privacy. Wildflowers dotted the opposite bank.

"The water's very cold, so take that into consideration when you bathe," Reno said.

As he started down the bank, he held out a hand. Libby hesitated only a second before she accepted his help. She would have been confident of her ability to navigate a mere bank, but the oversize boots might cause her to take a spill. She vowed not to land on her backside in front of Reno McCord.

When they reached an area of soft grass, he dropped her bag but continued to hold her hand. "If you need any help, yell." His gaze leisurely roamed over her. "Leave off the dress."

"You're an exasperating man, Mr. McCord." Whenever he looked at her, strange sensations flitted over her skin and made her extremely uncomfortable. "You know perfectly well why I won't do as you ask." He looked her over again. Wiggling her hand free of his, she said. "I don't think you have my safety in mind at all."

"You're wrong. Why else would I want you to take off the dress?"

The slight curve of his handsome mouth mocked his innocent words. "Truth be known, Mr. McCord, you want to ogle my legs, that's why!"

"What's wrong with that?"

Libby forced calm into her voice. "You have the wrong woman."

"Your legs aren't malformed, are they?"

"No, thank goodness." Flustered by his uncanny ability to set her emotions on edge, she fired back, "It's not your affair if they were."

A slow grin stole across his mouth. "I look forward to seeing if my imagination is right, that your legs are long and shapely."

"Mr. McCord!" She sought the proper words to chastise his forward behavior and failed. "Please leave this instant."

He aimed her a smart salute and then started back the way they'd come. "I'll be just up there." He pointed up the incline. "Where I can keep an eye on the animals, and an ear out in case you need me."

"I'll be fine."

"Stay alert." He smiled at her over his shoulder. "Wouldn't want a grizzly eating you for breakfast."

Her eyes grew large, until she saw his smile drift into a mischievous grin. "If a bear comes, I'll tell him he shouldn't settle for a scrawny chicken when he can eat a prime steer just by climbing a hill."

As Reno disappeared over the rim, his laughter floated back to her.

Dear heavens. Everything about Reno McCord affected her in one way or another. Something must be wrong with her. She was beginning to find him amusing. If she wasn't careful . . . Libby shook her head to clear her mind. If she didn't make good use of the time, Reno might worry something had happened to her and come back down.

The water was indeed cold. The gooseflesh which rose on her skin prompted her to hurry. After she'd finished her bath, she frowned at the man's shirt she'd been wearing under the dress. Today, she wouldn't make the same mistake. She buttoned the dress over her clean camisole and felt much more comfortable. The pants were another matter. There was no way she was leaving them off. Her unconventional employee had already whipped up her skirt once.

Half of her hairpins were gone. Being especially mindful of the several she had left, she tucked them into a pocket in the pants. She shook out her hair and, tilting back her head, ran the brush through the tangles. Her missing pins were probably still in the makeshift bed. She dallied for several moments more, making sure she'd seen to every private function necessary to begin one's day. Since Reno had said he could go all day without stopping, she was determined to last as long as he.

Libby picked up her satchel and began the

arduous trek up the steep bank. The heavy bag made travel difficult, as it seemed to want to drag her back the way she'd come. She reached the top by sheer will and released her burden. Unfortunately, she'd chosen an unstable spot. Several small rocks tumbled free. The bag began to slide, slinging more rocks out from under it.

She dashed after her belongings, tripped on the hem of her dress, and lost her footing. A shriek tore from her lips as she pitched forward. Over and over, she rolled down the bank, until her hip collided with the large rock.

A cry and a commotion behind him startled Reno from his musings. He spun around and ran the short distance to the edge of the incline, where he spotted Libby lying near the water's edge, smack against a rock. With a muttered oath, he plunged down the embankment.

He dropped to his knees, another oath on his lips. Gently, he tipped Libby onto her back. Relief flooded him. She remained conscious and appeared unhurt. "Lady, you sure are one helluva lot of trouble."

With a grimace, she pushed up on her elbows. "I was testing your reflexes, Mr. McCord."

He grinned in appreciation of her humor. Her hair trailed behind her, drawing Reno's attention. Much to his surprise, he wanted to run his fingers through it. "Did I pass?"

She attempted to move but groaned instead. "You were much too slow. I figured . . . you'd . . . catch me in midair."

"Where does it hurt?"

Libby eased to her side, then abruptly rolled

onto the other. She laid a hand on her left hip. "Here. I must've bruised myself when I hit the rock."

"You tripped on that damn dress, didn't you?" Her reluctance to reply convinced him he'd guessed right. He grabbed a handful of her skirt and whipped it to her knees. "You'll have to let me have a look. You might've broken the skin."

She slapped at his hand. "You'll do nothing of the sort."

"Well, someone has to make sure your injury isn't serious."

"It's a bruise, that's all." She snatched the dress from his hand and shoved it back in place. "You are most certainly not looking at my bare . . . skin."

"You will allow me to check your injury, Miss Chandler, after which we'll see about removing your dress."

"What you're proposing is scandalous."

He sat back on his heals. "You mean to fight me?"

"Every inch of the way, Mr. McCord."

He nodded, acknowledging her intention, but sure in his mind he would be the victor. Allowing her no time to prepare herself, he pinned her to the ground with his arm across the top portion of her chest. His gaze steady on her face, he began to pry open buttons on her dress.

"Take your hands off of me, you immoral, graceless . . . ruffian!"

Reno burst into a laugh and managed the remainder of the buttons. He dodged a slap, then he released her long enough to grab the neckline of the dress. He dragged it over her shoulders, halfway down her arms. He had her trapped now. "You might as well relax. I'll have my way. I don't want to hurt you."

She swung a leg and knocked her knee against his back.

"Are you trying to make me lose my temper?"

Libby quieted. Her gaze collided with his. He read determination in her eyes. The lady had enough grit for three women. Before she thought to fight him again, he jerked the dress lower, exposing her lace-trimmed camisole.

She wiggled in a frantic attempt to free her arms. "I was right about you in the first place. Why, you're nothing but a coarse barbarian!"

Despite his attempts to hold her immobile, she freed one hand. He snapped his fingers around her wrist before she could follow through and slap his face. "Now, Miss Chandler," he said softly, "there's no call to hit me. I'm not going to do anything indecent, just remove one damn dress before it causes you to break your neck."

She struggled against his hold for several seconds more before her arms went slack. "It's not your intention I question. It's your brutish method of accomplishing it."

"I'm much too strong for you to fight," he said, lowering his voice to a coaxing tone. "You might as well surrender the battle. Remember . . . I'm a graceless ruffian."

He could've sworn the corners of her mouth briefly curved upward. In a daring movement, he fell back, bringing the dress over her hips and legs. He tossed the ugly garment away.

Libby pushed herself up, her hair falling into a magnificent drape around and over her shoulders.

He got a glimpse of pale breasts swelling over the top of the lacy camisole. Women's clothes had always baffled him. They hid nearly every feminine curve. And Libby Chandler had curves that shouldn't be hidden.

She crawled to her knees and, quick as a flash, shoved her hands against his shoulders. Reno toppled over. She pushed to her feet and stood slightly turned away from him.

No wonder she had fought so hard to hide her body, he thought. Her waist nipped in above gently rounding hips, and her backside could tempt Satan. He couldn't stop staring at her. "Lady, you're sure no scrawny chicken."

Uncertainty on her face, she crossed her arms over her chest. A telltale blush crept over her cheeks, staining her neck as well. "I hope you're satisfied," she said, her tone laced with reproach.

"You don't know the half of it."

Reno climbed to his feet also. While he dusted off his pants, he took in the whole of her in one glance. "God never intended women to wear pants."

She sucked in a harsh breath.

Closing the distance between them in one long stride, he muttered, "Especially you, Libby."

"You were never supposed to see them."

She stayed put, which confused him until he reminded himself that she couldn't know how seeing her in such form-revealing clothes had awakened in him an awareness of her as a desirable woman. He forced his voice into a business-like tone. "I have to check your injury."

Her mouth briefly pursed. "You're as obstinate

as a mule. I suppose, if I refuse, you intend to resort to physical strength to have your way?"

He crossed his arms over his chest and gave her a curt nod.

She fumbled with the top button on the pants. "Very well, I'll show you. Look quickly, Mr. McCord. A glimpse is all you'll have."

He watched her lower the trousers over her hip, revealing the top of white drawers. Her gaze found his for a second and then darted over his shoulder. In a lightning fast movement, she dipped the drawers over her hip and back again. That split second, though, would live in his mind. Creamy skin, softly rounded, broken only by an ugly red scrape.

"That wasn't so hard, was it?" he asked, his voice sounding much lower than he'd intended.

She shot him a quelling look.

"It's just a scrape, Libby, but it might turn purple by tonight."

"It might very well turn orange for all you'll know," she snapped. "And don't call me Libby."

"Lady, I've seen more of you than any other man. The least you can do is allow me to use your given name." He contemplated the green sparks flashing in her eyes. "A little salve will help it heal faster."

She arched a finely shaped brow. "Administered by you, no doubt?"

"If you like."

"Absolutely not!"

A smile hovered on his mouth. "Now, who's acting obstinate?"

She searched for her dress. When she spotted it

half in the water, she brushed past him, bent low, and snatched it up.

Reno mouthed an oath at the provocative sight she made.

Libby abruptly straightened. She tossed the dress on the rock and then whipped a blue shirt out of her bag. "Kindly turn your back, Mr. McCord."

The smile hovering on Reno's mouth blossomed into a wide grin. "Little late for that, don't you think?"

"Be that as it may, I'm not in the habit of dressing in front of a man." She held the shirt in front of her. "Please . . ."

His smile vanished. He felt chastened for his rough handling of her. Gently, he took the shirt from her and held it out. "I'll close my eyes if you want. But allow me to help you."

After a short pause, she slipped her arms into the sleeves. "You didn't close your eyes."

"You didn't tell me to."

"I presumed you'd do as you'd promised."

"Did I promise? As I recall, I said I'd close my eyes if you wanted. You said nothing, so I thought you weren't serious."

She reprimanded him by clearing her throat.

He moved nearer and began to push buttons through holes. "At least allow me to make up for my behavior before."

She fell silent. He leisurely buttoned the shirt, his fingers brushing her skin, then the soft material of her undergarment. She smelled good. Too damn good. Like a woman. His hands lingered when he reached the bottom of the shirt.

Her breath sounded uneven.

"Feeling strange inside again, Libby?"

She shook her head adamantly.

"Liar," he whispered. "You should wear green, not blue. Green goes better with your coloring."

"My shirt's nearly as dark a shade as your eyes."

Her mouth sagged briefly, causing him to believe she'd spoken rashly. Amused by her distress, he tipped up her chin with a finger. "Is that why you bought it? Because the color reminded you of my eyes?"

"Most certainly not," she shot back. "It was . . . the only one that looked as if it might fit."

"My eyes are my best feature, or so I've been told." When he saw her gaze wander to his mouth, he smiled. "Of course, they usually get around to mentioning that my heart isn't exactly in the right place."

"I wonder why. Do you act this coarse when you court a woman?"

"I never court. I just—"

"Rob them of their virtue and then bid them farewell?"

"In a manner of speaking, but the women I've known had all lost their virtue long ago."

"I suppose by your standards, that makes it all right?"

Though he'd whipped a handkerchief from his pocket and strode to the edge of the stream, Libby saw Reno's frown. She'd asked a question he wouldn't answer, she thought. He wet the cloth in the water and, before he rose, picked up something from the ground. He crammed the article into his shirt pocket.

"You have dirt on your face," he said when he returned. His eyes swept to her hair and remained. "And grass in your hair."

She still felt quivery inside, a fact she had been desperately striving to hide from him. Why had she hired such a disturbing man? A bothersome man with a forceful nature. No man except Reno McCord had ever dared put his hands on her. She wove her fingers through her hair to remove the grass.

His gaze followed her movements. Tipping up her chin once more, he swiped the cloth over her forehead and one cheek. His ministrations were exceptionally gentle, considering that moments before he'd held her down and stripped off half her clothes.

There must be something dreadfully wrong with her, she mused. As hard as she tried to remain angry with him, she found herself warming to him.

He wore a smile as he dabbed a spot from her nose. "You missed some grass. Do you have a brush?"

"In my bag."

He left her to dig through her belongings. Libby took advantage of the time to tuck the tails of the shirt into her trousers. She hoped, if he noticed, he wouldn't make mention of her attire. Her hopes were short-lived.

"Definitely not a scrawny chicken. Didn't they have larger size pants?"

Libby swallowed hard. "No."

"When we return to town, you better wear the dress."

He appeared uncomfortable, as uncomfortable

as he seemed to take delight in making her. She couldn't pass up the opportunity to repay him for his frequent teasing. "But you insisted I not wear it, and you resorted to ungentlemanly behavior to see it removed. Now, you want me to wear the dress?"

"Lady, if you don't know why, I'm sure not telling you."

She extended a hand.

The brush disappeared behind his back. "Let me brush your hair for you."

She never knew quite what to expect from Reno McCord. The look in his eyes, and his manner, confused her. If she didn't know better, she'd suspect he found her enticing. Censuring her mind for conjuring up such an unbelievable notion, she continued to hold out her hand. He was still playing games, at her expense.

"Libby, I'm serious."

She arched a brow at him. "Why? Should we be wasting time here? We have miles to travel. I'm not paying you to dally at a stream."

The brush slapped into her hand. Startling her, he leaned close and captured a lock of her hair in his hand.

"Tonight then," he mumbled, his tone holding a promise. "I just wanted to touch your hair, Libby. It's . . . it steals a man's breath."

Flustered by his compliment, she blurted out, "It would be a shame, indeed, were you to be robbed of breath, Mr. McCord. However would you taunt me?"

Abruptly, he spun around. He grabbed up her bag, slung the dress over his shoulder, and stood ready to climb the embankment. "Trust me. I'd find a way. By now you should've learned how persistent I can be."

Libby dashed the brush through her hair, then she hurried to where he waited.

He nodded at the bank. "After you. I don't want to chance your falling a second time."

She noticed his stiff bearing and the furrows etched across his brow. His sudden change of mood puzzled her. But most likely the rogue would take advantage of his position and stare at her backside.

"Hold your vision heavenward, Mr. McCord," she said as she started up the hill.

When they reached their camp, Libby fell to her knees to hunt for her lost pins. Finding none, she stood and shook out the blankets and coat. Even a search of the ground proved futile. She did, however, stumble upon a small, rough piece of tree bark. She hid it in her hand and looked at Reno.

Squatted before the remains of their campfire, he was scattering ashes. His shirt had ridden up, leaving a space between his collar and his neck.

Under the pretext of finding her pins, she wandered close to him. He paid her no mind, which worked to her advantage. As she walked by him, she dropped the piece of bark into the gap left open at his neck.

Seeing him reach behind him, she said, "Goodness, there's an ugly bug on your shirt." She brushed at his back. "There, it flew away."

He rose. "Thanks."

Libby grinned while he walked to where he'd hobbled Charity.

Reno's movements were sure and efficient as he repacked the mule. She watched him stop several times to run his hand over Charity's side or neck. A warm feeling flooded through Libby. Though she heard him talking, he spoke so low she couldn't make out his words.

He might be brash and forceful upon occasion, she mused, but he possessed a caring nature.

As if he sensed her gaze, he asked, "Something wrong?"

"No," she returned. "I seem to have misplaced my pins is all."

When he inclined his head in commiseration for her loss, Libby frowned. He looked entirely too innocent as he led Charity to where he'd secured the horses. If she didn't know better, she'd think he knew what had happened to her hairpins.

"Come along, Libby."

Dismissing her suspicions, Libby went to her horse. It was time to mount again. Before she could figure out a way to climb back up on the horse, Reno stepped close.

He bent low and formed a cup with his hands. "Put your foot in my hands. Do it fast, before my back locks and I become stooped before my time."

Libby smothered a smile, grabbed hold of the pommel, and did as he'd asked. As soon as he began to lift her, she swung her leg over the saddle. She sent him an inquiring look.

Reno, however, climbed on his horse and came abreast of her. "Ready?"

She nodded.

"Your horse, by the way, is named Sugar."

"Don't tell me. Because she's sweet-natured?"

"So I was told. I can't imagine any other reason to call a horse by such an idiotic name." He dismounted and stood beneath Libby. "How did you get her going yesterday?"

"She just set out following you."

"Move up. I might as well give you a lesson."

Libby froze. Reno McCord couldn't possibly think to ride with—but he was! Seeing his body already in motion, she abruptly scooted forward. And not a second too soon. His large body settled behind her, his long black-clad legs flat against the outside of hers. His arm circled her waist as he wiggled tight against her.

"What are *you* doing? There isn't room for two of us."

"Don't get all fired up. We aren't going far this way, only until I'm sure you know the basics."

Libby felt certain her knowledge would cover much more than the basics of riding before he left her horse. Already, she knew how it felt to have his hard body pressed so close. Heavens, her backside rested right between his legs! "I hardly think it's necessary for you to . . . to go to this extreme."

"Hush, Libby. Pay attention."

While his hand clamped her left knee and pressed it to the horse's side, his warm breath fanned her neck. A most annoying rush of heat stole through her body.

He made a clicking sound as he walked Sugar a few steps. Close to Libby's ear, he asked, "Want to try it?"

"Yes. Yes, all right," she muttered.

Reno rested his hand on her thigh. Stunned by a jolt to her stomach, she sagged against him. His breath on her neck came faster and Libby felt close to swooning. At that moment, she didn't give a fig about learning to handle the horse. She was aware only of Reno, and his disturbing nearness.

Libby sucked in a ragged breath.

"You're not concentrating, Libby," he said, his voice sounding a trifle hoarse. "But, hell, neither am I. Not now."

His hand inched higher along her thigh. "You're too tense when you ride. Hell, you're too tense all the time. Don't fight the horse. Riding is like making love. You have to sense what move your partner is going to make and move your body in tune with him."

Fire instantly licked Libby's cheeks. "Mr. McCord, your methods of teaching leave much to be desired. And don't use vulgar descriptions."

"Vulgar? Lady, if that's your perception of lovemaking, you're in for a surprise."

The heat from his hand scorched her skin through her pants. His suggestive words were playing havoc with her resolve and her senses. Strangely, a peculiar languor stole over her.

"I wasn't being vulgar," he added, "merely attempting to give you the idea."

"Please . . . don't dwell on your unfortunate choice of descriptions. I understand." Closing her eyes, Libby willed her taut body to relax.

"Libby . . . it feels so good having you lean into me. Are you trying to arouse me on purpose?"

She lurched upright.

Reno chuckled and clamped his arm around her middle. Then, his hand rested on her leg again. "I was only teasing."

Her thigh felt even more branded. She imagined the imprint of his fingers deeply scarred into her skin. She wanted to grab his hand and shove it away, but a greater want kept her from doing the deed.

Dear Lord, she loved the feel of his hands, relished the fire whipping her insides from his intimate touch. "What of *your* motives, Mr. McCord? Are you trying to seduce me?"

The sound of his harsh breathing filled the air between them. "It's you who are doing the seducing, Libby."

She stiffened again. "I assure you I wouldn't know how to go about seducing a man."

He groaned low in his throat. "Lady, you underestimate yourself. Hardtack's more pliable than I am right now."

After a long, confused pause, she said, "I don't know what you mean."

"If I don't get down, whether you like it or not, your education will advance more rapidly than you want. Before I do . . ." His hand left her leg.

Libby nearly sighed with relief, until she realized he'd only given her a brief respite. He pushed aside her hair, baring her neck. Her first instinct was to jerk away in order to spare herself additional torment. She ignored the impulse, ignored the warning sent by her mind. Instead, she allowed her senses to dwell on Reno's nearness, anticipating his next move. When his lips seared a path from just under her ear to the tender spot where her shoulder began, she released a soft, anguished moan.

"God, you smell good," he said. "You taste even better."

She must have lost her mind along with her senses, she thought. The man who had just taken the liberty of kissing her neck was her brash, reckless employee. Libby lurched away. "Mr. McCord, you've forgotten yourself! Get down from my horse this instant."

His arms fell to his sides. "You know you liked it."

"I . . . I most certainly did not!"

He jumped down, still holding both sets of reins in his right hand. With an unfriendly twist to his mouth, he saluted her. "As you've reminded me often enough, you're footing the bills."

Libby touched her hair as she strove to subdue the heat still plaguing her body. "When we return to Denver, you may use your amorous skill all you want. Perhaps you'll even find a woman who'll welcome your advances."

"I've never had any trouble finding a *willing* woman before." His swung onto his horse. "But I think I know what has you so riled."

Libby slid back in the saddle. If the sun fell from the sky, she wouldn't give Reno McCord the response he obviously wanted.

"You like to act cold, Miss Chandler, but I know the truth. Water doesn't flow through your veins, like you'd have me believe. Your blood's as red and hot as mine. One day I'll prove it to you."

"You're mistaken, Mr. McCord, if you think you'll prove any such thing," Libby said calmly. "You are in my employ, certainly not the sort of man I would trust with my love. I would have to care deeply for a man before I would allow him to stir my blood. I know you're just amusing yourself with me because I'm the only available female."

"You must be right, Miss Chandler."

She glared at his broad back as he rode his horse in front and started out.

The man had just behaved forwardly and not only touched her thigh, he'd kissed her neck. She still felt gloriously flushed. She didn't feel like an old maid now, a woman doomed to live her life without ever knowing the thrill of a man's touch. This man's touch.

Reno McCord excited her beyond belief!

He'd sent her emotions reeling, overheated her body, and then seemed quite content to accept her erratic responses as rational. Thank goodness she'd found the presence of mind to call his arrogant bluff.

She hadn't been rational since Reno McCord had crashed through the door of the Crooked Creek Saloon and into her life.

Chapter 8

They hadn't spoken since they'd left the stream four hours ago. Reno knew they should stop. Libby must be getting tired or thirsty by now. Part of him wanted to keep riding, to get the job done as fast as possible. The other part of his mind, though, seemed determined to overrule his common sense—wanting to prolong their trip.

He'd set a slow pace, riding beside her when the terrain allowed. Libby had held up better today. He hadn't seen her bounce in the saddle. She was a sight to behold with her hair streaming down her back, her hat tipped low on her forehead. She possessed an alluring profile, among other things. As she held the reins loosely in her right hand, her left hand rested on her leg.

The memory sped across his mind. He felt his own hand resting in the same spot, felt again the heat penetrating the material of her pants. He had been playing with fire. Libby Chandler was off-limits to him, a wealthy woman who wanted to settle down. Yet, unmindful of the warning bells ringing inside his head, he couldn't maintain a proper distance from her. He'd come to relish her pithy responses and the sparks flashing in her eyes when he pushed her too far.

"How are you faring?" he asked.

"Just fine. How are you?"

"You're not manufacturing another of your small fibs, are you, Libby?"

"Certainly not. If I feel the need to stop, I'll tell you."

He smiled. She was the bossiest woman he'd ever met. "We'll keep going."

Until they came upon another stream, he mused. The sudden desire to take a bath and shave struck him. He scratched the stubble on his chin. And then cursed himself for a fool. Before long, he'd be acting like an untried schoolboy, flustered and stammering for words in Libby's presence. Women had always bragged they'd found him handsome.

He wanted Libby to find him handsome. The realization startled him.

"What do you intend to do with the money I'm paying you?" she asked suddenly.

Her question jarred him to attention. "Frankly, I haven't thought past the end of this trip."

"Have you no desire to see to your future?"

"The future has a way of taking care of itself."

"But what about when you grow old? How will you survive?"

He shrugged his shoulders. He ought to tell her to mind her own business. "I might not survive past this year. If I stash away all my money, who's to enjoy it?"

"You've never been married?"

"No."

"Don't you want a family someday?"

Feeling her scrutiny, he strangled the reins. "No."

"Now, that's where we differ. I yearn for a family."

"Well, I don't. I'm happy with my life the way it is," he said.

"But you have no one to love."

He thought of the many women he'd made love to. He'd never known the kind of emotional love Libby spoke about, but he did know how to enjoy life. "That's where you're wrong. Love is waiting in the next town."

When fine lines feathered across her brow, he knew she'd never understand the life he'd chosen. "Do you ever have any fun?"

"Fun?"

"Do you ever let down your hair?" When she touched her hair, he shook his head. "Having a good time now and again isn't a sin, you know."

"I imagine your idea of a good time differs from mine. Don't you want something more rewarding than brawling in saloons?"

"I happen to like brawling in saloons," he said with conviction in his voice. "Try it some time. You might surprise yourself."

"Me?" She gave him an incredulous look. "Go into a saloon? I think not, Mr. McCord."

They were as different as night from day, he realized.

"I know you don't believe in ghosts," she said, "so before we arrive at the canyon, I think you ought to reevaluate your thinking."

"Lady, you sure know how to change a subject. Do you actually believe that dumb story of a ghost?"

A slight flush on her cheeks, she admitted, "You'd think I'm crazy for sure. But . . . there's always a chance."

He raised a brow at her.

"I realize you don't understand my dreams about Clarence. I don't understand them myself. But the fact that I have them convinces me it might be possible to have a life after death." She looked off into the distance. "Many people have claimed to have seen spirits. Either they're all liars, or there's some form of existence after one dies."

"Hogwash."

When she looked at him, moisture rimmed her eyes. "You've already made up your mind. You think I'm crazy, don't you?"

She would ask him such a damning question. "What about you? You don't honestly think there's a ghost in that canyon?"

"I've never actually seen a spirit, so I'd be a fool to say I believe. I just . . . I prefer to— Anything is possible. I don't understand most of the world we live in, yet it exists." Her lips hinted at a smile. "I don't understand you, yet here you sit."

"Well, we have something in common. I don't understand myself, either."

"One thing is sure. When we reach the place I see in my dreams, and if there is a bad-tempered ghost, I'll feel much safer knowing I have such a fearless man to protect me."

Struck by an inkling that she'd just taunted him, he frowned.

"If a ghost does appear, Mr. McCord, you'll have to change your mind, won't you?"

"Lady, if some decaying phantom sprouting an

ax from his head appears at any time, I'll kiss your ass."

"If it's a wager you're after, I suggest a more worthy prize."

"Why, Miss Chandler, I'm shocked by your daring. Are you proposing a wager?"

"Normally, I wouldn't but I'm overcome by temptation."

Pleased to have discovered a very human failing in his proper employer, he grinned. "I've chosen a worthy prize. What would you have me put up as a stake?"

Mischief twinkled in her eyes. "Your hat. If we see a ghost, you'll eat your hat."

"I'd much rather kiss your ass."

"Reno McCord!"

"All right. You win. My hat it is."

"Oh, I do hope there's really a ghost."

The lady *did* know how to have a good time. Or maybe he'd finally worn away enough at her prim nature. "You would enjoy my misery?" he asked, his tone playful. "What stake are you willing to forfeit?"

"What would you have me wager? Perhaps I should rephrase that. What *modest* prize would satisfy you?"

"A kiss." He watched her tongue dart out and wet her lips. Unable to tear his gaze from her mouth, he squirmed in his saddle. The resultant squeak of leather echoed between them. "A kiss like none you've ever given before. I want your tongue in my mouth, and your breasts smashed tight against my chest."

"Mr. McCord!" A blush tore across her cheeks.

"Lady, if I have to eat my hat, the least you can

do is offer me a rousing reward. I won't settle for a quick smack on the lips."

Her blush blossomed from pink to crimson. "I doubt kissing me would be, as you put it, *rousing* to a man like you."

"A man like me?"

"A man of your vast experience," she said as she twirled the reins in her fingers.

She seemed so uncertain, he wondered if she'd ever been soundly kissed. "Don't worry, Libby, if I can't teach you how to kiss a man properly, I'll eat my socks as well."

"Your confidence is inspiring, Mr. McCord. I'll pray we see a ghost." Suddenly, she motioned with her hand. "We're coming upon narrower ground. If you aren't careful—"

Reno regained his senses when his horse ground to a stop. Since he hadn't been expecting the sudden move, he pitched forward. He jerked back in time, saving himself an ignominious ejection from the saddle. His hat, however, wasn't so fortunate. It sailed over the horse's head and disappeared. Past the animal's neck Reno saw the sharp drop of the land. A giggle lured his attention to his grinning employer.

"Your dinner has chosen not to chance being eaten," she said. "Either you'll have to go after it, or pick another item. Your boots perhaps?"

Reno dismounted and stood on the edge. He scowled. Down the precipitous ravine dotted with different sized rocks he spotted his hat. It rested on a rock ledge. Far below, however, water rushed at a violent rate. "Damn, Libby, you distracted me. It's a fine predicament I've gotten us into."

She appeared at his side. Casting him a worried

look, she pleaded, "Don't go after it. It's just a thing, whereas you aren't expendable."

"I happen to like my hat."

"Surely you're not going down *there!*"

"Concerned for my welfare?" He discovered he liked the idea that she was worried for his safety. No one had worried about him in a very long time.

"How can you ask such an asinine question? I—"

"Care what happens to me?"

She peered over the edge. "Of course I'm concerned for your welfare."

She seemed so preoccupied with the rugged landscape below, he couldn't resist the temptation to pursue her change of manner. "Because if I die, you'll lose your guide?"

Her gaze flew to his. "Do you think I'm so callous as to think that?"

Uncomfortable under her regard, he said, "No, Libby, I don't."

"Why, then, did you ask me such a thing?"

Rarely did he reveal his true feelings. Surprising him, the words tumbled out of his mouth. "I suppose because I wanted you to say you were worried because you cared about *me,* not out of some sense of duty, or because you'd be lost out here without me."

Moments passed while she stared at him. He regretted having asked her such a question. While he found her amusing, he wanted no permanent relationship with a woman.

Lord, he didn't know himself any longer. Part of him wanted her to care what happened to him.

"Yes, I do care about you for yourself," she finally said, her tone far too grave. "How could I not? You're so mannerly, and you flatter me so eloquently."

He smiled at her attempt to tease him. Despite a glimmer of devilment in her eyes, her next remark caught him off guard.

"But, to be totally honest, in lieu of our wager, your death would be most untimely and inconvenient."

"Why, Libby?"

"Should you die, you might become a hatless spirit."

"Go on."

"Don't you see my point? I will have won but you won't have a body." She retreated a step. "In order to eat your hat, you will have need of human form."

Reno swallowed a laugh. "If I became a spirit, I wouldn't play fair. We'll never know for sure whether a ghost can chew and swallow an object, but we'd know something else."

"What?"

"Whether a spirit can physically touch a human being." Her eyes widened slightly, encouraging him to continue. "I'd dare to claim much more than a mere kiss."

She heaved an irregular breath. "You would cheat?"

"I'd have nothing to lose. Aren't you curious about what I'd claim?"

"I am not."

"Liar."

"You will be careful when you go after your hat?" She went to his horse and returned with a coil of rope he'd looped over his pommel. "I have no desire to kiss a spirit, Mr. McCord." Green sparks glittered in her eyes. "I imagine it would be like kissing a very large icicle."

Slowly, he grinned. "Oh, I think I'd melt soon enough."

She grinned back. "All over me, no doubt."

Reno chuckled and took the rope from her. He was beginning to enjoy having her around. A disturbing thought lanced through his mind.

What if she was wrong? What if they found Clarence Trout alive and well and ready to marry her?

Could he stand by and watch her go off with another man?

Hell, yes! a voice in his head answered quickly. He'd be doing her a favor. Trout was the man she was meant to marry, decent, hardworking.

The staying kind.

Confusing emotions coursed through Libby as she watched Reno tie the rope to the pommel on his saddle. She'd warned herself not to become attached to him, yet she'd done it anyway.

But her feelings for him weren't love. One didn't fall in love with a man so quickly, especially with a brash, reckless man who lived only for a good time. She knew what love was. She'd loved her first fiancé, or at least she'd thought so at the time. Could she have simply been infatuated? She also loved Clarence. The emotions swirling inside her now were different. She must feel only a physical attraction for Reno because, despite his faults, he was not only handsome, he excited her.

Reno unbuckled his gunbelt and carefully laid it on the ground. With nimble fingers he tied the other end of the rope around his waist.

He might fall. "Are you sure the rope will hold your weight?" she asked with a catch in her voice.

"It has in the past."

"You've done this before?"

He looked up. "I'll be fine, Libby. My hat isn't down far. Besides, you'll be up here in charge."

"In charge of what?"

"Making sure my horse doesn't decide to follow me."

"Oh! He won't, will he?"

"He wouldn't be as smart as I know him to be, but animals sometimes do the unexpected." He lifted a brow at her. "I'm counting on you to stop him if he decides to act dumb."

Libby rolled her eyes heavenward. "You expect me to stop a powerful horse when I haven't been able to stop you? And you, Mr. McCord, are supposed to be abundantly more intelligent."

"I want my hat, Libby. I've become attached to it."

"Obviously." The man was an enigma, ready to risk his life for a silly hat. "Be careful."

He saluted and then disappeared over the edge. Libby's heart slammed against her ribs. If something happened to him—

Libby dashed to the spot where she'd last seen him and peered down. For a man his size, he was quite dexterous. He scaled the side of the rock face as though he'd been born to it. Feeling dizzy, she retreated a safe distance away. A glance at his horse reassured her. The well-trained animal hadn't budged an inch, even though the rope had grown taut.

"I'm coming back up," Reno yelled.

Borne on a breeze, sent by what she presumed

must've been a mighty toss, his hat soared past Libby.

She realized she'd been twisting her fingers together. Reno McCord was entirely too fearless, she thought. Hearing a noise behind her, she spun around, and found Charity's face inches from hers. "Bad mule! You frightened me nearly to death," she chastened the animal. "Go away."

The mule nudged Libby's arm and stepped forward instead. Libby reached for the lead rope, but Charity ran smack into the rope supporting Reno, causing his horse to neigh loudly. Libby darted in front of Charity. Determined to stop the mule from following Reno, she pushed hard against Charity's shoulders.

"What's going on up there? Libby!"

Libby couldn't answer. She was deploying all her strength to hold back the mule, and her arms were weakening from the exertion. Without warning, Charity retreated. The mule's sudden move caught Libby unaware. She stumbled forward. She tried to maintain her balance, but the next instant she lost the struggle to remain on her feet.

Libby sat on the ground so hard that she nearly went over the cliff. Then the ground began to crumble beneath her. A scream tore from her throat as she plummeted after Reno, her life flashing before her eyes. But instead of falling to her death, she struck a sturdy object. Air rushed from her lungs. A strong arm locked around her waist and she found herself flattened against Reno's side.

"Bring your feet down!"

The masterful command spurred Libby to action. She wiggled her legs free of the cliff.

"Miss me?" Reno asked. "That why you flew down to see me?"

Libby looked up and noticed he used his other hand to strangle the rope. They dangled in midair, high above rushing water. Libby's heart raced wildly, until Reno dug his feet into rocky soil and found a foothold. "How can you joke at a time like this?"

"Lady, it's either joke or . . . say, you sure feel good all mashed against me. Wiggle like that against me again and—"

"You impossible jackass," Libby ground out. "Be serious."

"I would if I could. Might I remind you, the hand I was using to climb is presently holding you. Any suggestions about how I should proceed now?"

Terror gripped her heart. "No!" She glanced down and her head began to spin. Immediately, she pinched her eyes closed. Seconds passed before she could speak. "I'm paying you well, Mr. McCord. Earn your pay. Get us out of here."

"I'd be happy to," he grated out. "But you'll have to turn around."

"Turn around? Are you daft?"

"I need both hands."

"I can't," Libby squeaked. "I'm afraid of heights."

"Fine time to tell me."

"Can't you signal your horse to drag us up?"

"He would at that," he said, a note of disgust evident in his tone. "But he'd probably drag me on top of you. In case you hadn't noticed, I'm heavier. I can't chance hurting you."

"All right!" Her head was still spinning, and a

queasy feeling invaded her stomach. Reno held her so tightly that she could barely breathe.

"When I let loose of you, turn around."

"When you let loose? Don't you dare!"

"I'll do it a little at a time. You start twisting. When you're turned far enough, lock your legs around my waist, and your arms around my neck."

Libby felt giddy from fear and lack of air. The absurdity of their predicament struck her motionless.

"Move!" he commanded.

Libby flipped an arm over his shoulder. They were both going to die and she felt light-headed. "You aren't planning on taking liberties again?"

When Reno burst into a pained laugh, he relaxed his hold on Libby.

Libby's scream echoed over and over down the ravine. Faced with the prospect of plunging to her death, she twisted her body and clamped both arms around his neck, her legs around his hips.

"Damn," he shouted in a strangled voice. "You're choking me."

His arm left her, and she shifted lower. Libby gasped a breath. But, wedged between his upper arm and the rope, she suddenly felt safer than she should.

Reno grabbed hold of the rope with both hands.

Once more, Libby's life flashed before her. She tightly closed her eyes. At least she wouldn't have to see death happen. She tried to remember a prayer. Any prayer.

She'd just thought of one when a sharp tug lifted them a foot higher. Then another foot. Until the movement changed into a crawling pace. She wanted to ask Reno how he'd managed to raise them. Fear held her silent. She didn't want to distract him.

One final jerk had them lying on their sides on solid ground. Pain sliced down Libby's leg. Not allowing her time to think, Reno flipped her onto to her back. They were safe, out of the ravine. She dared to open her eyes and spellbinding blue eyes met her astonished gaze. A large, hard body pinned her to the ground.

Reno pushed up on his elbows. "Are you all right?"

His impetuous, daring nature had nearly sent the both of them to the Hereafter. Now, despite the danger they'd just lived through, his devilish look hinted at his amusement. "No, I am not! You nearly got us killed."

He brushed a lock of wayward hair from her brow. "My horse took it upon himself to drag us up."

"We owe our lives to a horse who has more intelligence than its owner."

"You forget I trained him."

A pained expression pulled his features taut. He pressed his lower body harder against her than he had in front of the saloon. Her legs remained around his hips, making their position far too intimate.

"Please, let me up," Libby said.

As Reno's eyes narrowed slightly, they burned with a foreign glow. "Not this time."

Chapter 9

"**W**hat do you mean, not this time?" Libby asked hesitantly.

He touched her cheek, then drew a line to her chin with a finger. "Libby . . . you might have died. What were you thinking getting so close to the edge of a ravine?"

"It was Charity. She wanted to follow you, and I had to hold her back."

"She pushed you over?"

"Not exactly. To my misfortune, she failed to inform me before she moved. I lost my balance."

The weight of his body made her warm all over. It felt good having him so close. Her brush with death had reinforced a truth. She hadn't lived enough yet. There were too many things left to experience.

He laid his hand squarely in the middle of her chest. "Your heart is still racing."

Too startled to speak, she nodded.

"It was exciting, wasn't it?"

"What?"

"Knowing you could easily fall and die."

"It's not an experience I wish to repeat. Ever."

Wicked lights danced in his eyes. "Maybe we should renegotiate our contract."

"Renegotiate how?"

"If I'm going to be saving your life, you should add a little something to what you owe me."

"Is this to be in the order of the *warming fee* you mentioned last night?"

"Not necessarily. I enjoyed warming you. But if you're intending to leap over cliffs, it changes things."

"I did *not* leap. I accidentally fell." Recognizing his efforts not to grin, she said, "Might I remind you of the foolhardy person who went into a ravine after a hat!"

A smile tipped up the corners of his mouth. "Bet you felt more alive during those moments than you've ever felt?"

She felt abundantly alive at this minute. But she wasn't about to admit any such thing to him. "Your hand's quite heavy."

He regarded her intently. "You still feel alive, Libby. I feel your heart pounding."

When he ran his hands down her sides, Libby's heart skipped a beat. His mouth hovered over hers, their breath mingling. She couldn't answer. If Reno suspected that *he,* not the terror of falling, had caused her heart to race, he would be insufferable. He might also take her reaction as an invitation.

He moved so quickly, Libby's eyes flew open. His hands rested under her hips! She felt the hard proof of his desire between her thighs. Too shocked to speak, she pushed at his shoulders.

"Let me kiss you," he said, his voice deeper than she'd ever heard it.

His mouth grazed hers.

"No!"

He withdrew but only an inch. "You're quivering, Miss Chandler. Admit you want me to kiss you. Are you burning all over?"

"No, I most certainly am not. I want you to let me go."

One corner of his mouth lifted. "You're not very convincing. We just shared a life-threatening experience together. Do you want to go to your grave not knowing what it's like to be with a man?"

Libby seized handfuls of his shirt and tried in vain to push his shoulders away. But he was much too strong. "You will never be that man, Mr. McCord."

Their eyes met for a long, silent moment. Libby cursed the heat swirling through her body from Reno's nearness. Dear Lord! To her shame, she did want to know what it would be like if he were to kiss her passionately. The unsettling realization weighed on her conscience, and her heart.

"I'll forgive your unseemly behavior," she rattled off, "if you release me now. I'll take your actions for what they were: excess exhilaration brought about by a dangerous situation."

"You're a desirable woman, Miss Chandler. I wouldn't be much of a man if having a hot-blooded woman squirm under me didn't inflame my passions."

Libby's throat grew thick from his admission. Reno McCord was a man in every sense of the word, a man who greatly disturbed her mind, senses, and body. However, she would be a fool to give him her heart. She nearly laughed. He hadn't asked for her heart. Obviously, he wanted a woman. *Any* woman would serve Reno McCord's needs at this moment.

"We better be on our way," he said, his tone clipped.

She allowed him to yank her to her feet, after which she busied herself by dusting off her arms and legs. One day soon she'd show him the proper way to help a lady up so as not to rattle her teeth in the process.

"Damn."

When Libby followed Reno's gaze, she had to bite her lip to ward off a grin. His hat, for which he'd risked life and limb, resided in an inauspicious location, directly under Charity's right forefoot.

Reno briskly strode toward the mule but jerked to a halt. He mumbled unintelligible words as he worked at the expertly formed knots in the rope which held him in place.

Libby covered a laugh by slapping a hand over her mouth.

Within minutes he'd freed himself. Upon reaching Charity, he bent down and tried to lift the animal's leg. Content to nibble at Reno's hair, the mule refused to budge. No longer able to control her amusement, Libby laughed aloud.

Charity lowered her head and chewed on his neck instead.

"I think . . . she's . . . kissing you," Libby stuttered between giggles.

He brushed the mule's head aside, then grabbed the brim of his hat. The action cost him his balance, and Reno landed on his backside. Charity took advantage of the opportunity. She sedately walked over his legs to stand a short distance away. Reno snapped his hat against his thigh, sending dust flying.

The hat sported a dent in the center. Despite Reno's attempts to return it to its former condition, the dent popped back in.

Perhaps it hadn't been inconceivable for Reno to go over a cliff to rescue one very used hat. The few belongings he'd brought with him might represent his total worth. She would willingly wager that, though he spent his money without a thought to tomorrow, he regarded his possessions as priceless. Curious now, she said offhandedly, "You can always buy another."

"I happen to have broken this one in. I don't own much, Miss Chandler, so when I grow attached to something, I prefer to hold on to it as long as I can."

She wondered if his statement applied to people as well, then scolded herself for the ridiculous notion. Reno McCord held strict control over his heart. He would probably never allow a woman to sneak past his defenses.

She watched him climb to his feet. He wound the rope into a coil. When he paused two times to scratch his back, Libby grinned. Reno probably wouldn't find the piece of bark until he changed his shirt.

Reno had slightly altered their direction, Libby thought several hours later. They were heading directly south. She hadn't wanted to dwell on the ways in which he affected her senses, so she'd concentrated instead on the breathtaking scenery. The landscape varied so greatly, it was hard to remember exactly where and at what moment she'd seen particular features. First the plains, then foothills about twenty miles wide which had narrowed considerably as they'd traveled. Peaks, valleys, small parks covered with luxuriant grass and flowering plants, and an assortment of pine, larch, and aspen trees. The soil, too, became fertile-looking in some locations.

A short time ago they'd passed an area of serried lines, fantastic outlines in which she'd imagined both human and animal shapes. The magnificent creation had held her entranced until it had faded from sight.

And, now, a series of peaks which would have been imposing if not for the distant giant, purple mountain towering over them. She had always loved Pennsylvania's mountains, especially in the fall when the leaves turned and splashed vivid colors over the treetops, but they paled in comparison to what she saw in Colorado.

While navigating a rather steep passage up a canyon, her thoughts veered to her lost intended. Clarence had deserved better than to have been stabbed in the chest, if that had truly been his fate. He was such a dear man, so kind and solicitous of her feelings. Tears welled in her eyes. Not wanting Reno to see her moment of melancholy, she swiped her sleeve over her eyes.

Shortly, they left the canyon and encountered flatter ground.

Coming abreast of Reno, she understood the reason for the satisfied curve to his mouth. Another stream. Though it was fast-moving and at a greater altitude, she saw no dangerous ravine. She realized her body ached in places she hadn't known existed. It had been a hard, long day, and she desperately wanted a rest.

"I'm craving a big, fat trout," he said.

Libby's mouth watered. "Do you think there are any?"

"If I don't catch at least a dozen, I'll eat my hat twice."

She wearily slid from her horse. When she eased her head in a circle, her bones cracked. "Considering your partiality to that particular belonging, I find it amazing how easily you gamble it."

"It's a sure bet. How many can you eat?"

"If you're referring to trout, depending upon its size, I imagine I can manage a half of one."

"That all?"

Libby removed her hat, shaking her head afterward. "Women don't generally eat as much as men."

Reno's eyes moved to her hair. "When they're downright hungry, they do."

"All right. I'll order one whole fish."

Reno's rapt preoccupation inspired a warm feeling to invade her stomach. The memory burst across her mind. *Tonight then.* He had threatened to brush her hair. The idea caused a prickle of sensation to skip down her back. He had been teasing her. Hadn't he?

"I better get cracking if I want to land five before dark." He headed for the mule. "There's a nice-looking spot ahead. It should provide enough cover to set up camp."

"Five?" she said as she followed him. "You're going to eat four fish?"

"Unless they're small. Might need six or seven then."

Libby rolled her eyes at his exaggeration. Back in Denver she'd seen him devour enough food to sustain a bear for the winter. But six or seven trout? "I pity the woman you marry. She'll need to order special pans in order to cook enough to fill you."

His head snapped to the side. "Who said I'd ever marry, Libby?"

Libby groaned. "Certainly not I. Only a crazy woman would have you."

He grinned at her comeback, confusing her.

With his normal efficient manner, he had their camp established and the animals settled with remarkable speed. Then, armed with several oddly shaped hooks, a length of string, and a burlap bag, he aimed her a confident smile. He set off for the stream. "Get my pan out and have it hot when I get back. Shouldn't take long. I'm not only the best scout west of Missouri, I'm the best fisherman!"

Cocky braggart, she thought as she rearranged the supplies to her liking. She threw more sticks on the fire. Reno hadn't allowed her to do anything. Well, he wasn't here now. She intended to surprise him.

Damn if she hadn't made biscuits, Reno thought. He stood a short distance away, admiring the image of Libby squatting beside the fire.

The minute she spotted him, she quickly stood. Though she rubbed her hands nervously on her pants, he saw no trace of flour on them.

"Smells good," he said. "You *can* cook."

She chewed her lip briefly. "I think they would've come out better in a stove. It's the first time I've used a pan and an open fire."

She dropped to her knees, spread a clean towel on the ground, and tipped the pan. Out rolled six fluffy pan biscuits. With a hesitant smile, she asked, "Do you think they're all right?"

"Best darn biscuits I ever did see."

She stole a glimpse at the sack he carried in his hands. "Catch any fish?"

"Five, just like I promised." He grinned. "Biggest darn trout you ever did see."

"Are they ready for the pan? Cleaning fish has never been my favorite pastime." She grimaced prettily. "They're slimy and scaly, and prickly, and they have foul-looking innards."

He resisted the temptation to tease her, motioning to the pan instead. "Lop in some grease and put the pan in the fire. I've cleaned the fish."

She sighed. "Oh, thank goodness."

"Move aside, woman. I'll fix your supper for you, again."

"You don't have to." She reached for the sack. "It's not necessary for you to cook every time."

He noticed how sunlight lighted her hair, creating a crimson halo around her head. He didn't want Libby cooking. He didn't want to get used to having her do for him. A man might become too attached to her. "You run down and fill the coffeepot."

As she walked away, she swung the enameled pot at her side. "Don't dally, Mr. McCord. I'm ravenous."

Reno didn't immediately begin his task. The sight of Libby striding away held his interest. He shook his head, censuring himself for succumbing to the enticement. She sure as hell filled out a pair of men's trousers nicely. Several minutes passed before he summoned the strength to tear his vision from her. Had he known she'd turn out so wildly provocative, he would've left her in Denver.

In his mind's eye, he saw her lift the ugly dress she'd been wearing and drop her pants. His imagination ran wild, supplying an image of creamy white, shapely long legs. He thought of her dipping into the jar of salve, and he grew hot all over as he imagined her smearing the salve over the petal-soft skin of her thighs.

Had her skin been hot enough to warm the salve? If Libby hadn't been so straitlaced, he would've helped her tend her thighs, and they might have ended up having a good time. But she wasn't just any woman, he thought. Libby Chandler was his employer, his very rich employer.

Reno groaned. Having sexual fantasies about Libby would get him nowhere. She'd made her feelings clear enough. She wanted a family and babies, lots of babies. She was also bound to another man.

If he valued his sanity, he would stop playing games in order to amuse himself.

But his play had somehow gotten out of hand. He shouldn't have ripped off that damn dress. He wondered how much longer he could be with her and temper the attraction which had suddenly sprung up between them.

* * *

Libby lay on her back, close to Reno, though her mind wouldn't allow her to sleep. They'd shared an enjoyable meal and watched a spectacular sunset. He had actually behaved decently the entire time.

His irregular breathing pattern told her he remained awake, also. She wondered if disconcerting thoughts meandered through his mind as well. Earlier, she had found his overly long, heated glances disturbing. Two layers of clothing no longer protected her from his penetrating blue eyes, instilling in her an awareness she'd never before known. But how could she not notice he looked at her differently now?

He'd seemed especially preoccupied with her legs. He had bragged he'd seen many women's legs. She knew he'd spoken truthfully. His unbridled interest, while embarrassing, had left her with a warm feelings of anticipation and excitement.

"Why aren't you asleep?" he asked. "I know you must be tired."

His voice sounded low. Far too seductive. "My body's exhausted, yet my mind refuses to settle down."

"Yeah. I've the same problem."

"What are you thinking about?" she asked, and then reprimanded herself for voicing her curiosity. She had been musing about him. Had he been thinking of her? "Forgive me. I didn't mean to pry."

He chuckled softly. "My mind was on you. I thought you'd be a bother, but sometimes you're nice to have around."

Libby gaped at him in the dark.

"I've spent most of my life holding people at a distance."

"Do you want to talk awhile?" she asked hesitantly.

"Tell me about yourself."

Although it wasn't what she'd had in mind, she respected his reluctance to talk about himself. "There isn't much to tell. I'm afraid you'll find my life boring compared with yours. An old . . . an unattached woman is limited in what she's allowed to do."

"What do you do with your time?"

"Teach piano," she returned too quickly. "To children. I adore children. They're so innocent and give freely of their love."

After a long pause, he said, "To occupy your time, I suppose. Being wealthy, you don't have need of payment."

Not wanting to lie to him, she phrased her words carefully. "Rich or poor, I'd still cherish the hours I spend with my students."

"But you wish they were your own?"

Libby released a sorrowful sigh. "Yes."

"That's why you accepted Trout's proposal, wasn't it? Because you want a family so bad."

Abruptly, she attempted to veer their conversation from the troubling subject of her lost intended. "How long has it been since you've seen your family?"

"I visit them whenever I'm in Kansas."

"Not very often, I suppose."

"I left when I was fifteen, Libby. I had an itch to travel. If I stay in one town too long, the itch comes again."

"What did you do after you left home?"

"I joined the army."

"Is that where you received your education?"

"Some. My mother taught me a lot. My commanding officer had a sweet wife, though, who wanted to mother me."

"But you were determined not to allow that," she said, her tone amused.

Ignoring her comment, he added, "I did, however, allow her to teach me. She'd been a schoolteacher. It became a nice arrangement. She was lonely, and I craved knowledge. Hell, I even let her hug me once in a while."

"Because you felt sorry for her?"

He sighed heavily. "Yeah. Guess so. It was the only way I had to repay her, and she seemed happier for it."

His kindness toward his commander's wife seemed out of character with the Reno McCord she knew. "You aren't angry with me for prying?"

He rolled to his side, startling her. "If I'm angry at anyone, it's myself."

She felt his presence, sensed he was staring at her in the dim light afforded by the embers remaining from their fire. "Why would you be angry at yourself?"

"For telling you things I've never told anyone. Why do you suppose that is, Libby?" He squeezed her arm lightly. "Are you a witch? Able to cast a spell on a man's tongue?"

She laughed softly. "I'm not a witch. I just want to know more about you."

Her arm tingled. She closed her eyes for several seconds to better savor the delicious sensation.

"Why, Libby? Why do want to know more? I'm not a person you would want to know."

But she did. She wanted to know everything about him. "You don't think much of yourself, do you?" she asked with what she hoped sounded like playful banter.

"On the contrary. I like who I am. I have no desire to change, either."

An ache clawed at her heart. "The life you've chosen must be lonely."

When he pulled back, she felt the loss of his tender touch. She'd hit upon a truth.

"Lady, you're getting mighty nosy."

His abrupt withdrawal and unfriendly remark betrayed his true feelings and Libby had just gained another bit of knowledge. "I suppose you've known many women."

"More than my share."

"Did you care for them at all?"

"Some I did . . . until morning came."

"What a shame."

He moved suddenly, seizing her wrist. "Don't feel sorry for me, Miss Chandler. And don't try to make me into something I'm not."

Libby wiggled her wrist free. "You flatter yourself, Mr. McCord. Why would I feel sorry for a womanizing ne'er-do-well who will never have a penny to his name? Furthermore, no woman in her right mind would try to reform you. It would be an act of futility!"

He said nothing for seconds. "You have the tongue of a viper, Miss Chandler."

"And you, Mr. McCord, have the grace of a three-legged mule, and the manners of a . . . a . . . boar!"

"Are you through?"

"Quite."

He gripped her arms so suddenly, Libby gasped. A moment's regret swept over her. She shouldn't have allowed him to rile her. Again, he'd acted out of character. Usually he found her retorts amusing. Now, though, she felt his tension, and anger. And something more. Some indefinable sensation which left the air between them charged.

"Lady, you sure are a helluva lot of trouble. Trout is welcome to you."

He shoved to his feet and strode off into the night.

Libby sat alone and miserable, wondering what had just happened between them. She'd asked him a few innocent questions, and ended up insulting him. Tears stung her eyes.

How *could* she cry over Reno McCord?

Chapter 10

Reno awoke with a start. And a headache.
He'd slept fitfully. If he'd made his bed far
away from Libby, he would've spared himself the
torment of lying beside her soft, warm body.
Under normal circumstances, she would never
have allowed him this intimacy.

She lay half on top of him, her leg thrown over
his, her arm across his stomach. Her head rested
on his chest. Despite his morose mood, he smiled.
He had held her in his arms during the night, and
she'd held *him* back—a *womanizing ne'er-do-
well*. Were she to awaken, she would turn beet red
and deny her embarrassment. Her provocative
fragrance had played hell with his willpower all
night. He'd never spent the night with a woman
and not made love to her.

A prick to his back just above his belt momentarily distracted him, so he wiggled several inches
to the right.

Libby snuggled closer, her leg sliding farther
over his hip. She would blush for sure if she awoke
and saw herself now. But he wasn't about to
awaken her just yet.

The sun had risen some time ago. He'd already decided he wanted to prolong their time together. Whether he found Trout or not, their lives weren't meant to travel the same road. When they parted, he would miss Libby's mocking banter, even her curt censure.

The thought distressed him. He shouldn't have noticed how green sparks flashed in her eyes, or how silky her hair felt. He shouldn't have noticed a lot of things about Libby Chandler. Her grit and quiet determination topped his list.

Gently, he lifted her. She was limp and warm and reluctant to let him go, which he found not only amusing but damned tempting. Were she any other woman, he would take advantage of her affectionate mood. Perhaps he wouldn't leave Libby for a few more minutes.

He traced the line of her jaw with a finger, then tipped up her chin. She looked lovely asleep. Long lashes touched her cheeks and her mouth begged to be kissed. Heat ripped through his body. The sudden wave of desire left him wretched. He wanted her, wanted to kiss her, hold her, make passionate love to her for as long as she allowed.

To fight his weakness, he reminded himself of the many reasons why he should keep his distance. But when he slipped free of her and knelt to reach above her head for his gunbelt, he inadvertently brushed Libby's hair.

Again, a prick to his skin stole his attention. With a curse on his lips, he yanked his shirttail free of his pants.

* * *

She had been cushioned in warmth. Now, though, a feeling of loneliness crept into Libby's drowsy mind, causing her to shiver. She hovered on the brink of wakefulness, unsure whether she wanted to surrender to oblivion or to rouse herself. Still tired from yesterday's travel, she fought the lonely feeling and surrendered to sleep.

A man, followed by a horse and a dog, left a cabin in an area of fallen red rock. But instead of dragging his feet, he walked with a purposeful stride. She couldn't see all his features, which greatly disturbed her.

Libby thrashed against the cover pinning her to the ground. Her dream had never varied before.

Another man appeared and turned in her direction. Dear Lord, he had no face. A scream worked its way to her throat. A struggle began between the two men, more fiercely this time because the man who had left the cabin appeared larger and stronger, deadly intent upon winning. When their combat advanced to a life-and-death struggle, Libby's throat seemed paralyzed. Her scream wouldn't come out.

Both men spun around. Sunlight glinted off metal seconds before the dagger plunged into the first man's chest, a man with magnificent eyes the color of a midnight sky.

The man who had been stabbed was not Clarence Trout this time. It was Reno McCord!

The scream she'd been unable to voice tore from her throat, echoing over and over and over in her mind.

Libby bolted upright. Her pulse was racing, her heart hammering her ribs. She swallowed hard but found her throat had gone dry. In the dream, she'd been screaming; however, she knew with certainty no sound had come out.

Reno had left her alone. A moment of panic nearly sent her fleeing after him. Then common sense returned. It had been a dream. Reno was safe, probably at the stream.

A piece of paper lay on the ground beside her. Her fingers trembled as she read the brief note. *Stay here,* it said. *Back soon.*

She felt calmer.

Libby pushed hair from her brow and realized it must be all tangled and wild. Where had the rest of her pins gone?

She folded the note and saw writing on the opposite side. She hadn't missed the list of supplies Reno had given her at the beginning of their travel. She'd tucked the paper inside her bodice. How? Why, she must've dropped it at the stream and Reno had found it.

Libby frowned. Sure enough, a bottle of whiskey had been added to the necessary supplies. She didn't condone Reno's reckless life, yet it wasn't her place to try to change him. She nearly laughed. She doubted *any* woman could put bonds on Reno McCord.

With the intention of hiding the list in her shirt, she opened a button in the center of her chest. Only then did she feel a foreign object in her camisole. Fearing she'd find an insect, she jerked both her shirt and undergarment free of her pants. She hopped in a circle. An ugly, brown, oddly shaped creature fell to the ground at her feet. Libby shrieked and jumped back.

The creature didn't move, so she kicked it. Upon closer examination, she discovered it wasn't an insect after all. She clicked her tongue as she scooped up the piece of tree bark which should've been in Reno's shirt.

Evidently, Reno had found the bark and retaliated. Her eyes widened. He must've slipped it into her camisole while she slept. The rogue *would* choose an unseemly hiding place, but she put nothing past him. Suddenly, she grinned. She was beginning to know what he meant by having a good time.

Not knowing how long he'd been gone, she decided to postpone breakfast and see to her morning ablutions first. A check of the animals showed his absent saddlebags. He might have gone to bathe.

Armed with clean unmentionables, soap and brush, Libby set out for the stream. The morning was still and pleasant, the water cold. She sat on a large boulder to tug off her boots and pants. As she unbuttoned the shirt, she surveyed the area. She could have been the only person for miles. Reno might or might not be near, but she didn't care.

Only three hairpins remained. Using them judiciously, she piled her hair off her neck. She'd just finished washing her face when a faint rustling noise brought Libby to her feet. Her heart skipped a beat. Deciding the sound must've been made by a small animal, she bent over.

Cold air brushed her neck.

With a harsh gasp, she rose again. Her first instinct was to turn and run. Feeling silly for letting her imagination run wild, she slowly turned her head to the right. To make certain, she repeated the movement on the opposite side. When she saw nothing out of the ordinary, she leaned down and sloshed her hands in the water. A breeze. That's all it had been. Just a cool breeze.

But there wasn't a breeze.

Libby froze. She wasn't crazy. She had felt cold air on her neck!

Unease channeled through her, until a sudden thought tripped across her mind. Reno enjoyed taunting her. He had probably crept up from behind and blown on her neck. Satisfied she'd arrived at the solution to the mysterious noise, she moved her hands in the water once more.

If Reno had blown on her neck, wouldn't his breath have been warm?

And wouldn't she have seen his reflection in the water?

Nonsense! Her very active imagination was playing tricks on her.

But if she did, indeed, find Reno lurking about with a wide grin on his face, she intended to lecture him soundly. First for spying on her. And then for daring to frighten her.

The rustle came again. This time, terror gripped Libby's heart. It wasn't Reno. She was sure of it. He wouldn't be so cruel as to taunt her twice. Would he? Afraid to glance to either side, afraid not to, she slowly stood.

Something cold and bony gripped her neck.

She couldn't move, couldn't even think of screaming. It hadn't been a breeze, or anything even remotely resembling air. It had been . . . felt like . . . *icy fingers.*

It *had* been Reno. Words of censure on her lips, she whirled around. And choked. No one, no thing was there.

Forgetting she wore only her camisole and drawers, forgetting everything sane or logical, Libby broke into a run along the rugged edge of the stream. She shoved bushes out of her way as she leapt over fallen limbs. Branches tore at her hair. One snapped and struck her arm. Libby squealed and quickened her pace. She was gasping for breath when she reached what appeared to be an end to the stream. She dropped to the ground and stared behind her.

Her mind refused to give credence to the idea. Reno would think she was insane. But she would swear on a Bible something . . . inhuman . . . had seized her neck.

Her harsh breathing echoed in the quiet. Seconds ticked by. Still nothing. She crawled to her knees and brushed dirt from her hands. Staring back the way she'd come, she waited.

The sound stopped her heart cold.

Singing. She actually heard singing—a colorful ditty with obsene lyrics about a saloon girl.

Libby searched the area. Instead of ending, the stream cascaded over an abrupt drop in the land. The singing guided her and she discovered that the stream became a waterfall, descending to a shallow pool below. He must be there, she thought. On the chance that she'd find Reno, she tiptoed along the edge. None of the straggly bushes, however, afforded her a good enough view.

She detoured slightly, to a spot where the

ground wound down without the impediments of dense underbrush and trees. Close by, water pounded. Libby sat on a smooth ledge and inched forward. A conveniently located bush offered a sturdy branch, which she grabbed for support. She saw a thirty-foot fall of water over a granite face. Rocks jutted from the shallow pool and littered the entire area. Thank goodness she hadn't run farther earlier. She might've plunged to her death.

Curious whether the man was Reno, she held a hand above her eyes to cut the sun's glare. Minutes later, she saw a form in the center of the waterfall. She slid closer, until she remembered her state of undress. Also, she couldn't be sure of the man's identity, since cascading water covered him.

Libby attempted to inch back up. The rock, which had been easy to navigate downward, proved too smooth. She would have to remain here until he'd left.

Lifting her knees, she placed her feet flat, half beneath her backside. Her position secure, she pushed thoughts of what had happened at the stream from her mind, concentrating instead on the figure under the falls.

Libby sucked in a breath.

Mercy! She hadn't meant to spy on anyone, particularly a naked man.

And *what* a man.

As he pivoted under the falls, water formed a wall around him. She glimpsed a broad back, well-formed arms, a trim waist, and a flash of a white backside. Dark wet hair clung to his head and face.

When he turned and lifted his arms above his head, the breath Libby held whooshed from her throat. His broad chest, with a heavy furring of hair that dipped into a dark band as it progressed lower, was spellbinding.

Shamelessly, she stared at the rest of him. If a man could be called beautiful, *he* was. Reno would look like this, she thought.

Ashamed of herself, she covered her mouth with her free hand. An old maid had no business ogling a naked man, even if he looked like a god. She watched him reverse positions, presenting his back again. She'd always wondered what a man would look like without his clothes. She had heard women's whispers of spindly, hairy limbs and, on one occasion, of a fleshy protrusion. But those underprivileged women hadn't been describing *him*.

She considered the possibility that Reno had cut his hair.

He stepped out from under the water and sluiced a hand over his hair, then down his chest. He looked up, straight at the sun, probably to gauge the time. Sunlight struck startlingly blue eyes.

Reno!

Libby slapped a hand over her mouth again. Color drained from her face. She'd been spying on Reno, and she hadn't even been sure of his identity.

A barely audible, ungodly sound came out of nowhere.

Libby snapped her head to the side. Cupping her ear with her hand, she listened. And gasped. A man's hideous laughter carried from a distance, from about the exact location where she'd felt icy fingers on her neck!

A violent shudder shook through her, causing her to release the branch.

The water felt good, cold and refreshing, Reno thought. It had also cured his desire for Libby. A glance at the sun told him he'd been gone longer than he'd intended.

A flash of white caught his attention. Reno faced the wall of the small canyon in time to see Libby slide downward over smooth rock. To his amazement, she landed on her feet.

As swift as a deer, she ran a zigzag course toward him. Her knees lifted to her waist as she leapt and dodged various-sized rocks. Water splashed in all directions from her frenzied flight, and her untidy hair flew about her. Clad in underclothes spotted with dirt, she showed no intention of stopping when she reached him. Sure she meant to plow him down, he braced himself for the full brunt of her impetuous charge. But instead of ramming him, she leapt straight at him.

Reno stepped back to maintain his balance. His heel, however, struck a sharp object and toppled him flat on his back in the pool at the foot of the falls. They sank beneath the surface of the water. Reacting swiftly, he anchored his hands on the slippery bottom and sat up . . . with Libby straddling him.

She shook uncontrollably and couldn't seem to catch her breath.

"What the hell?"

Her eyes were wide as she stammered, "I . . . I—"

"Leaping from cliffs again, Libby?"

"No, I—" She heaved a breath. "I was frightened."

He spared a grin. "Of what? What could have frightened you enough to make you jump on a man in the altogether?"

Her face immediately took on more color.

"I suppose you got a good look first?" Judging by the two bright dots of red on her cheeks, he'd guessed right. "Were you spying on me, Libby?"

"Certainly . . . not."

"What a charming liar you are," he said. "Did you find me so irresistible you couldn't wait to join me?"

"Reno McCord! That isn't what happened at all."

Water dripped from her hair, over her brow. He watched her dash a shaky hand over her face. "What frightened you, Libby?"

Suddenly, she threw her arms around him, muttering, "While I was bathing, something very cold and bony grabbed my neck."

He captured her wrists and broke her strangling hold. Terror flashed in her eyes, alarming him. "Did you see what it was?"

She slowly inhaled. "I thought it was a breeze, or that you were playing tricks on me. Only there wasn't a breeze, and you weren't nearby."

"Libby, playing a trick on you is one thing, frightening you to death is another."

"It wasn't a breeze, either." She shivered. "The air is calm."

"Maybe you took a chill."

A shiver shook her again. "It felt like icy fingers grabbed my neck."

"Icy fingers?"

She dipped her hands in water and strangled his neck, nearly choking him. "This is what it felt like. Any sane explanation you supply will be appreciated and accepted."

He cupped her cheeks, using his thumbs to stroke her lips. Her hair dripped water, her mouth trembled. He should have been there to protect her, he thought guiltily. "If you say you felt icy fingers, I believe you."

"You don't believe me," she accused.

"All right. I apologize. I haven't an explanation for what you experienced."

"It makes me shiver just thinking of it."

"Do you think you saw a ghost?"

Her mouth dipped briefly. "If I had seen an apparition, I surely wouldn't tell *you*."

He bit back a grin.

"I saw nothing." Another second of terror flashed in her eyes. "That's what frightened me. I ran until I found you. I wouldn't have come down, but I heard laughter." She tensed. "*Demented* laughter."

"I wasn't laughing, Libby."

She stared at him. Jerking free of his hands, she said, "Maybe not then, but you are now!"

Reno held his mouth in a somber line. "I'm sorry. But, if I told you the same story, what would you think?"

One of her shoulders shrugged as she lowered her eyes. "I would presume you were telling the truth."

He used a finger to tip up her chin. "Come now, Miss Chandler. You'd think I was crazy."

Moisture filled her eyes. "I'm not crazy," she

said in a soft, distressed voice. "And I'm not in the habit of imagining things."

He bound his arms around her. Crushing her against his chest, he searched for words to soothe her. "You're an intelligent woman. I believe you saw or heard something which frightened you. There's a logical explanation. When we go back, I'll search the area. Maybe I'll even find the cause of your unease."

Her arms wound around his back. Pressing tight against him, she sighed raggedly. But, just as quickly, she went rigid in his arms. "You're naked!"

Reno chuckled. "And you, Miss Chandler, are wearing wet underwear."

Abruptly, she shoved at his chest. As he gripped her shoulders and held her away, he looked lower. The wet camisole showed more of her breasts than it hid. Despite the cold water lapping at his hips, an unwelcome heat surged through his veins. "You're sure no scrawny chicken."

She gasped and crossed her arms over her chest.

"Don't hide yourself from me, Libby." He angled his head, trying to see her eyes. "Whatever your reasons for interrupting my bath, I don't mind if you sit on my lap." When he heard her suck in a breath, he smiled. "My ego is soaring."

"Your ego, Mr. McCord, is lower than a snake."

Belying her sharp retort, she seemed entranced with the sight of his bare skin. Her gaze drifted over his shoulders, arms, chest, and lingered on his abdomen. The heat in his veins escalated into a raging fire. Scornful of the reprimand sent by his conscience, he slid his hands to her waist.

"Like what you see?" he asked.

"No," she returned breathlessly.

Though he held her loosely, she made no move to rise. The pulse in her throat throbbed against her creamy skin. He wondered if her blood was as warm as his. Reno shut his eyes against the temptation Libby unwittingly offered.

"You know you're handsome," she said in a shaky voice. "Especially since you shaved and cut your hair."

"You noticed."

Her fingers slid over his chest, until they reached his shoulder. Reno held his breath, counting seconds. If he surrendered to the desire which licked at his insides, he'd be a fool. Libby wasn't herself at the moment. She wasn't aware of how her innocent exploration strained his willpower. He caught her fingers before temptation got the best of him. "Lady, I haven't had many good intentions in my life. If you don't get off of me and hurry back to where you left your clothes, I can't promise anything."

Immediately, she attempted to stand. Her legs, though, must've grown numb from the cold water. She plopped back down.

Water splashed his body and face. "Damn."

Another attempt to rise had worse results. Losing her balance, she fell forward. Her forehead knocked his face. With a curse on his lips, Reno clapped his left hand over his throbbing nose. His right hand locked around her arm and held her fast. "Don't move!"

"I'm sorry, but you always say such scandalous things."

He closed his eyes. "Lady, I'm beginning to see why you're regarded as ill-fated."

She tugged his hand away. "I barely bumped your nose, Mr. McCord. It looks fine. You will no doubt live."

His eyes met hers. The fine lines that feathered across her brow contradicted her unruffled remarks. He ached to rattle the prim control she exercised over her emotions. Once again, his mind warned him of the folly of messing with a rich woman who wanted different things out of life. "Thanks to you, my nose will probably be crooked," he said, his voice pained.

"I'm sure women will still find you quite handsome." She bit her bottom lip. "What I mean is, if you mind your manners, a woman might not notice your misshapen nose."

Reno scowled. "If I mind my manners, Libby, how is a woman to know I'm on fire for her?"

Crimson tore across her cheeks. "Perhaps you might regale her with an eloquent compliment."

He arched a brow at her taunt. When had he begun to like her? He wanted to kiss her so thoroughly that she would lose her senses. "I usually take a direct route to what I want."

"Do you, indeed?" She frowned as she stuck out a hand. "If you help me up, your nose will be spared another bump."

Instead, he chose to court danger. He dragged her into his arms.

Lord, she hadn't been herself the past minutes, not the retiring old maid she'd always been. Reno made her heart race, her pulse pound. Trapped in his strong arms, her senses went wild.

"Dammit, Libby, I know this is a mistake, but I

just can't help myself this time." His mouth slanted over hers with skilled purpose.

Libby forgot how to breathe.

His kiss swept her inhibitions far, far away. She drowned in the tide of emotions and pleasant sensations which skipped along her nerve endings. He'd always brought her emotions to life. Now, they whirled out of control. When she heard his moan, her own ego soared.

The pressure of his mouth escalated as his hands roamed her body, leaving her skin tingling and hot, aching to be touched again. Yet, as urgently as he devoured her, he remained gentle.

Wanting to touch him, too, she explored his body. His moan came again, longer and more anguished. He tore his mouth from hers and stared at her for an interminable amount of time. Gold sparks glittered in his eyes, emphasizing their dark blue color. She felt cast under a spell.

"Had enough, Libby? I'll stop if you want."

Shame washed over her. She didn't want him to stop, though logic dictated otherwise. She meant to nod, but shook her head, instead.

His laugh startled her, almost as much as his awkward attempt to stand with her in his arms. After two tries, he managed the feat. He carried her toward the waterfall.

He strode through the cascading falls, drenching them both. It was private, and pounding water created a thunderous ovation. He set her on her feet. Against her hip, she felt cold, wet granite.

His breath-stealing blue eyes roamed her face, then strayed lower. "You're beautiful, Libby."

The most beguiling tremble darted to her toes.

Realizing his gaze had settled on her breasts, she stammered, "They're not . . . very big."

When his hands replaced his gaze, his satisfied smile and sensual caress sent another tremble through her. Her knees felt wobbly.

He seized her wrists and pressed her hands to his chest. "Touch me," he said in a husky voice.

She had no mind to disobey his command. His skin stretched taut over his ribs, and his strong shoulders were exactly the right width. The muscles bunching in his upper arms lured her to drag her fingertips over their expanse.

A shudder ripped through Reno. She hadn't imagined she could affect him the same way he did her. Suddenly his large hands found her bottom and jerked her against him.

Her stomach lurched from his sudden move. Through the thin layer of her cotton drawers, he burned hard and hot against her stomach. The excitement she'd felt before paled in comparison to the tumult slashing through her now. A strike of lightning couldn't have ignited her more completely than Reno.

Chapter 11

He had lost his sanity.

But he was human, at this moment the weakest human alive. A man whose self-control had abandoned him. He should never have brought Libby behind the falls, to the private world he'd found earlier. He should never have kissed her in the first place, or touched her, or—hell.

His fingers tangled in her hair. Another mistake.

Despite her wet underclothes, heat penetrated the thin material, scorching him. He hungered to possess her, to show her the passion that dwelled within her. Reno surrendered to the blinding desire waiting to consume him.

He splayed his fingers deep in Libby's hair. Cradling her head, he captured her mouth with more pressure than he'd intended. When her lips opened in astonishment, he seized the advantage. He delved his tongue inside and ravished the tender recesses of her mouth. The splinter of sanity which remained in his passion-clouded brain warned of Libby's innocence.

But remembering the way she'd held on to him in a stranglehold back at the ravine, the way she clung to him as if her life were in jeopardy, his reasoning shattered under the sizzling effect of her fiery response.

Libby learned quickly. Her tongue met his, thrust for thrust, her sweet, hot mouth plundering his in return. Fire ripped through him. He swelled to a painful erection. Even that blatant demonstration of his desire failed to daunt her. As she pressed tighter against him, a low, ragged moan came from the back of her throat.

He swallowed her moan. With every measure of strength, he willed a semblance of control and regained a measure of command. Instead of ravishing her mouth, he began a slow, torturous seduction which mimicked the way he would make love to her.

If he dared tempt fate.

She wilted and he had to support her physically. Then her moan became a whimper. Blood pounded so hard in Reno's head, he feared fragile veins would explode.

He wasn't consuming Libby. She was consuming him.

His body burned, yet she made him all too aware of her own feelings. Her response seemed an almost joyful acceptance of what he'd previously regarded as merely a prelude to gratification of his lust.

Kissing Libby vanquished any such notion. His lust be damned. He felt as if their souls were entwined in a dangerous dance that would forever leave him branded.

* * *

Reno was making love to her with his kiss. The feelings shifting through her were so exquisite, Libby feared she'd swoon. She never wanted him to stop. No man could make her feel this way, no man except Reno. She knew it in her heart as surely as she knew that, beyond the waterfall, the sun still shone.

The thought sent a chill down her spine. Reno wasn't a man she should want. She knew that even as he kissed her into a sweet, paralyzing languor. He couldn't stay put long enough to have a home.

When his kiss waned into a gentle stroking of her mouth, she leaned against him for support. Whispers of spring danced in her mind, soft breezes and scented wildflowers.

His breath came in great, heaving gasps as he finally pulled his mouth from hers. "I can't do this!"

She still felt dizzy and weak, barely able to remain upright on her own.

"Libby," he mumbled as he brushed his fingers over her cheeks, "you surprised me. You kiss like a damn sorceress."

"You surprised me, too." Tears welled in her eyes and she dashed the back of her hand over her face. "No one will ever kiss me like that again."

Closing his eyes, he remained silent for seconds. "There's a man for you, maybe your Mr. Trout. He might be alive, waiting for you to come to him."

How could he remind her of her intended after he'd just kissed her senseless? Anger replaced the sweet languor she'd felt only seconds earlier. "How very chivalrous of you."

"Hell. Your virtue's safe."

He had changed her forever, she thought. "I disagree, Mr. McCord."

He released a ragged sigh as he sat her on the ledge behind him. "Lady, you still have me on fire. Only a thread of sanity is keeping me from taking you here, on a lousy bed of rock. You should be grateful I stopped before I'd ruined you."

"I am."

"What happened between us was lust. Don't read anything more into it."

Her shoulders sagged with despair. She should have known better than to think he'd felt anything. Another shiver ripped along her spine. She had blossomed when he'd kissed her, felt so alive and warm. But perhaps he'd been right. He probably treated every woman the same.

He brushed his mouth over hers before he held her away from him. "It's pointless, remember?"

She laid a hand on his cheek, gazing deeply into his eyes. Dear Lord, her lips tingled with remembrance. "How well I know."

"Keep looking at me like that, and I'm liable to kiss you again." He moved back a step, allowing her to see his arousal. "I'm still on fire for you. I can't guarantee I'd find the strength to stop." He nudged apart her knees and stood between them. Searching her face, he asked, "Are you shocked, Libby?"

Her face felt on fire, and her body ached in unmentionable places. She should have closed her eyes when he'd boldly displayed himself. Had she always been this wanton deep down? Libby steeled herself to speak in a cool, calm voice. "Nothing you say or do shocks me anymore, Mr. McCord."

As he drew a finger over the tiny buttons on the front of her wet camisole, amusement flickered in his eyes. "Are you challenging me, Libby? If so, it's only fair to warn you. I like to win."

Libby's breath turned shallow from his rapt attention and his husky tone. A rush of cool air on her chest caused her to gasp. "Heavens. How did you open my camisole without my knowledge?"

"Experience," he returned with a lazy grin. He covered her breasts with both hands. "Will you heed my warning now? Do you need further proof?"

Libby sucked in a tortured breath. Tremors rocked her from the ardent glow in his eyes. Before she could mutter another word, or even exhale the air trapped in her lungs, his mouth replaced one of his hands. His tongue reminded her of a lick of fire as it circled each of her nipples in turn, then laved them into taut points. Desire trickled through her. She writhed, fighting the unwanted emotion.

He was a devil. Or a god. At the moment, she didn't know or care which. No one had ever told her such delicious torment existed. Even Mrs. Peabody's descriptions of spiritual bliss with the right man failed miserably. So quickly, Reno had turned her into a quivering mass, unable to move or think.

She braced her hands on the ledge beside her hips.

Suddenly, he bowed his head and mumbled an obscene oath. When he straightened, his dark expression made her wince.

"Hell, I must be loco," he said, his voice bleak and full of self-contempt. His hands a bit shaky, he shoved her undergarment closed. He pushed buttons through the holes. "But, you, Miss Chandler, are either exceptionally cunning. Or crazy. Which is it?"

Libby tensed.

"You'd let a womanizing ne'er-do-well who'll never have a cent to his name nearly have his way with you? What do you want from me?"

Stunned by his accusing tone, she slapped him.

He barely flinched. "Now, you're acting like the woman I've come to know."

"You don't know me at all, Mr. McCord." She felt bereft, unsure of what she wanted. He muddled her mind and set fire to her insides. "You kiss me like the very devil himself, and then dare to blame me?"

He ran his fingers through his hair, leaving wide parts across the top. "I'm worse than the devil, Miss Chandler. I would take anything you offered and feel no regret."

"I hate you," she whispered harshly.

"I don't know what's running around in your head, but it's not hate."

Libby stiffened. He'd come so close to the truth.

"I kissed you, lady. And you kissed me back."

"You're insufferably conceited, Mr. McCord. Why should I be different from any other woman? As you've said, it's not a sin to have a good time."

His eyes widened briefly. "Do you want me to go back and get your clothes?"

"But I thought—"

"I'm not in the mood to swap insults, Miss Chandler," he snapped. "For your information, I've never kissed a woman like I kissed you. Do you want your clothes, or not?"

Her hands shook. Hiding her distress, she said, "Yes, please go for my clothes. You can't miss them as I wasn't far from our camp."

He swept her from the ledge, onto her feet. She watched him plow through the falls. Unabashedly, she considered his proud back, trim waist, and backside. Libby shook her head. He should have giant warts all over his body. Instead, he'd been gifted with perfect proportions and features. No decent woman would allow him to stir her emotions, and her body. She must not be decent. She wanted him. But his words and manner grew more confusing as the days passed.

Reno McCord would be the ruination of her yet.

He reappeared, drenched, his manner strictly business. He tossed her a bar of soap. "You might as well have your bath while I'm gone."

She stared at the spot where he'd just been. He'd vanished again. She remained dazed, unable to still the wayward yearnings he'd brought to life. Reno McCord acted like a drug in her system. But at least he'd tried to warn her of his wicked nature.

"Get cracking, Libby. We have miles to travel."

The masterful command had come from behind the waterfall. Shaking her head clear of her lethargy, she skirted the smooth wall of rock. Soap in hand, she peered past the falls. She spotted him right away, near a drooping bush. She watched him attempt to tug on his pants with the hindrance of a wet body. Impatient, he hopped several times. She shouldn't spy on him. Strangely, remorse evaded her.

Reno's mouth slanted in an annoyed line as he buttoned his pants. Was he still swollen with passion? It might explain his apparent difficulty, and his developing scowl.

When he buckled his belt, she found the sight stimulating, and far too suggestive. She felt wickedly sinful as she continued to watch him. He picked up his shirt but apparently had second thoughts. He hung it on the bush. After he'd draped his gunbelt over his shoulder, he climbed the embankment barefoot.

He wouldn't be gone long. Realizing she'd wasted precious time, she dashed under the waterfall. She soaped her body from head to toe, shivering all the while. With Reno, she was never cold. He heated her from the inside out.

Angry with herself for sparing him a thought, she applied more vigor to her task. Perhaps, if she scrubbed her skin raw, she could wash him out of her mind as well.

She'd just finished when she heard him say, "You can come out now. I've closed my eyes."

True to his word, he held his eyes pressed shut. He held out a blanket with both hands and she stepped into the circle of warmth. After he'd wrapped the blanket around her from behind, he tightened his arms for several heart-stopping minutes.

"Thank you," she said with a catch in her voice.

Close to her ear, he returned, "For what?"

"For being so considerate." She angled her head, attempting to see his face over her shoulder. "I know you must've seen all of me through my wet underclothes, yet you're pretending you haven't. Dare I question your motives?"

"I don't want your gratitude. And don't give credit where it isn't due."

"Your *rare* kindnesses are certainly reason for comment," she remarked.

"I'm not being kind!" He moved away. "I know what you look like, all right. I brought the blanket to preserve what sanity I have left."

She reveled in his testy mood. She felt equally as frustrated. He'd taken her to the brink of some ecstasy about which she could only wonder, and then left her curious and unfilled. Holding the blanket tight, she faced him. She wanted to hate him. Why couldn't she? At least she could dish him some of his own medicine. "You're even handsome with a fierce scowl," she said sweetly.

A faint smile tugged at the corners of his mouth.

"I know what you meant, now."

He lifted a brow.

"When you were teaching me to ride." Though she ordered her eyes to remain on his face, of their own volition they darted lower. "About hard-tack."

A long minute passed before he spoke. "I've thoroughly corrupted you. You wouldn't have come out with such an unseemly remark before."

"Unseemly?" she asked as she devoured his bare chest. "I see nothing whatsoever unseemly. My breath quite escapes me when I look at you." An intense desire to touch him threatened her. He was so masculine, so enticing when he behaved himself. Why did she find him much more enticing when he didn't? "I wonder exactly how many women have succumbed to your kisses."

"Dammit, Libby. You don't make it easy. Are you purposely trying to arouse me again?"

"Certainly not, Mr. McCord. Your mood seems to deteriorate when you're in such a state."

Holding her gaze high, she noted faint color tinged his neck. Had she been cruel to taunt him? Judging by the wrinkles radiating from the corners of his eyes and across his brow, she had succeeded.

"I can't count the number of women who have succumbed to my kisses. I assure you, my mood has never *deteriorated* with them. But no other woman has—" He scowled again. "Your clothes are over there," he said. He pointed to the bush under which he'd dressed earlier. "You have ten minutes. I don't like leaving the animals unattended much longer."

He'd assumed an all-business manner again, but his brusque tone barely fazed Libby. He'd masked his feelings, or embarrassment, over an admission he'd almost let slip. Though she hated to admit to a weakness, she would give her last dollar to know what he would've said.

Libby dressed quickly and found his back to her. She wondered if he sought to guard himself against unwanted passion again. Surely he hadn't allowed her privacy out of some sense of decency. Neither had he stopped kissing her because of an attack of honor. A man like Reno McCord took what he wanted without a thought to the consequences.

Suddenly the memory of her nightmare returned in full force. Had it been a dire warning? Had her intended grown angry because, despite her best intentions, she'd failed to distance herself from Reno?

She snatched his shirt from the branches of the bush and went to him. "Cover yourself, Mr. McCord."

He spun around and took the garment. As he pushed his arms into the sleeves, he looked her over. "You've lost the rest of your hairpins, haven't you, Libby?"

Wet hair trailed over her shoulders, dampening her back. She gave him a curt nod.

"I like it down." He fumbled with the bottom button of his shirt. "It's more becoming than the way you wore it when we first met."

Feeling peculiar inside again, she brushed away his hand and worked on his buttons herself. "Let me."

She shouldn't have offered her services, she thought. Being close to him had an intoxicating affect. Though she felt a physical awareness, as usual, the act of helping him dress, of performing such a simple deed for him, left her with a warm glow. When they parted, there would be a void in her heart. If he met with a tragic end, she'd feel even worse.

"Let's not go any farther," she said in a rush. "Clarence must be dead. He wouldn't want me to hunt for his remains."

She reached the third button. But he trapped her wrist, stilling her movement. "Why the sudden change of heart? I thought he was calling out to you."

The fate which had befallen Reno in her dream sped across her mind. "It's turned out a much longer trip than I intended."

"You're lying again, Libby."

"Yes, I am," she retorted as she lifted her chin. "I think the icy fingers I felt at the stream might have belonged to a ghost."

"Another lie?"

She glanced up and drowned in his gentle look. She had expected him to mock her. "Not precisely. I was frightened out of my wits."

His thumb caressed her wrist. "The truth, Libby. Why have you suddenly decided to call a stop to the search? Is it because of what nearly happened between us? What might still happen before we find Trout?"

"Heavens, no." Realizing how her response must have sounded, she said, "As you pointed out, you haven't done much more than kiss me."

A wry smile pulled up one corner of his mouth. "I told you I'd let you know when I had designs on your innocence."

"You did," she stammered as heat touched her cheeks. "In the future, though, you mustn't kiss me. It will only complicate our deal."

His eyes slightly narrowed as his smile deepened. "You're evading my question. Why have you changed your mind about searching for Mr. Trout?"

Libby frowned. "You're much too stubborn for my liking."

"Tell me, dammit!"

"All right, if you must know. I had another dream in which *you,* not Clarence, died."

"Dreams don't frighten me."

"Even if we find Clarence, I can't marry him now."

He touched her cheek. "Libby, your virtue is intact, a bit tarnished, that's all. He'll never know I laid a hand on you."

"I'll know." She lowered her gaze. "I'll know how you made me feel. I would always know I'd cheated him."

"You'll feel the very same with him, or with any man."

She said nothing. Reno was wrong. The glorious emotions, the fiery desire that rippled through her when he touched her, would never happen with another man. Desolation swept over her. She should never have begun this journey or met Reno McCord.

"You've hired me to find Trout. Find him I will."

Dark hair curled on the skin still visible in the open section of his shirt. Quickly, she fastened another button. "Libby," he said roughly, as if the words were torn from his throat. "I'm not the marrying kind."

"I'm not dense, Mr. McCord," she retorted crisply. "But, as your employer, I have a right to worry for your welfare."

Reno tucked his shirttail into his pants, all the while considering Libby. His employer. She never failed to remind him of their differences.

Leaving her, he pulled on his boots and used the time to reclaim his resolve. He'd come too close to losing himself in her. Worse, she had hit so close to the truth, it frightened him like hell. He hadn't just kissed her. He had been making love to her.

When he was ready, he helped her climb the bank downstream, where it rose more gently. He tried but failed to put what had happened at the falls from his mind. Things wouldn't be the same between them now that he'd tasted her sweet, savage response to his kisses. She'd seared her brand on him.

Determined to master the desire still simmering

in his blood, and the unsettling emotions she made him feel, he looked at everything except Libby. It was useless, of course, but not for lack of effort on his part.

Upon reaching the spot where the stream fell into the falls, she stopped so abruptly that he plowed into her. "What's wrong?"

She held her spine as rigid as a post. "Nothing."

He sensed that whatever had scared her lingered in her mind. "I don't know of another way to return. I might overshoot our camp."

Her steps slower and shorter, she stared out again. "I'm not afraid with you here with me."

He grabbed her arm and turned her to face him. "Trust me, there are no ghosts. Your imagination got the better of you."

"I know I heard a man's demented laughter."

"The wind sometimes plays tricks on people."

"There was no wind."

Reno fell silent, at a loss for a comeback. "Well, there must be an explanation."

"Obviously, we won't find it here, will we?" She forged ahead, saying, "Are you coming?" She glanced over her shoulder, daring him with a look. "I'll have need of your expertise if the owner of the chilling laugh does happen along."

The lady had grit. And a certain way of taunting him which, to his dismay, he found far too exciting. He hadn't been bored in *her* company.

As he followed her, he watched the subtle but very feminine sway of Libby's hips. Her backside curved with a man's downfall in mind. His temperature shot a degree higher. He should've taken the lead, he thought.

Without warning, she stopped, nearly causing

him to trip over her. "I'm surprised you—" Her eyes narrowed as her lips pursed together. "Enjoying yourself, Mr. McCord?"

Heat rose to Reno's face. He cursed the telltale proof. "Hell, I'm only human. I can't help it if you've been blessed with a fair behind."

"Only fair, Mr. McCord?"

Shocked to his core by her remark, he struggled for a reply. "I should've said exquisite."

Hands on her hips, she subjected him to a thorough scrutiny. "Exquisite is the precise word I'd use to describe yours, also. The rest of you isn't so bad, either." She whipped around and set off at a fast pace.

Reno was slow to follow, slower to close his gaping mouth. Sometimes, he didn't know what to make of Libby. When he came alongside her, he said, "I'm not sure if I approve of your forward manner. You never acted this way back in Denver."

"Blame yourself."

"I've done nothing, Libby," he protested with an innocent air, "except give you one measly kiss."

"I'm curious." Her gaze shied from his. "When you kissed me the first time, you said you could kiss better. I suppose you save your best for special occasions."

Reno coughed and successfully covered a laugh. If he'd accomplished nothing, apparently he'd taught Libby how to have a little fun. "It's unwise to mock a man's prowess."

"Indeed? I was very serious."

Her eyes flashed with green sparks. Reno lost his train of thought. Long, dark and curling gently, her lashes made an enticing fringe. Why did her eyes have to be such an alluring combination of colors? He must've been blind not to have noticed them in Denver. He shook his head. "Had I given you my best kiss, Libby, we'd still be at the waterfall."

She swallowed before she said, "You're very smug, Mr. McCord, to think that."

He leaned close and inhaled the scents of fresh air and the soap he'd given her. She was downright provocative. And tempting him beyond his endurance. But he suspected her playful banter masked her unease. They must be close to the place where she'd thought she'd felt icy fingers touch her neck.

They reached the spot where he'd found her clothes, and Libby's pace picked up. Because of his longer stride, he adjusted his step easily. She'd seen or felt something here. Though he doubted it had been anything as unlikely as an apparition, he wondered what could have disturbed her enough to send her into a panic.

She had run to him in fright.

A surge of protectiveness rose within him. He'd never before wanted to protect a woman from harm. From himself.

He had felt more, physically and emotionally, during those fevered minutes at the waterfall than in his entire life. He forced the thought from his mind. He wanted no bonds to Miss Libby Chandler.

Little fool. She was entirely too trusting. *He* was a greater danger to her than a being returned from the grave.

Chapter 12

❦

They had ridden for several hours. She'd grown used to sitting a horse and could've kept up with Reno, Libby thought. Well, almost. His sedate pace aroused her curiosity. Was he intentionally prolonging their travel?

There could never be a permanent relationship between them. He loved a good time, probably owned nothing of value, and couldn't stay in one town too long. He loved women and brawling in saloons far too much to ever change. Perhaps if she reminded herself of his unsuitability more often, she would find him less attractive.

Fat chance of that ever happening, she mused.

As she followed behind him, she admired his broad back. His kisses at the waterfall had been emblazoned into her soul. Her own brazen behavior, the wanton manner in which she'd responded to him, played in her mind. A decent woman would be grateful he had mastered his passion.

Lord, she must be a shameless hussy. She would always regret the sudden control he'd found. Reno confused her. She confused herself more. How could she long to be close to him, to recapture the wondrous feelings she'd discovered in his arms? Contrary to his words, lust had played only a minor part in her delirium.

If he had made love to her, she would have been ruined. The thought, which should have mortified her, had the opposite result. Her hopes of finding Clarence were quickly evaporating. No other man would ever come along, certainly no one as exciting as Reno. At least she would've had intimate knowledge of Reno to savor during the long, lonely years to come. And if the townspeople had whispered behind her back and called her an ill-fated old maid, she would have pretended not to have heard.

She would have known that, for a few brief moments, Reno McCord had belonged to her.

Libby gasped at the wayward thoughts which had meandered through her mind. She was definitely no longer the same woman who had left Denver.

Reno stopped in a high area dwarfed by spectacular mountains. Trees thickly dotted the landscape, affording a canopy. She watched him dismount and unpack Charity, as he spoke softly to the mule. He did possess some fine traits.

Libby followed his example and led Sugar to the spot Reno had chosen to secure the animals. She retrieved her extra set of underclothes and the blanket from the pommel, where she'd looped them to dry, and put the underwear in her bag.

He hadn't spoken much to her since they'd left their previous camp. Maybe it had been his way of dealing with what had happened between them. But she had missed his company.

"I'm not as tired today," she ventured as she circled the pack animal. "I suppose I'm getting used to having my bones jarred for hours on end." He gave her a barely perceptible nod in return, so she waited while he unsaddled his horse. "Or maybe a certain portion of my anatomy has grown numb."

When he moved to drop the saddle, she thought she detected a slight curve to his mouth.

"Is that how you've managed all these years?" she asked. "Has a portion of your body ceased to exist in your mind?"

He spun around. "No, Libby, it hasn't. My ass hurts just like anybody else's if I ride too far."

She smiled. She'd sparked some reaction from him.

"What? You aren't going to criticize my choice of words?"

"It's futile to try to change you."

"Ah, you've learned a lot about me, after all."

"Not as much as I'd like to learn," she blurted out. Libby promptly bit her tongue. "You're an interesting individual. Colorful, I should say."

His brows furrowed together. "How about gathering some sticks for a fire. I could drink ten cups of coffee right about now."

Libby roamed the area and found the wood he'd requested. At least he'd allowed her a chore. As she dropped the collection of sticks, her eyes lingered on his body. She noted everything about him. How his shirt drew taut across his broad back when he reached for something. The way his black pants hugged his long, muscular legs. Mostly, she appreciated the lock of hair which fell forward on his brow, softening his features.

Libby inhaled a shaky breath. He was intoxicating. His cheeks looked as if they'd been sculpted by a master craftsman. His jaw rounded with perfection. Despite the times she'd bumped him, his nose no longer boasted the slightest hint of swelling. It descended in a straight, fine line. Were he dressed in evening wear, no woman would be able to resist him.

Women couldn't resist him now, she thought. Reno needn't marry. He would never want for female company.

"I'll see if I can find water," he said so suddenly that Libby nearly jumped out of her boots.

Coffeepot in hand, he disappeared into the thick foliage which surrounded them.

She wondered if she'd ever know his quicksilver change of moods. Or her own.

During his absence, she collected enough wood to last the night. Afterward, she ventured off to tend nature's call. When she returned, Reno sat with his legs crossed before a roaring fire.

"My, you are certainly efficient," she said as she seated herself beside him. "I thought you'd be gone much longer."

He aimed her a confident smile. "It seems I've a knack for finding water."

"You have a knack for a lot of things." Uncomfortable under his penetrating look, she stared at the coffeepot in the fire. "I'm not hungry yet."

"Neither am I."

She felt his avid scrutiny. A warm glow invaded her. Had he known of her fervid examination a short time ago?

"Your hair's tangled."

Libby promptly ran her hands over the bushy mass.

"It looks all wild," he said. "If you get your brush, I'll brush it for you."

"No!"

She was as shocked as he looked from her adamant response. She didn't trust herself. If he performed such an intimate act for her, she'd grow weak and hot all over and probably embarrass herself.

"Brushing my hair isn't a chore I expect you to do," she said in a softer voice. "Why, you'll probably expect me to pay you something extra."

"No extra charge, Libby." He chuckled and captured a handful of her hair. "I didn't think you were such a coward."

His light touch brought her gaze to his for a very long minute. "You're a strange man. You ignore me all afternoon, then want to brush my hair. Why?"

"I can only be strong for short intervals, that's why. Did you think I was made of granite?"

Memories of their passionate embrace at the waterfall floated in her mind. Libby smiled. "Granite you're definitely not."

His eyes drifted over her face, finding and lingering on her mouth. "Are you thinking of the waterfall?"

She sat straight. "Definitely not."

He released her hair instantly. "You are a witch. You cast a spell over me when I least expect it."

She cast him a curious gaze. "You're addled. I've rarely seen an old maid witch. If I truly had such powers, I'd have men begging for my hand."

He grinned. "The men you've associated with

were blind and ignorant. If they had taken time to get to know you, they would've seen what a remarkable woman you are."

A butterfly batted its wings in her stomach. It wasn't like Reno to spout flowery words. Adopting a teasing tone, she said, "Flattery will get you everywhere, Mr. McCord."

"A tempting observation if ever I heard one." All trace of amusement faded from his expression. His mouth grim, he said, "Playful banter of this sort is exactly what I hoped to avoid."

Libby sighed. "If that's how you feel, you shouldn't have spoken to me at all. But . . . I've grown rather fond of your teasing."

"Hell, Libby, I'm not teasing. That's the problem. I want you, and I don't trust myself."

Libby lowered her vision. She wanted him, too. They were partners in misery. Her eyes strayed to his mouth, upon which hovered a faint smile. "Rest assured, I have no desire to kiss you again."

"But you *would* like to redeem me."

"I suppose most respectable women would see you as a challenge."

His lips grazed hers, as if he were merely sampling her. "You can't change me."

Libby shut her eyes against the warmth he inspired in her traitorous body. "So you've said. Many times."

"Yet you allow me to kiss you. It gives a man ideas."

An image of Reno being stabbed with a dagger loomed in her mind. Abruptly, she lurched away. She drew in a steadying breath. Had Clarence sent the image to bring her to her senses?

Reno stood so fast, Libby nearly fell backwards.

He held his gun. And she hadn't even seen him draw.

He mouthed a foul oath as he dipped his fingers into his pant's pocket. "Someone's coming."

She darted a look behind her. "Who? I don't hear anything."

"Two if I'm not mistaken."

He helped her rise. Pressing something into her hand, his voice sounded urgent. "Put up your hair, Libby."

"Oh, you skunk! You had my pins all along."

A sheepish grin on his face, he confessed, "I wanted to look at your hair. I planned to give them back. Eventually."

She heard the intruders now. They made an ungodly amount of noise, which sounded like pans clanging together. "Do you think they're friendly?"

"Friendly or not, I'm not feeling sociable at the moment."

Libby stuck the pins between her teeth. While she hurried to pull her hair into a knot at her nape, Reno's gaze followed her movements. Her task became more difficult.

"If it weren't for them," he snarled, "I'd be kissing you right about now. It's a bad omen."

"Your confidence amazes me, Mr. McCord. I was not about to kiss *you*. But maybe they're just passing through."

"They'll stay. They probably smell the coffee."

He looked so disgruntled, Libby thought it best not to smile. Reno had stolen her hairpins. She might have been angry if not for his confession.

He kept track of the men's progress and studied her at the same time. "If I were sure we had enough time, I'd tell you to put the dress back on."

"Perhaps you have a flour sack handy as well." His mouth thinned at her remark, so she added, "It's acceptable for you to stare at my . . . shape, but not other men?"

"Exactly right, Libby."

She could've sworn he'd sounded possessive of her.

Reno swung around.

Two very different men came out of the trees. One short, portly, and shabbily dressed. The other, of medium height, wore more costly clothes. Even their choice of animals differed. The smaller man rode a mule, his partner a spirited dun horse. The horse pawed the ground when they stopped. Behind them, another mule had been loaded down with shovels, picks, pans, and the like.

The coffeepot chose that second to boil over.

Mumbling beneath his breath, Reno holstered his gun. He squatted and swooped the pot from the fire. A louder mumble escaped him.

When he stuck several fingers into his mouth, Libby smothered a grin. For such a competent man, Reno was certainly prone to accidents.

"Told ya," the smaller man said to his friend. He swung one leg over the front of his mule and dropped to his feet. Snatching off a tattered, dusty hat, he flashed Libby a smile. "Archie, here, said I was plumb loco. I knew I smelt coffee."

The man had no front teeth on the top, lending an occasional whistle to his words. His thin, gray hair stuck out in tweaks.

"You were right," Libby said. "If you have cups, you're welcome to help yourself."

With a grumble, Reno came to his feet. A grimace pulled at his mouth.

She shot him a pointed look. "Be nice," she whispered. "I like the little man."

Reno rolled his blue eyes heavenward as he skirted around her. He held out his hand to the second man who had remained on his horse. "Reno McCord. As my woman said, you're welcome to join us."

His woman? Though Libby blinked at his remark, she let it pass.

"Archibald McGovern," the man said as he shook hands with Reno. He nodded at his toothless friend. "This is Snake Walton. We're much obliged."

Snake hurried to the pack mule. Within seconds he shuffled to the campfire with two dented tin cups. Libby mastered a smile. His well-worn, overly large pants gaped between taxed suspenders which had lost a hook. His faded brown shirt had lost two buttons smack in the center. Red underwear peeked through the opening. Instead of squatting, he bent from the waist to fill the cups.

McGovern had also dismounted. She found Reno and he engaged in a lively conversation.

While Snake gulped swallows of the coffee, Libby peered past him at McGovern. A much younger man with pleasant features, sandy hair, and a thin, slightly darker mustache, he noticed her right off. He glanced past Reno's shoulder. Though layers of dust hid the color of his trousers, they had been tailored from good material. Likewise his shirt. The two men made an odd pair, she thought.

Reno brought McGovern to the fire, where Snake handed over one of the cups.

"It's mighty agreeable of you to share with us," McGovern said. His brown eyes drifted to Libby. "You haven't introduced us to the lady."

Libby offered a hand. "Libby Chandler. It's a pleasure to meet you, Mr. McGovern."

"Libby." He gripped her fingers and held them seconds longer than propriety demanded. "It's been a long time since we've come across a woman in these parts. Call me Archie."

A glare pinching the corners of his eyes, Reno interjected, "*Miss* Chandler to you."

Libby considered the censure she'd heard in Reno's voice. She hadn't been mistaken. He *was* acting possessive of her.

"Forgive me, Miss Chandler," Archie said quickly. He followed Snake's example and gulped the coffee. "Been in the wilds too long. Forgot my manners. This sure is good. We ran out a week ago."

"Are you mining for gold?" Libby asked.

"Ain't found much to talk of," Snake volunteered. "But we didn't stay long in the last place. We aim to try west of here."

Reno eyed the men suspiciously. "Why did you leave the last place? Gold run out?"

Snake's eyes bulged. "No sirree." He shuffled his feet. "There was this screaming banshee what scairt me sh—, what scairt me."

Archie grabbed his friend's arm and pulled him back. "You'll have to forgive Snake. He imbibed too freely one night and thought he saw a transparent fiend. Cured him of his drinking for a day."

Libby's knees went weak. She sidestepped to maintain her balance. She looked at Reno. Ignoring his cynical smile, she said, "The editor of the paper in Denver told me that many people have seen strange things in a canyon near here."

Reno narrowed his eyes at her. "Nothing but hearsay."

Snake shoved Archie aside. "I seen it. I did. Howled at me somethin' awful. Weren't the drink, neither."

Unable to restrain herself, Libby aimed Reno a smug look.

"Snake hightailed it, leaving me to pack up our supplies."

"You said you weren't scairt!" Snake shot back.

"You might as well share our supper," Reno said, his tone lacking enthusiasm.

The men nodded in response. When Reno left them, she lowered her voice and asked, "At any point did you feel a cold rush of air?"

When Snake opened his mouth, Archie punched his shoulder to silence him. But the fear she saw in the shorter man's eyes was answer enough. A chill shook Libby's composure.

Reno pried open two cans and dumped beans into a pan. Though his expression betrayed little, she detected a distinct hostility in his movements.

Throughout their supper, Reno controlled the conversation. He asked questions about the area, then regaled them with his experiences as a scout.

Libby felt excluded, so she retired a distance away. As she sat on her blanket, a moment of worry troubled her. Reno seemed determined to ignore the importance of Snake's frightful experience.

Then she noticed someone had produced a deck of cards. Reno, in turn, brought out the bottle of whiskey. Soon, all three looked and sounded intoxicated. Hoots and exuberant yells erupted at the end of each hand of poker. She suspected Reno was gambling the money she'd paid him. Worse, he seemed unconcerned when he lost. She thought it inconceivable to gamble so freely without conscience. If he lost all of his money, he would have only the half she still owed him.

Reno McCord loved a good time, she reminded herself. However, as she watched him now, she realized exactly how difficult it would be for him to change. His eyes fairly glowed, his grin came easily, as did his laughter. With an especially loud hoot, he slapped down five cards. He raked the money close to his feet.

"That was the devil's own luck, McCord," Archie complained.

"The hell it was!" Reno fired back.

Libby frowned. Both of their voices sounded slurred. Before long, they'd all be drunk. She collected her blanket and moved as far away as it was safe. If she went to bed, when she awoke she might find the three of them passed out.

Despite the frequent shouts, and Reno's absence at her side, she drifted into a restless sleep. After a while, the noise abated until only small sounds drifted to her.

An image of Clarence floated through her mind. In the familiar area of fallen red rock, another man appeared, his manner hostile.

Libby squirmed, moaning in her sleep.

Some part of her foggy mind registered a difference, the warmth of a body fitted against her back. A strong arm fell around her. Despite the odor of whiskey, she welcomed Reno's presence. It dispelled the nightmare and sleep claimed her.

She waited on the sidelines of Maryville's church hall, at a social. Men decked out in their Sunday best tapped their feet to music supplied by local musicians. Women, also wearing their best frocks, chattered gaily and tittered behind their hands.

But not her. She stood, alone, watching couples dance. An old maid no man wanted.

It wasn't a dream she'd ever had before, but it had happened more than once. She had always felt alone at gatherings, even the one time when Clarence Trout had escorted her.

Something was about to happen. She gazed around the room. She felt peculiar, as if she were under scrutiny. But no one paid her any mind. It was as if she weren't really there, as if she were merely an onlooker.

The people who clogged the dance floor slowly moved aside to open a wide space. She couldn't imagine why.

Had something dreadful happened?

All eyes turned to her. Libby looked to each of the townspeople in turn, questioning them. The feeling that someone was staring at her became intense.

A tall man dressed in elegant evening attire stood across the hall. He could've been a prince. From his smart top hat to the toes of his polished shoes, his outfit spoke of refinement. A crisply starched white shirt drew attention to his sun-darkened skin. A dignified gray-striped waistcoat added the perfect touch to his black coat and trousers. When he started toward her, her breath lodged in her throat.

Only when he came close did she notice the color of his eyes. Blue. A deep, dark, mesmerizing shade which could only belong to Reno McCord.

But it couldn't be he.

He looked dashing as he swept off his hat and bent into a charming bow. Then, tossing his hat to a man, he stepped right up to her. "Dance with me, my love," he said.

Libby's head began to spin. He whirled her around on the dance floor, eliciting gasps from the people they passed. She tried to speak to him and found she could not. He said nothing more as they danced. And danced.

She tried to focus on faces. She spotted Mrs. Peabody, who laughed and clapped her hands. Libby desperately wanted to tell the kind lady it was a dream. Reno McCord wasn't the sort to dress in grand attire and squire a lady around a dance floor.

She swung her gaze back to Reno and drowned in his devastating smile. "You're not real," she urgently whispered.

"I'm real, all right. Marry me, Libby, and I'll love you forever."

"Now, I know this is a dream."

"I can't live without you. I've given up my reckless ways. I want what you want: a family, home, and babies. Lots of babies."

Someone shook her. "No," she mumbled. She didn't want to awaken. Her mind tried to recapture the wonderful thoughts she'd had only a second before.

"Libby," a sleepy-sounding voice said close to her ear. "Stop mumbling."

Libby cracked open one eye and saw darkness. "Reno?"

His arm tightened around her middle. "You were dreamin'." A loud, prolonged yawn rustled her hair. "And talkin' in your sleep."

"It was a wonderful dream," she said, a touch of sadness creeping into her voice.

"Dreamin' of me?"

The temptation rose to admit the fanciful things she'd dreamt about him. Pride held her silent. "You've been drinking," she said softly.

"Yeah."

"You don't sound drunk, though."

"I wanted to be. I'm sober enough." After a short silence, he asked, "Did you think I'd get falling-down drunk with two strange men near?"

"I wasn't sure. When last I heard, all of you were enjoying yourselves."

She lay quiet. She relished the comfort of having him so close. She'd gotten used to sleeping near him much too fast. When they parted, her nights were bound to be lonely beyond belief. "Did you lose everything?"

"Ten dollars." His hand slid across her stomach and settled on her hip. "I could've just as easily won a hundred."

Tingles skipped down her leg even as her mood dipped lower. How casually he spent his hard-earned money. "You might have lost a hundred, also."

"That's why it's called gamblin'." His hand lazily roamed her leg then stilled when it encountered her hip again. He nuzzled her ear. "You'll never know how much fun gamblin' is 'til you've tried it."

Her breath turned shallow from his warm breath on her neck. "I couldn't possibly . . . risk . . . my money on such uncertainty."

"I'll teach you how to play poker, and you won't have to wager a cent." His caress grew bolder, his palm sliding over her stomach again before venturing higher. "Tomorrow, maybe."

Intellect told her to push him away. Her body, however, craved his touch. Dear Lord, she was doomed. She could no more relinquish his comfort than she could stop breathing. "You won't have any incentive to win."

"Who says I won't?" His fingers molded around one of her breasts. His breath sounding as strained as her own had been, he whispered, "You can wager your clothes."

"My . . . clothes?"

He chuckled. "One item at a time."

Seizing his hand, she lifted it far enough to tuck it under her chin for safekeeping. She felt entirely too flushed. And weak all over. God only knew where their two guests had chosen to sleep. "You said yourself I'm smart. Why, I just might win all of *your* clothes instead."

With a chuckle, he slipped free and rolled her to face him. He brushed his lips over hers. "That sounds good, too. Look what nearly happened earlier when you saw me in all my glory."

A retort danced on her tongue. But she was too warm and amused to chastise him. Besides, he probably would have forgotten by morning. The thought dared her to say, "You were *exquisite*."

"Damn, Libby. You have me on fire again."

"You woke me and began your own misery," she accused as she weakened to a temptation. She kissed his cheek. "What have you done with Snake and Archie?"

"They're dead to the world. It appears they can't hold their liquor."

"And you can?"

"Need you ask?" He slid her closer, until she took his meaning. "I'm not dead to the world. I'm very much alive. And I'll probably not have another second of sleep tonight. Neither will you."

"How can you say that?" she asked breathlessly.

"You're trembling, Libby. If we were alone, I'd do more than kiss you this time."

"You're not sober, Mr. McCord, or you wouldn't be saying such things." The moment the words left her mouth, she frowned. Reno needed no incentive to act brashly. "Go to sleep and stop tormenting me."

"I haven't begun to torment you, Libby."

He rolled her under him and tangled his fingers in her hair. His mouth slanted across hers. Tasting whiskey, Libby jerked her face aside. But he didn't retreat. Hot kisses rained across her cheek, down her neck and settled beneath her chin. Dizziness assailed her.

"Your pulse is racing, again," he said against her throat. "You want me."

"It's the liquor talking, Mr. McCord. Let me go."

"You sound breathless."

"No," she said. Dismayed because her voice had, indeed, come out breathless, she sighed. "You're drunk!"

"My name's Reno. Say it."

"Reno."

His lips seared a path lower, to the open vee in her shirt. Heaven help her, she did want him. She was powerless against him, and if he refused to stop, she knew she'd be lost. If any other man dared take such liberties, she'd fight him with her last breath. She *was* doomed. She no longer had the strength to resist him.

He released a ragged sigh. "If you have a lick of sense, you'll stay away from me tomorrow." Abruptly he released her. Rolling away, he snarled, "I have no good intentions where you're concerned. Not anymore."

His words held a promise. Unease channeled through her, making her heart skip a beat. Well it should, she mused.

Tomorrow she might very well lose much more than her heart.

Chapter 13

❦

L ate the following morning Libby peeked over Charity's head and saw Archie hunkered down by the remains of their campfire. Reno and Snake had been gone an hour. A glimpse of the men's animals told her they'd be on their way shortly.

She liked their visitors, particularly Snake, but she wanted them gone. She felt they were intruding on her time with Reno. Were they to remain, they might also tempt Reno into another card game. With nothing to occupy her time, she headed to the spot where she and Reno had spent the night. As she shook out the blanket and folded it, the preposterous dream she'd had about Reno skipped across her mind.

It had been folly to imagine Reno McCord in evening attire, behaving like a polished gentleman. He was a different sort. If would be more sensible to imagine him as he'd looked this morning with a well-used hat, a gunbelt strapped to his hips, and a day's growth of dark beard. Were he to appear at a social function, he'd most likely grab her hand before he unceremoniously yanked her into his arms.

She went to Charity and tucked the blanket beneath the sack which held their supplies. Wisdom told her to do the same with her dreams of Reno.

"We'll be leaving soon as Snake gets back."

Libby sucked in a startled breath. She hadn't heard Archie approach.

"As will we," she said, facing him. Though she thought him an attractive man, she sensed a softness about him. Perhaps it wasn't fair to compare him with Reno. "I hope you find the gold you're seeking."

"We might get lucky."

Libby averted her gaze from his intense brown eyes. Though he had looked overly long at her several times yesterday, she had thought nothing of it. Any woman dressed in man's clothes attracted attention. She returned to the open area where they'd sat last night. When she stopped, she realized he'd followed her.

Where were Reno and Snake? "Do you know where your partner and Reno are?" she asked, her tone surprisingly composed.

"Snake took Reno to see something."

Suspicion crawled through her mind. "What?"

"I don't know," he answered. "Might be he was showing him the way to that canyon Reno mentioned when we were playing cards."

His reply sounded feasible enough. Had her imagination caused her unease? She wasn't normally a suspicious person. Under the pretext of watching for Reno, she moved several feet and stared at the line of trees beyond the clearing.

Again, Archie followed her, apparently determined to dog her heels, and escalated her unease. She felt like a defenseless animal pursued by larger, relentless prey. To occupy him during Reno's absence, she asked, "Where are you from?"

"Been many places." His thin brown mustache grew thinner when he smiled. "Don't stay in any one town long." He ran a finger over her shirtsleeve. "You his woman, like he said?"

Libby's heart fluttered wildly. "Reno said so, didn't he?"

"I wanted to hear it from you. Thought you might give me a little kiss before we go."

A gasp jumped to Libby's throat. She quickly swallowed. Intending to catch him off guard and then flee, she eased a foot behind her.

His mouth lifted on one side.

Libby tensed. Her instincts about this man had been right.

"All I want is one little kiss." He looked her up and down. "Bet you've given *him* more than that. A man like McCord wouldn't be happy with just your kisses."

Instantly furious, Libby splayed her hands on her hips. A voice in her mind urged caution, but she ignored it. "What's between Reno and me is none of your business. Stop following me."

When he gave a low laugh, Libby nearly stumbled. But perhaps he merely sought to bluff her, to see if she were willing to grant his request. Her unseemly attire might have given him the wrong impression. He made no move to stop her, so she darted past him. She waited until she'd reached the line of trees before she glanced over her shoulder.

Her heart jolted. Slowly, surely, he walked toward her.

This couldn't be happening. Not to her. Plain women had no need to fight off a man's unwelcome advances. Leastwise, *she'd* never had the need. She could scream. If Reno were near enough, he would hear and come to her rescue. But then Archie would no doubt attack Reno.

What if Archie was merely toying with her? Amusing himself at her expense.

She had one option: to run. But in which direction? Running the wrong way might take her too far to be heard. Instead, Libby waited. Her heart pumped much too fast, sending extra blood to her head. Within seconds Archie stood near her.

"Are you daft?" she asked him. "Think twice before you anger Reno McCord. Why, he's liable to sever your head and feed it to a grizzly bear."

"I'm willin' to take that chance." He gripped her upper arms. Slowly, he pulled her against him. "McCord didn't look so tough to me."

"You aren't very smart, then, are you?" she bravely taunted. Her gibe had no outward effect on the man. Desperate, she tried another tactic. "A man as good-looking as you must have women vying for your attention. What could you possibly hope to gain by terrorizing me?"

"Terrorizing? I want a kiss." He lowered his head. "You'll like it."

His breath brushed her cheek. Libby feigned dizziness or compliance. She wasn't sure which she hoped to achieve, only that she lead him astray. When she thought he intended to kiss her, she kicked his shin hard. He yelped and straightened. Then she awarded him a sound slap. Anticipating his anger, she turned to flee. However, he moved too fast. He caught her wrist.

Libby stared into seething, cold dark eyes.

A muscle ticked on one side of his face, the side reddened from her slap. "Can't blame you for hitting me. That kick hurt, though. You kick like a mule."

Libby's mind worked furiously; she had to find a way out of this dilemma. "Let me go, and we'll forget this ever happened."

"I really want that kiss." He grabbed her other arm. "And I'm done playing."

Terror gripped Libby's heart. He looked so deadly earnest, she knew he meant to take more than a kiss. Allowing her no time to think, he grabbed her, wrestled her to the ground, and fell on top of her. Fright lent Libby strength. She kicked and squirmed, trying to throw him off. She bit his shoulder. She knocked her head against his. She even got out a bloodcurdling scream.

But she only managed to enrage him more.

Swearing profusely, he shook her. "Don't make me hurt you. I will if you keep fighting."

Libby went limp briefly, just long enough to lead him to believe she'd surrendered. She gouged her nails into his cheek.

Following another litany of curses, he swung back his arm. He would've struck her—if his hand hadn't been stopped in midair.

"Sweet Jesus," Archie cried.

His expression alarmed her. His eyes bulged, and his mouth gaped open. He shook violently as he shoved himself to his feet. Abruptly, he began to back away. Though he muttered words, they came out garbled.

Archie looked *horrified,* she thought.

A foul odor made Libby wrinkle her nose. A frigid blast of air swept over her. She thought of a door opening in mid-January. When Charity began to bray and one of the horses screamed, Libby clapped her hands over her eyes. She felt boots pound the ground. Archie had been so frightened of something, he'd broken into a run.

Why couldn't *she* move?

Seconds later another vibration traveled through the earth. A body hitting the ground?

A pained grunt spurred Libby to move. She sat up and uncovered her eyes in time to see Reno fall onto a prone Archie. The two men rolled in the dirt, pummeling each other with their fists.

Libby scrambled to her feet. Snake appeared at her side. Poking his side, she shouted, "*Do* something!"

The little man gave her a bewildered look.

She jabbed his side again. "Stop them!" With a hand against his spine, she pushed him. "Reno will kill Archie if you don't stop him!"

Snake rushed forward, grasped Reno's arm, and tugged with all of his meager might. His face soon grew mottled. Reno shook his arm, attempting to shake off Snake's hands. Archie took advantage of the opportunity and landed a punch to Reno's jaw.

Seeing Reno's head snap back, Libby wrung her fingers together. Reno, however, recovered quickly and with a powerful jerk, broke Snake's hold and tossed the smaller man onto his back. Before Libby could blink, Reno gave Archie a taste of his fist.

Snake crawled to his feet. He grinned sheepishly as he toddled toward Libby. "Ain't no one gonna break them up," he said when he reached her. "No use a body gettin' kilt over it."

She shoved him aside and dashed to Charity. The jittery mule danced in a circle. Visions of Reno being beaten to death hovered in Libby's mind, making her hands tremble. She spoke quietly as she ran a hand over Charity's nose. It seemed an eternity before the animal stood still. Libby tore at the ropes that secured their supplies, but it was no use. Reno had tied the knots so expertly, she'd never find a weapon in time.

Libby darted to Snake's mule. As she'd hoped, their supplies were not so neatly tied down. She tossed utensil after utensil aside until she came upon a cast-iron frying pan. She balanced it in her hand, testing its weight.

Finding both men still rolling over and over, throwing wild punches, she cautiously crept forward. She lifted the pan over her head. Reno, who had been on top, suddenly flipped Archie beneath him. The action threw them against Libby's legs. A yell escaped her as she collapsed to her knees.

The pan grew heavy so she lowered her arms. She gritted her teeth and heaved the weapon high again. Her eyes steady on Archie's head, she brought the pan down onto Reno's temple.

Her target had moved at the last second!

Reno cursed and shook his head. His eyes took on a glazed appearance.

With a groan, Libby sat back on her heels. To her dismay, Archie rose. He snatched a handful of Reno's shirt. His other hand balled into a fist. Sure he meant to punch Reno, she sent the pan crashing down a second time.

Despite an ominous thump, Archie didn't fall. He remained as he'd been, one arm ready to throw a punch, his other hand still clutching Reno's shirt.

Libby scrambled to her feet and hopped in front of the two men. Only then did she notice that Archie's eyes stared straight ahead. Slowly, he slumped on top of Reno.

The frying pan slipped from her fingers. She knelt and, grunting from the exertion, shoved the unconscious man off Reno. Using strength she didn't know she had, she pulled Reno upright.

Blue eyes slowly focused on her. His hand went to the bump already forming on his temple. "Damn, Libby. You nearly cracked my skull."

Relieved that Reno seemed fine, she said, "You look terrible." In the background, she heard Snake hauling Archie away. She didn't care. Blood trickled from one side of Reno's nose, his left cheek was red and scraped, and his chin looked equally abused. "What's a woman to do with a man like you?"

He gingerly touched a finger to his nose. "You might try helping me up."

While Libby eased an arm under his to lend him support, she glanced nervously around the area. Something had frightened Archie. She had felt frigid air, and smelled a foul odor, too. She dared not give credence to the thought forming in her mind.

"Run and get the rope from my saddle." Reno winced as he fingered the bump on his temple. Then he turned to Snake, who had been attempting to rouse Archie. "Don't bother waking him. Miss Chandler will have to pound him again with her pan."

Duly intimidated, Snake froze.

Though loath to leave Reno, Libby went for the rope and returned within minutes. "You're going to tie Archie?"

"I sure as hell am." He touched her cheek. "Frankly, I'm not in the mood to continue our dispute." He stepped forward but nearly stumbled. "It appears I'll need your help. The crack you put in my head has made my ears ring."

Libby swung her arms around his waist. "I never meant to hit *you*. I was aiming at Archie."

"I'm glad you were on my side." Reno fell silent, his gaze tender on her face. "Did he hurt you?"

"No," she returned. She hugged him tighter. "You came in time."

His hands settled on her shoulders. Pressing her far enough away, he searched her eyes. "Why didn't you yell sooner?"

A violent tremble rocked her. "I was afraid."

He brushed tendrils of hair from her forehead. "That's understandable. I can't bear to think of what might have happened if I hadn't gotten here in time."

"I was afraid of him, but mostly for you."

His hand stilled against her hair. "You were afraid for me?"

"I didn't want Archie to hurt you."

He grimaced. "You didn't think I could take

him? Hell, Libby, I've fought men twice his size and come away the victor."

She slid a finger down his swelling nose, then over his frowning lips. His right eye had already begun to turn colors. "If you could see yourself, you'd have more compassion for my concern. You'll have a shiner soon enough, not to mention a bulbous nose. Have I deflated your ego beyond redemption?"

"My ego's indestructible."

"Obviously. Though most likely, you'll hurt all over later."

"Every time you touch me, I hurt all over."

Libby swallowed. His deep, sensuous tone made gooseflesh pop out all over her skin. "Thank you for saving me." To repair any damage she'd unwittingly done to his masculine pride, she added, "You were exceptionally brave. I have every confidence in your abilities as a fighter. If I hadn't interfered, you would've had Archie unconscious in no time."

"Flattery will get you everywhere, Miss Chandler." He reached behind her back and stole the rope from her hand. "However, I want you to promise you won't come after me with your frying pan again. By tonight I'll probably have two heads."

Libby grinned and said softly, "Or one very big one?"

He narrowed his eyes at her.

She reached out to touch the goose egg on his temple. "Does it hurt very much?"

He deftly caught her wrist. "Hell, yes. Lucky for you, I have a hard head."

"Nevertheless, I believe you should tie Archie before he comes to. I suspect he'll have a raging headache."

Reno paused to look at her over his shoulder. "Don't get the wrong idea. I'm only hog-tying Archie for Snake's safety."

Libby smiled. "I *have* dented your ego."

He aimed her an exasperated look.

"I'll feel much happier knowing Archie is bound. Otherwise, you might forget yourself and injure him irreparably."

Reno's mouth quirked up on one side as he unlooped the rope. He tied Archie proficiently. At the same time, he spoke to Snake.

Grateful the ordeal was truly over, Libby hugged her arms at her waist. She watched Reno lift the unconscious man, stand, and plop the inert body over his shoulder. Despite the bruises he'd incurred, and an egg-shaped lump on his temple, Reno had the stamina to hang Archie over his horse.

Reno clapped Snake's back. "Don't let him loose until tonight."

"He'll be mad as a hornet long before that."

"Yeah," Reno agreed. "By then you'll be far from here. Should your partner decide to trail us, I won't be as forgiving the next time." He looped the ends of the rope under the horse's belly and tied them together. "I might have to shoot first and ask questions later."

"I . . . won't . . . let . . . him go," Snake sputtered. "No sirree, I'll keep Archie tied until we're done clear of these parts."

"Good man. In that case, you're free to leave."

Reno crossed his arms over his chest and kept track of the men until all sight and sound of them had faded away.

Silence grew ominous. They were alone again. Heaving a sigh of relief, Libby went to Reno.

The sound of Libby's oversize boots dragging the ground brought Reno away from his hateful thoughts. He'd wanted to beat McGovern to within an inch of his life for daring to assault Libby. If she hadn't knocked the man over the head with the pan, he would've probably done just that. He had never possessed a violent nature, even during the frequent brawls he'd engaged in after hours of drinking and gambling in saloons. Hell, altercations of that sort, though occasionally rough, had been in the nature of fun.

For the first time he wanted to kill a man. Libby had saved him from himself. Damn. The man had deserved much worse. Only a spineless bastard would force his advances on a defenseless woman.

Well, maybe not so defenseless, he thought with a smile. Libby had sent the bastard away with a helluva headache.

Feeling her hand on his arm, he turned too fast. Pain splintered through his head, a reminder that he, also, had suffered at her hands. Without thinking, he pressed his fingers to his injury.

"I've hurt you more than you've let on," she said.

He laid his hand over hers. "I've had worse. Like I said, I have a hard head." He lifted his arm over her shoulders, luring her closer. "You're really not hurt?"

"I'm fine. I think he took exception to some-thing I said."

She flattened her hands on his chest and tenderly checked him over. Several spots hurt when she moved her fingers over them, but he stoically bore the discomfort.

"What did you say, Libby?"

"I told him it wasn't wise to annoy you. I said you would sever his head and feed it to a grizzly bear." Her gaze flitted from one injury to another on his face. "Your poor face. If you don't give up brawling, one day you might not be as fortunate. You're so handsome, it would be a shame to see your beautiful nose crooked."

"It might be worth it to have you fuss over me and tend my wounds."

She leaned into him and laid her cheek against his chest. Reno closed his eyes, absorbing her heat and womanly fragrance. He had planned to stay away from her today. Instead, not only was she in his arms, he found himself savoring the tender qualities he'd found in her. She should have lots of babies. She'd make a wonderful mother.

When had she become important to him? He tried to recall the exact moment his defenses had fallen. Perhaps it hadn't happened all at once but in small moments of tenderness. When they finally said good-bye, he'd suffer for his weakness.

"I don't want to stay here any longer," she said. "I don't want to think about Archie and what he almost did." A shiver swept through her. "When you came back . . . did you . . . see anything?"

"The scratches on McGovern's face told me all I needed to know."

"That's not what I meant. Reno, something scared the daylights out of Archie. One minute he was about to hit me, the next he cursed. Then, he couldn't retreat fast enough."

"He probably heard me. Snake and I made no effort to approach quietly." When she gripped handfuls of his shirt, he tipped up her chin. "Let's leave this place and never return. I know which way to go now, thanks to Snake."

She nodded. Suddenly, her lips curled into a wry smile. "Are you recovered enough from the whack on the head I gave you?"

He felt more than recovered. He considered kissing Libby. However, Charity's loud brays helped him regain his senses. She kicked out with her back feet as she strained against the rope with which he'd secured her. "What do you suppose has gotten into that crazy mule?"

The rope snapped. Still braying, Charity ran straight at Reno. She would've plowed him down if he hadn't leapt to the side. He caught the end of the rope.

"I think she missed you," Libby said. "Apparently your appeal extends to females of all species."

"I think she's frightened." He looked back to where he'd left the horses. Neither seemed unduly agitated. Without warning, the mule broke free and trotted across the small clear area, into the trees. "Do you still think she's enamored of me?"

"I think you were right. She's frightened." She cast a worried look to her left. "Charity made a fuss earlier, too."

"Come with me," he bade as he headed for his horse. He swung to his saddle, then he searched the area while he waited for Libby to catch up. "Stay with your horse. I'll find Charity."

Not waiting for a response, he galloped after the mule.

Libby gripped the reins. She should have protested, not allowed Reno to go off and leave her alone. What if Archie had gotten loose and was hiding in the trees, waiting to lunge at her? Or if whatever had frightened Archie had returned?

Sugar stepped nervously and neighed. Shivers crawled over Libby's skin. Reaching up to grab the pommel, she tried to slip her boot into the stirrup, but the horse moved just far enough to prevent her from accomplishing the deed. On the third attempt, Libby managed to mount. Her hands shook uncontrollably.

Sugar resisted Libby's efforts to turn her. The horse inched backward instead. Seconds later, the animal refused to budge. Libby remembered the icy fingers which had touched her neck at the stream. Her heart leapt at the thought. She'd felt cold air then, too.

She darted a glance behind her. She saw nothing out of the ordinary, so she glanced to her right. And gasped. At the edge of the clearing stood a riderless horse.

Libby's mouth fell open as she drew in a slow, shocked breath. Sure her vision must have suffered during her scuffle with Archie, she blinked twice. She decided there was nothing wrong with her sight. Her mind, however, must be playing tricks on her.

The horse was transparent.

Chapter 14

L ibby still looked pale.

Reno frowned. The past hours plagued him. No matter how adamantly he'd questioned her, she had politely refused to tell him what had happened while he'd gone to find Charity.

Determined to have it out of her before they'd traveled another mile, he stopped in the middle of the mountain road they'd been following. It would be dark soon, anyway. Snake had warned him not to travel the road after sunset. The man had sounded so sincere, Reno trusted his advice.

Libby stared ahead. He followed her gaze to a jutting cliff. "What are you looking at, Libby?"

She drew in a breath. "The rock is red."

"Was it in your dream?"

"This place doesn't look familiar, but it feels strange. I feel strange. Are we stopping here?" she asked, her tone betraying her anxiety.

He spotted a creek hemmed by cottonwoods, juniper, and pine on a ridge, and thickets of scrub oak. "It's as good a spot as any. Unless you really want to go on."

"No, I want to stop here. Tomorrow's soon enough to find out what's ahead."

Reno dismounted and stood below Libby. Although her fingers still strangled the reins, he saw they trembled. He held out his arms. "Come on, Libby. Tell me what's bothering you."

A resigned look on her face, she tilted toward him. She allowed him to pull her into his arms. "If I tell you, you'll scoff."

He held her against him before he lowered her to her feet. "You aren't going to admit to having seen a ghost, are you?"

As she played with a button on his shirt, she held her gaze lowered. "Not of a man."

"What's that supposed to mean?" He tipped up her chin. "What did you see?"

She released a weary sigh. "You'll think I'm crazy, but I want to share it with you. I believe Charity must have seen the thing, too."

Growing impatient, Reno growled under his breath. "Dammit, Libby, I promise I won't think you're crazy."

She inhaled a deep breath and said, "I saw a horse."

He waited several minutes before he responded. "And you thought I'd think you were crazy? There *are* miners scattered about. The horse might've wandered off."

"I saw through it."

"Saw through what? The horse?"

Her arms slipped around him. "It was transparent. Now, do you think I'm crazy?"

Her admission left him speechless.

"I thought I might've been imagining it, or that

my eyes were playing tricks on me. But the vision never wavered. It was a phantom horse."

Words escaped him. He knew she'd fibbed to him before. This time, however, no one could've convinced him she wasn't telling the whole truth. Whether he believed her or not weighed heavily on his mind. There were no such things as ghosts.

"Your silence gives you away, Reno." She eased away from him, removed her hat and hung it on the pommel of her saddle. "You want to believe me, yet you don't. Maybe the next time, you'll see it."

"It could've been the light. The sun has a way of filtering through trees and creating forms and shadows."

She whipped around. Fine lines webbed across her brow. "I saw a transparent horse. No excuse you manufacture will convince me otherwise."

He pulled her into his arms. "I believe you think you saw just that, Libby. Rest easy. Okay?"

"I knew you wouldn't believe me."

"Would you believe *me* if I claimed the same?"

"Well . . . I would want to." She fell silent a moment before she begrudgingly admitted, "I suppose not. I'd do exactly the same as you, search for plausible reasons to explain the sight."

"We've reached an agreement, haven't we? I won't think you're crazy, and you won't think I'm an ogre for being skeptical." He grazed his cheek over hers, intending to kiss her neck. When she drew slightly away, he ran his fingers over his face. "I didn't have time to shave this morning. I was more interested in getting our visitors on their way."

"You are a bit prickly." She considered him.

"As soon as you've set up camp, I'll tend your injuries." She angled her head, staring intently at his right eye. "That's an impressive shiner you have already. Actually, your nose is swelling, too. Maybe you should allow me to shave you."

He raised a brow at her. "I've never let a woman near my throat with a razor."

"Oh? And why is that?"

"You don't need to know."

"I can well imagine. You, however, haven't given me any cause to dispatch you to the Hereafter. In fact, you've just saved me from harm. Besides, it's safer if I do it. I have two good eyes."

He aimed her a knowing grin. "You win. This might prove very interesting."

The devilish twinkle in Reno's eyes hinted at mischief. "Any movement on your part will be at your own risk. Startle me at the wrong minute and I might accidentally slit your throat."

"I have every confidence in you, Libby."

She looked around the area. Despite Reno's teasing banter, she still felt uncomfortable in this place. "Will you will be sure to tie Charity so she can't run?"

"I'll do it first thing." He brushed a kiss on her lips. "Once you've finished tormenting me, I have plans of my own."

Libby's heart skipped a beat. "Should I inquire as to the nature of these plans?"

"I'm going to brush your hair. When you're all relaxed and purring, I might kiss you."

Tingles of anticipation darted over her skin at the provocative image. "Are you expecting to be overcome by a weak moment?"

He grinned. "Sharpen your claws, just in case."

"But you warned me to stay away from you. Have your intentions changed?"

"No, Libby, they haven't. But I figure I've duly suffered today while I was saving you from McGovern. Will you take my sacrifice into consideration?"

Though she suspected he'd been trying to take her thoughts from ghosts and her intended, she grew warm from his teasing banter. "I have already considered your sacrifice. I've agreed to tend your wounds."

He growled with impatience. "I believe you've jinxed me, Miss Chandler. Before I met you, I'd never been injured as many times in so short a period."

"You should be more careful," she said, her tone serious.

He shook a finger at her. "Tonight you're not to offer any protest about having your hair brushed. In fact, you *will* purr."

"You're awfully confident. Why, I've never purred in my life."

His laugh was low and sensuous as he slipped past her. She smiled. She watched him unpack their supplies at a brisk pace a good distance from the trail. By the time she'd selected a smooth, cozy spot to place their bedding materials, he had hobbled Charity, tended the other animals as well, and gathered wood for a fire. The immense pile of sticks told her he intended to have a roaring fire.

She thought she knew why. Although skeptical about her sighting of the transparent horse, Reno knew of her unease. She had to admit she would feel much safer with the light afforded by the flames.

Reno cast her a look over his shoulder. With a seductive wink, he asked, "Do you want supper now . . . or later on?"

"Later," she stammered too quickly.

"Good." He paused to smile. "I'm not hungry now, either."

He stood and came to her. His hands disappeared behind her head as he gave her a melting look. "I've been wanting to do this all day."

Several deft movements and her hair tumbled free. He dropped her pins into his shirt pocket.

"Have I lost my hairpins again?" she asked.

"Knowing your tendency to misplace them, I think it best if I guard them for you."

"By all means," she said, her voice a breathy whisper.

"I owe myself this."

His lips were gentle as they moved over hers, gentle yet searching. A second passed before she moaned with pleasure, craving more. Her knees sagged under his sweet assault. Libby slipped her arms under his. She moved her hands over his chest until they reached his shoulders. In response, his arms swept around her. Reno bound her so close against him, she could barely breathe.

His kiss deepened, stole the remainder of her breath as his hands roamed over her. She locked her arms around his neck, caught up in the heady power he exercised over her senses. And her heart. She'd done the inexcusable.

She'd fallen head over heels in love with Reno McCord.

And she didn't care. He was all she'd ever want. Even if she could only have him for a short time, she'd grab those moments and revel in them in the years to come. She poured her heart into her kiss, wanting to prove to him that he belonged to her.

Earth-shattering minutes passed before he slowly withdrew. His breath came in pants as he brushed tendrils of hair from her brow.

"It'll be dark soon."

"Is that significant?" She gazed at his handsome features which had taken on a warm hue from the setting sun.

"Let's go down by the creek."

She waited while he fetched his saddlebags, then she followed him partway down the embankment. He chose a large, flat rock close to the water, took out his shaving implements, and passed his straight razor slowly back and forth over a leather strap. She spared a grin. He must trust her implicitly to sharpen the razor.

His lazy movements held her gaze. He'd threatened to brush her hair several times, but he hadn't followed through with his threat. This time, she hoped he did. As she watched him slide the razor over the strap, she imagined him brushing her hair with the same methodical, mesmerizing rhythm. Flitters of pleasure skipped down her spine.

Then she felt icy fingers touch her neck.

Libby released a squeak and dashed the rest of the way down the embankment. She skidded to a halt beside Reno.

His razor froze in mid stroke. He looked up.

Libby inhaled a quivery breath and stared back at the spot where she'd stood seconds before. She saw nothing strange, no invisible horse, no ghost belonging to the icy fingers which had gripped her neck. Not wanting to burden Reno more, or give him additional reason to question her sanity, she dropped to her knees silently. She took the razor from him.

"You're shaking like a leaf."

"I am not," she said. Knowing her feeble protest must've sounded ridiculous, she added, "I'm just nervous. I've never shaved a man before."

He grimaced. "There's a comforting thought if ever I heard one."

Despite his remark, he appeared calm as leaned over. After he'd wet his face in the creek, he used his soap to work up a lather. He straightened and stuck his legs out on either side of hers. When he wiggled closer, his features were solemn.

Libby shoved thoughts of the icy fingers from her mind. Reno was near. She trusted him to protect her. She considered the comical sight he made with lather covering the lower half of his face. "You'll have to show me where to start."

He pointed beneath his chin. "Might as well do the risky part first. If you're going to slit my throat, I'd rather not be held in suspense any longer than necessary."

"If you're so apprehensive about me shaving you, I'll find another chore."

"No," he said quickly. "I'm not worried. One thing though." Lights flashed in his blue eyes. "When you get near my nose, please don't lop it off."

"I wouldn't dream of it. I happen to like your nose."

"We're in agreement." Lines at the corner of his eyes creased as he offered her a smile of encouragement. "The soap's drying, Libby. I'm going to close my eyes. I promise I won't move or say a word to distract you."

Libby's confidence soared. Shaving Reno would be fun, she thought. True to his word, he remained still as a statue during her first attempt to graze the razor from his neck to his chin. To Libby's amazement, her hand never wavered. Inch by inch, his throat came into view, smooth and free of stubble. Tempted to press her lips on the tantalizing display, she thought better of breaking both of their concentration.

"Very good," he complimented when she paused to admire her handiwork. Using his finger as a guide, he showed her how to do the rest. "Your touch is much softer than the last barber I trusted. He scraped off half of my skin."

She aimed him a dubious look. "I wouldn't brag on my capabilities until I've finished."

"Yes, ma'am. Proceed."

Saving the area around his precious nose for last, Libby rested the palm of her other hand on his forehead. She swiped a path down his cheek to his chin. She stopped to wipe the lather off on a small towel he'd laid close, then repeated the procedure again and again. When she felt ready to maneuver around the sides of his nose, she bit her lip. She slid the razor ever so slowly along the smile line that dipped from the area of his nose to the corner of his mouth. The left side proved more difficult, since she was right-handed. Remarkably, she performed the deed without a mishap.

She sighed with relief and leaned back to study her handiwork.

Reno opened his eyes. He ran his hands over his

face. "You're an excellent barber, Libby. Not a nick."

Unable to resist, she said softly, "I hope you aren't too disappointed when you look in a mirror."

"Why do you say that?"

Libby bit back a smile. "One very tiny edge of your nose sort of got in the way of the razor. I'm afraid I lopped it off. Of course, most of it remains, so you shouldn't worry you'll look odd."

Reno's fingers immediately shot to his face to check for blood.

Libby released the laugh she'd been holding in her throat. Carefully, she laid the razor on the rock beside him.

"Libby, that wasn't funny."

"Perhaps not. But consider it repayment for stealing my hairpins."

"Guarding your pins," he corrected.

"You stole them for your own nefarious motives."

He fingered a lock of her hair. "And I have them now."

An eerie, chilling sound reverberated down the embankment—a man's demented laughter.

Reno gripped Libby's shoulders, preventing her from shooting to her feet. A tremble rocked through her. The same grotesque, inhuman laugh had sent her fleeing to the waterfall.

"What was that?" he asked.

A terrible odor assaulted Libby's senses. She realized Reno, too, had smelled it. Instead of horror, she felt relieved. She wasn't alone this time.

Reno snorted. "Good God. What's that putrid smell?"

"Rotting flesh?" she ventured timidly.

Her preposterous suggestion gained her a shocked stare. "Are you suggesting something dead made that sound, and is giving off that foul odor?"

Libby shivered. "I feel much better knowing you heard and smelled the same things as I did."

He shoved to his feet, bringing her with him. Deftly, he drew his gun and checked his ammunition. "Wait here."

She seized his arm in a death grip. "No! Don't leave me alone."

He patted her hand in a comforting gesture. "All right. It's probably best if you stay with me. It's obvious whoever is up there is trying to frighten us."

"He's doing a pretty good job of it."

He pushed them away from the rock and stepped in front of Libby. Over his shoulder, he gave her a pointed look. "It's not a ghost, Libby. It's a man. I hope Snake hasn't let Archie loose."

"He wouldn't. He was too timid." She reached out for his arm but grabbed a handful of his shirt instead. "Don't go. I have a bad feeling, Reno. Please."

He pivoted and swung his arm around her. Pressing her close against his side, he whispered, "There's nothing to be afraid of. Stay behind me. I have to go. The animals are there."

When the loud braying of a mule echoed, Reno pulled away from Libby and loped up the bank. He stopped so suddenly, his heels slid loose dirt from under his boots, undermining his foothold. Before Libby could think to follow him, he'd retraced his steps down to her. He stood still as death, blocking her view.

Charity continued to bray to the accompaniment of horses' neighs.

Wondering what had happened to force Reno to retrace his steps, she hopped to the side to see around him. Not twenty feet above her, something white and transparent hovered. Libby didn't trust her vision. She rubbed her hands over her eyes.

"You're not seeing things, Libby."

Reno's voice had sounded rough and low, as if his throat had gone dry. Libby tried to swallow but discovered her tongue stuck to the roof of her mouth.

The thing took on more substance, a form. A bearded man with an ax protruding from his forehead!

Libby's knees buckled. She would've fallen if strong fingers hadn't gripped her arm. Reno pulled her close, then he shoved her behind him. Although she appreciated his self-sacrificing action, she doubted even hiding behind Reno's strong body would protect her. A being with no substance could pass through objects. Couldn't it?

Reno inched backwards, forcing Libby to do likewise. She met resistance. Sensing he'd forgotten the obstacle and meant to keep coming, she stepped onto the rock. The additional height allowed her an unobstructed view over Reno's head. A fresh wave of panic made her heart beat at a furious pace.

The apparition started to move, slowly, drifting straight toward them. Reno cursed under his breath, then louder.

Libby prepared herself for an attack. When the spirit suddenly picked up speed and flew at Reno, she leapt from the rock. As she fell on her side on the edge of lapping water, she watched with stupefied fascination as Reno brought up his arm. He emptied his gun at the ghost.

Confronted with the prospect of an ill-tempered apparition flying through him, Reno rushed back, tripping over the rock and falling flat.

Libby realized she'd been holding her breath. The ghost swept over trees and bushes, circling the immediate area. She darted a glance at Reno. His face had turned pale. His wide-eyed gaze followed their inhuman visitor.

When the thing hovered again at a distance, Libby rose to her knees.

"Stay down," Reno warned as he crawled to her. "I don't know what he has in mind but—"

The apparition bellowed a grotesque, bone-chilling laugh. The odor of rotten flesh permeated the area.

"He's transparent. Do you think he can hurt us?" she asked.

"Maybe I should go and ask him."

Another hideous laugh floated to them. Libby shuddered.

The ghost suddenly took flight once more, aiming for Reno. She felt Reno's fingers dig into her upper arms as he covered her with his body.

The apparition stopped a foot away from them. This close to the thing, the odor became intense, nauseating.

"Good God, you smell foul, man," Reno shouted.

Libby held her breath, positive he'd further enraged their attacker. But, throwing back his ruined head, the ghost of Henry Harkins bellowed a laugh and disappeared.

Libby trembled and threw her arms around Reno's neck.

"Is he gone?" she asked in a quivery voice. "He seemed determined to attack you."

His hands slid over her cheeks as he gazed deeply into her eyes. "He's gone for now."

Libby realized an amazing fact. "Why, Reno McCord, you were just as frightened as I was."

Dark brows slanted ominously. After a minute, he nodded.

"I'm surprised you'd admit such a thing."

"One thing's sure, Libby." A strange, intense expression flashed across his face. "You didn't imagine what you felt. The icy fingers probably belonged to *it*." He glanced up the embankment. "I suppose you want to gloat?"

"No. Not yet, anyway." Seeing his grimace, she decided not to taunt him. "I'm glad you were here with me when *he* came." She trembled again. "At least you know I'm not crazy."

His thumbs slid from her cheeks to her chin, then grazed her mouth. His head lowering, he whispered, "I didn't think you were crazy, just overly imaginative."

"Liar."

"I have to see to the animals," he muttered against her lips.

"I'm not staying down here alone."

Taking hold of her hand, he led her with him as

he collected his saddlebags and shaving utensils. Then he cautiously led her back up the embankment. "Make us a comfortable bed."

"We can't sleep here, not after what happened."

Reno shrugged his shoulders. "Hell, this spot's as safe as any."

"Or as dangerous?" she muttered.

Chapter 15

The fire flamed high, snapping and hissing. Libby sat on the blankets, her gaze tuned to Reno's every move. Though food had been the farthest thing from her mind, he'd made their supper. She'd eaten halfheartedly, merely to keep her strength and her wits.

Behind her, a large boulder offered a sturdy support. With the fire positioned a safe distance away, the spot seemed warm and homey. Which it was not since Henry Harkins might decide to visit them at any given moment.

She shoved the thought from her mind. She didn't want to think of the terror she'd felt earlier. They were close to the place she'd seen in her dreams, close to where Clarence probably had met a tragic end. Tears of sadness welled in her eyes. At that second, she remembered the phantom horse. Though she hadn't made the connection then, somehow she knew the animal had belonged to Clarence.

Had he sent it to lead her? Deciding her imagination was, indeed, running wild, she hugged her knees to her chest. Surviving the next few days would be hard enough without dwelling on today's bizarre events.

She watched Reno instead, adoring his profile. Even with his wounds, she thought him handsome. Purple tinged the skin around one eye and gave him a roguish appearance. The lock of hair falling on his brow drew her. He squatted before the fire, staring into the flames. His mouth was set in a severe line.

Libby cleared her throat. Her action registered in the barely perceptible tilt of head. Reno was perfectly aware of her, she thought.

She cleared her throat again, then said, "Why don't you come over here?"

His lips lifted at the corners for a second. Then, looking straight at her, he released a ragged sigh. "If I do that, Libby, I can't guarantee your safety."

Her heart beat faster. "Am I in danger? You've built such a roaring fire, I doubt even a ghost would cross its boundary."

"You know very well where the danger lies."

"I don't regard you as dangerous," she said, her voice dropping low. "Please. I'll feel safer with you close."

She heard a muttered oath. He looked back at the flames, but not before she noticed how the flickering light reflected in his eyes. A long moment passed before he stood and walked over to her. His mouth thinned as he unbuckled and dropped his gunbelt. Then he tugged off his boots. He stared down at her for a long moment.

"Sit down, please."

Instead of doing as she'd asked, he walked around her. He swung his leg over her back and slid his back along the rock face. "Move up."

His husky tone sent heat to her toes. She scooted forward. When his arms came around her, a tingle tore down her spine.

She felt an object bump her back and decided he'd hidden something in his shirt. His fingers tangled in her hair. "You stole my brush," she accused softly.

"Earlier. When you were fixing our bed."

"Sooo . . . you were intending to do this all along?"

"I'd hoped to muster enough self-control to stay away from you."

She wilted against him. "I'm glad you failed."

He didn't respond with words. He delved his hand behind her, into his shirt.

Libby stiffened with anticipation. He pulled the brush from her temple to the ends of her hair. The long, leisurely, sensuous stroke scattered her thoughts. Over and over he performed the ritual, and she would've sworn her bones were melting. It was the most luscious torture, almost as luscious as his kisses.

"Did I just hear you purr, Libby?"

She hadn't the strength to argue. "Yes."

She sat in the crook of his legs. The heat from his body enveloped her, while the gentle brush strokes brought her senses alive. She wanted to protest when he paused and she tried to straighten, but his fingers grazed her neck. He lifted the fall of her hair off her shoulder.

"Feels like silk," he whispered against her skin. He kissed a trail of fire up to her ear. "But you taste even softer."

She heard a small groan. Could it possibly have come from her?

His fingers trailed across her shoulder, down her arm. He leaned back, leaving a space between their upper bodies.

Libby felt bereft at the loss of contact. She twisted around to search his eyes and saw creases furrowed across his brow.

She twisted the rest of the way around until she knelt between his legs. As she rested on her heels, she dipped her hand into her pocket and brought out the small jar of salve she'd sneaked from his saddlebags earlier.

His gaze dropped to the jar. "Been rifling through my belongings, Miss Chandler?"

Amused by his teasing tone, she nodded. "I presumed you wouldn't mind."

He chuckled and sat still while she touched her finger to the salve. Gently, she smeared it over the scrapes on his face. The fire crackled. She thought the same could be said of the tension sparking between them. Carefully, she circled his eye, which he closed during her ministrations.

"You're so gentle, Libby. A man could get used to having you around."

His voice sounded tormented, as if he were fighting a war within himself.

He caught her hand and caressed it. "As a child I was called Joey."

Reno's abrupt revelation took Libby by surprise. "But your name's Reno."

"Joseph Reno McCord. I stopped going by Joey after I left home." His thumb rubbed her wrist as he studied her face. "I figured Reno sounded more grown-up."

Using her free hand, she capped the lid on the jar and laid it aside. As soon as he released her wrist, she rested her hands on his shoulders. His fingers crept along her arms and halted at her shoulders.

A wry smile pulled at the corners of his mouth. "You're damned tempting. I want to kiss you again. But kissing you complicates things."

She touched her lips to his. When he failed to participate, Libby drew back with a frown. As hard as she tried to cover her chagrin, she lacked the sophistication.

"Are you trying to seduce me?" he asked with a catch in his voice.

His blunt question startled her. "I . . . don't . . . know what I want anymore."

He dug his fingers through her hair and spread the mane around her shoulders. "Well, you've damned well confused me, too. Libby, you know I can only be strong for short intervals. I haven't changed, either."

"I know that only too well. Unfortunately, I *have* changed since I met you."

He cupped his hands over her cheeks. "Aren't you afraid your ghost will come back?"

"Not with you beside me." A smile hovered on her mouth. "You can always shoot him again."

He groaned as color crept up his neck. "You'll never let me live that down, will you?"

"Afraid not."

"I suppose when we return to Denver I'll be the main feature in all the newspapers?"

"Absolutely not! It's a memory I plan to cherish. I'll never share it with anyone."

He looked relieved.

"When we part, the memories I'll have of you will be special," she said.

"I'm not a bit special, Libby."

"You are to me." Aghast because she'd almost betrayed her feelings with her quick response, she dropped her gaze. But maybe she should tell him. "I—"

He cut off the rest of her words with a finger over her mouth. "Don't."

She'd been about to confess her love for him. Perhaps it had been wise of him to hush her.

Reno's shoulders slumped, a look of pain clouding his expression. "Libby," he nearly groaned, "you've become a fever in my blood. When you look at me with such tenderness and compassion in your eyes, I'm powerless to resist you."

She hadn't tried to hide her thoughts from him, but his sensitivity to her mood surprised her. She had decided it would be futile to try to change him. Now, though, she wondered. "Exactly how powerless are you?"

He flashed a wicked smile. "If I say I'm weak as a kitten, will you take advantage of my infirmity?"

She touched his hair, brushed it off his brow. "Maybe if I pet you a little, you'll regain your strength."

He chuckled as he slid away from the rock. His action brought her with him. His eyes twinkling with mischief, he reclined on the blankets. "Why don't you pet me and see."

Firelight danced over him and glowed in his eyes. She saw no blue in them now. They reflected flickering flames of desire. Her bold taunt had left her feeling inadequate in view of his challenge. Though he'd shown her she possessed a passionate nature, she cursed her inexperience.

With another chuckle, he seized her about the waist and slid her on top of him.

Libby's breath lodged in her throat from his quick move. He'd opened his legs. Her lower body lay between his thighs. The rest of her sprawled across his stomach and chest. Libby spread her hands on either side of his waist to lift herself. Her eyes met his.

"I didn't mean to shock you," he said, his voice sounding much lower than before. "Are you too uncomfortable in this position?"

The heat of his skin burned through her clothing. Against her abdomen the bulge of his manhood felt hard and hot. A vision of Reno naked at the waterfall shot through her mind. Libby blushed. In response to his question, she shook her head.

"Good, because you have me blazing hotter than a raging fire."

Libby swallowed against her embarrassment and countered, "You certainly don't require much kindling, Mr. McCord."

Her words had barely left her mouth before he rose. He locked his fingers around the back of her thighs and pulled her into a sitting position.

"Not with you, I don't," he grated out. His fingers went to the top button of her shirt. "The question is, do you want me to continue? There's no one to interrupt us." He opened the button and paused. "I won't stop this time, Libby."

"Do you care for me at all?" she asked in a hesitant voice. "I need to know you're not still playing games with me."

He cradled her cheeks again with his rough

palms. A long moment passed before he answered. "I do care for you, Libby, much more than I feel comfortable with. But don't read more into it. I haven't it in me to settle down. I only know one thing. I want you. And, lady, your virtue is definitely in danger."

Straddling his hips, she knew for certain he'd meant what he'd said. An ache began at the juncture of her thighs from their intimate position and disturbed her train of thought.

"What do you want, Libby?"

She attempted to answer but her voice faltered. He had been honest, not lied to her as she imagined some men would. On the second try, she managed one word. "You."

He opened one more button. Before she could suck in a breath, her shirt hung open. Their cheeks touched as he reached around her to pull the tails out of her pants. Unable to resist, she pressed her lips to his cheek and slid them to his ear. "I want you to make love to me. It's a memory I'll cherish all the rest of my life."

He moved his head slowly, until his mouth trapped hers. His kiss, though brief, made her blood sing through her veins. He tugged the shirt over her shoulders and used it to drag her against his chest.

"I hope you aren't sorry tomorrow," he murmured.

Wiggling her bottom, she giggled. "Tomorrow is a long way off."

He gave a ragged sigh. "Damn, Libby, I wish you'd been with a man before. I'd be inside you in an instant."

"Perhaps it's best that I've never been with anyone else. I want you to love me all night."

He kissed her again, giving a miserable moan afterward. "On second thought, I prefer to test my stamina. I couldn't bear the idea of another man making love to you."

"Me either. You're the only man I'll ever want to touch me."

Another pained moan whispered against her mouth. "Libby, you defeat me."

Libby wiggled her arms until they were free of the shirt. She retreated long enough to work on Reno's buttons. His warm breath brushed her temple as her trembling fingers struggled with holes which seemed too small. Finally, with a laugh, he lent his assistance. He whipped off the shirt and tossed it over his head.

His skin gleamed in the firelight. Shadows played over muscles in his arms and the striking contours of his chest. She couldn't wait a second longer. Of their own volition, her hands explored his bare chest, her fingers tunneling through a thick mat of black hair. When he inhaled harshly, she exulted in the heady feeling. It pleased her to know she could affect him so acutely with such a simple touch. Over his broad shoulders, down the center of his chest, then around his ribs, she ventured. She reveled in his sheer raw masculinity.

Until he captured her wrists.

His eyes found hers. The fiery look he gave her sent blood racing through her veins at an alarming rate. "You stopped me," she accused, disappointment in her tone.

"Yeah," he bit out. "It's a torture I'm not up to handling right now. Let me torment *you.*"

His intention, the impact of his hoarse voice had a dizzying effect on her. Before he'd made a move, a quiver darted to her toes. He fumbled with the tiny buttons on her camisole. Impatient, he muttered an oath.

Libby shivered as pleasure rippled through her.

An abbreviated low laugh escaped him. "I haven't touched you yet, Libby."

"I know. Aren't I awful?"

"My ego adores you." A shameless grin slid across his face. "But not as much as *I* adore you."

He spread open the camisole. With infinite gentleness, he slipped it over her shoulders, letting it fall where it might. Libby closed her eyes. He was looking at her and she knew bright color must be staining her cheeks. Because she couldn't see him, the first touch of his hands on her breasts brought a sharp gasp from her. A quickening quaked to life deep inside. Shiver after delicious shiver darted down her legs.

"God, you're beautiful. More beautiful than I deserve."

His husky murmur plundered her senses. His heated caresses robbed her of thought and sanity. She had to remember to breathe. She gulped a breath, and his lips replaced his hands. The moist heat of his mouth scorched her skin as his tongue laved her nipples, lavishing each with devotion before, he suckled one, then the other.

Within minutes, as he kissed a fiery path to her throat, he whispered against her skin, "You're making strangled sounds in the back of your throat, Libby. Does that mean you like what I'm doing to you?"

"Yes," she said in a breathy whisper. "Oh, yes."

"Has your mouth gone dry?"

She nodded. He detoured around her neck. When he tried to unfasten her pants, he fumbled. "Dry as dust," she creaked out.

"Maybe I should kiss you now."

She threw her arms around him and slanted her mouth over his. She heard a half laugh, half moan when he took her obvious hint. Easy confidence marked his manner as his tongue dipped inside her mouth. It was a sinful, plundering exploration that stoked fire in her belly.

He ceased fumbling with her pants. His hands slid up her back instead. He applied pressure and forced her breasts tight against his chest. The intimate contact with his fevered skin heightened Libby's pleasure to such a degree, she whimpered. Back and forth his lips slid over hers, his tongue performing a demanding, sensual dance with hers. She felt light-headed, as if she floated far beneath the surface of a body of water.

Close to swooning, Libby wouldn't have called a halt to his tender assault if her life depended upon it. The way he kissed her wasn't merely an onslaught on her body and senses. The impression came to her that, despite his reluctance to share his heart, he was showing her in his own way he did, indeed, have strong feelings for her.

Her heart swelled. His mouth made a meal of her, yet emotion warred with passion in the gentle but savage intensity of his kiss.

Heavens above! She loved him to distraction, more than anyone or anything on this earth.

Then she tilted forward, descending with him, and sprawled on top of him again. He moved her up so he could continue to devour her mouth.

Against her lips, his voice sounded raspy and laced with desire. "I'm beyond all reason, Libby."

She smiled against his lips.

His fingers and palms scorched her skin as they moved with purpose over her hips, down to her thighs. Libby's eyes opened. The rascal had not only opened her pants, he was wiggling his fingers under them. Not even the thin barrier of her drawers dulled the wicked sensation of his branding touch.

"Stand up," he said.

The amused command registered in her foggy brain. On wobbly legs, she did as he asked. Towering over him, she swayed. She prayed her knees continued to support her weight.

He aimed her a sinful smile as he yanked her pants down until they met the resistance of her stomach. He offered her his hand, which she hurried to accept. "Careful now. You'll have to lift one leg at a time."

She eased a foot up, then tottered to her right. But Reno appeared more in control of his faculties. He had her free within seconds. Libby reversed her position. She kicked her other foot out of the pants.

His hands moved from her ankles and skimmed over the light weight of her pantalets. Reaching her knees, a devastating smile captured his mouth. "You're fetching in your drawers, Libby. But I want them off."

His suggestion brought a deep flush to her face. She knelt quickly and dropped over him. She wasn't about to disrobe completely in plain view. Lying down at least offered a small amount of privacy. "Then you'll have to remove them yourself."

Again his fingers fumbled, this time with the knot at her waist. To his credit and her amazement, she barely had time to contemplate his agility before he'd wiggled the garment over her hips. Cold air, mixed with heat from the fire, swept across her bare bottom. A soft gasp escaped her. "You sound surprised, Libby," he said, his warm breath rustling her hair. "It was a fairly simple feat."

"But you managed it far too easily." She lifted her arms over his shoulders, wanting to be as close to him as possible. With her breasts smashed flat against his chest, his heart pounded in tune with hers. "Should I ask how you gained such a talent?"

Laughter rumbled through his chest. "Stripping off a woman's underwear?"

After she'd grazed her teeth over his shoulder, she gently nipped his skin. "Precisely."

"Experience." A tremble quaked through him. "Damn, Libby, what are you doing to me?"

"Biting your neck." She nibbled a path from his shoulder, along his throat. She stopped at the corner of his mouth. "I can't get enough of you. I love being this close, and I think I'm going to like having you make love to me."

His mouth swooped over hers in fiery response and devoured her much the same as he'd done at the waterfall. She knew there would be no more banter, because he'd lost the ability to control his passion. Her heart leapt at the thought. She wanted him so much, wanted him to be part of her.

His kiss increased in intensity, grew powerful and erotic, leaving her quivering and yearning for more. She lay weak atop him. She loved having his tongue delve inside her mouth, the way his breathing became labored. His fingers dug into her bottom as he pressed her down, against the hard proof of his desire. His hips rose against her. Finally, growing extremely restless from the fire which licked her insides, she became an active participant in their kiss. She imitated his movements, met his adventurous, insistent tongue with her own. Strangled sounds welled in the back of her throat again, but the same sounds came from him.

His mouth still locked with hers, he abruptly rolled her half under him. Both of his hands slid down her sides, scorching her skin. Her pantalets swept along her legs. When they tangled at her ankles, he used his foot to push them away. Rising slightly, he grunted as he released the waist of his own pants and slithered out of them. Reno then began a feverish exploration of the inside of her thighs. His rough fingertips rendered Libby insensible.

The most pleasurable sensations engulfed her. Though she trembled, heat spiraled through her from his double assault. While he continued to kiss her, his feverish exploration of her tender thighs became her main concern. When his fingers strayed higher, she would've gasped, but her mouth was otherwise engaged. Wave after wave of bliss stole through her, leaving her a quivering mass.

His lips gentled on hers as he fitted himself between her legs. The first searing contact with his throbbing manhood caused her to stiffen.

"Rest easy," he mumbled, his voice thick and hoarse. "I'll try not to hurt you."

Allowing her no time to question his intent, he came inside her. He moved no more, merely placed quick, impassioned kisses all over her face. The feeling was incomparable, she thought with the part of her mind that still functioned. He was truly part of her. The pleasure distracted her so much, she wished she weren't enjoying his love-making so much. She wanted to distance her senses in order to cherish his every touch. The glorious moments while he was deep inside of her. She knew it wasn't to be. Already, her traitorous body wanted to draw him even deeper. Her muscles tightened of their own accord.

He muttered an oath against her mouth. "I gather I haven't hurt you?"

"No . . . pain," she managed. "You feel good."

"Ah, Libby, you're driving me insane. Where did you learn to move like that?"

"I'm not doing anything."

"The hell you aren't." With his hands under her bottom, he withdrew. Very slowly, he came inside her again. "Damn. You're a natural-born witch. I'm trying to be gentle but you're tightening around me."

She knew what he meant, though her body had reacted instinctively. "I'm sorry."

He laughed but it came out more of an anguished cry. "Don't be sorry, sweetheart. When I move, do it again."

He moved slowly, beginning a sweet friction

that drove her wild. The most exquisite heat began and developed into a mind-boggling tension which held her entranced. She didn't know what to expect. Instinct told her it would be beyond anything she'd ever experienced.

She clung to him, command of her body stolen from her by this reckless man who had robbed her of her heart. She imagined herself as a finely crafted musical instrument. Reno was a master musician who created a symphony destined forever to haunt her. When his movements generated into fleet, penetrating thrusts, the symphony burst to a grand finale.

Magnificent colors exploded across Libby's mind. She raked her nails into Reno's back, wanting to bind him to her eternally.

Chapter 16

⌒─◯◯─⌒

Reno reached his own blinding climax seconds after Libby's nails had scored his back. Long minutes passed before his mind cleared. Tremors still racked his body. He'd never climbed to such a glorious height with any other woman. But never before had he allowed a single trace of emotion to enter into his lovemaking.

Libby clung to him, her breath warm and fast in the crook of his neck. His back stung in places. Despite the minor pain, he felt wonderful and miserable at the same time. She'd done the impossible, stolen past his defenses.

Soft sounds came from her as her hands left his back and climbed to his shoulders then into his hair. Her lips, also, slid up his throat to his chin. His recently banked desire flickered to life. Still embedded inside her silky sheath, he unconsciously pressed deeper. He'd never recovered so quickly with another woman, which surprised him. Not wanting to overwhelm her, mindful of her inexperience, he shut his eyes. He willed his passion to wane.

"You were marvelous," she whispered close to his mouth. "I truly felt as if we were one."

"We still are," he grated out. "Did I hurt you?"

"Was it supposed to hurt?"

"Maybe just a little at first."

"You must be a master at lovemaking then," she said, trailing a nail along his jawline. "Because I felt only a little pinch, then the most joyous pleasure. Will it be that good every time?"

He groaned from her innocent praise and enthusiasm. "Even better."

"I think I couldn't bear anything better."

He brought her hand to his mouth and kissed her palm. When she shivered, wiggling beneath him, he held his breath to dispel the rush of blood through his veins. "Me either. You've branded me."

A soft laugh escaped her. "I sincerely doubt any woman could put her brand on *you*."

He wanted to argue but controlled himself in time. Libby had indeed burned a brand on him. Unfortunately, he wasn't sure what, if anything, he wanted to do about it. She was too good for him. He couldn't give her what she wanted and deserved. Hell, tomorrow was just another day to him, to be lived as he saw fit.

"It's just as well you aren't arguing with me," she said. "I expect nothing from you."

Her eyes looked lovely in the faint glow left from the rapidly dwindling fire, smoky and affectionate as they roamed his face. He considered her mouth instead. Surely she must see the agony he felt over his inability to love her.

"You look regretful."

"Do I?" he asked.

"I wish you wouldn't feel sorry. It was I who tempted you."

"It would've happened either way," he admitted. "If you hadn't been so sweetly persistent, I probably would've seduced you instead. I'm not a very honorable fellow."

"You are certainly good for an old maid's ego, Reno McCord."

Unable to stop himself, he met her gaze and smiled. "No longer an old maid, at least technically."

"No. You've made me a woman at long last." Her eyes gleaming with pleasure, she grinned shamelessly. "You . . . will you . . . can we do it again?"

"If I possessed a shred of decency, I wouldn't have touched you at all."

"Once will never be enough," she said softly, her voice breaking. "Neither will a thousand times. But I want as many memories to cherish as I can."

He made to pull away, but she held him fast. "Dammit, Libby."

She tangled her fingers in his hair, holding his head in place. As she brushed her lips across his, she whispered, "Mine until we return. If you'll recall, Mr. McCord, I'm paying you well."

"Libby! You're making it sound as if I'm your paid stud, when that's not the way it is at all."

"How is it then?"

He smiled in appreciation of her devious mind. He'd forgotten how clever she could be. But if she intended to make him admit he loved her, she could think again. Maybe he had fallen in love. Maybe. The strong urge to protect her, to keep her safe and by his side forever floated in the back of his mind. If that was love, he reviled it. He wouldn't protect her or save her from harm.

He'd squander her money in search of a good time.

He'd never be happy being tied down.

"I love you," she said with such devotion, he shuddered. "I wouldn't expect you to change. I know you—"

He clamped a hand over her mouth. "Don't say words you'll live to regret." When she clawed at his hand, he released her. "Libby, I can't give you what you want."

"I'm sorry. I never meant to tell you of my feelings. Lord knows, I tried so hard not to fall in love with you. I know you aren't the man I should want, but I love the man you are."

He moved his hand, intending to quiet her again. But she sank her teeth into his thumb. "You bit me!"

"And I'll do it again if you try to cover my mouth."

He grinned at her ferocious demeanor. "Lucky for me, there isn't a frying pan handy."

She grinned back. "There's no use hitting you. I cracked your head hard enough already. Apparently it had no result."

"None whatsoever. You might as well surrender the battle, Libby."

She heaved a sigh. "It was worth a try. I'm glad, though, that I told you I loved you. One day you might think of me and remember. And you might change your stubborn, granite-hard mind and decide you love me back." She aimed him a secret smile. "After all, stranger things have happened.

You, Mr. McCord, did not believe in ghosts. Well, I guess you do now. And, by the way, I haven't forgotten about our bet. Tomorrow, I fully intend to see you eat your hat!"

Splaying his fingers under her backside, he lifted her and thrust his throbbing arousal to the depths of her hot core. "I think I've found a sure way to silence you."

She inhaled sharply and hugged his neck. As his mouth descended to trap hers, she got out, "You have, indeed."

Reno awoke in the middle of the night. The temperature had gone down; so had the fire. He could barely see Libby in the dark. The one part of his body which remained warm gave testament to the fact that she lay curled at his side. Though loath to disturb her, the fire needed tending.

After he'd slipped his arm free, he tucked the blankets around her so the cold wouldn't sneak inside. Then, careful not to bump her, he crawled across her. Thank goodness he'd gathered plenty of wood.

Cold rarely bothered him. Tonight it shot straight to his bones. He accorded his sensitivity to the warmth he'd taken from Libby. Sleeping with her naked body tight against his would spoil him. It was a luxury he couldn't allow himself to like too much. His movements brisk, he tossed branches and twigs onto the embers. He used a stick to stoke the fire to life, shivering all the while. He usually slept in his clothes. Tending fires naked left something to be desired.

A rustle beyond their campsite made his heart lurch. Good God, he was jumpy. Damn Harkins.

Until he'd come face-to-face with the apparition from hell, he'd never once believed in ghosts which flew at people. Reno scowled. He'd made an ass of himself in front of Libby. She must have enjoyed herself immensely when he'd emptied his gun at a damned apparition.

Some guardian he'd turned out to be, Reno mused. Libby hired him to protect and guide her, and he hadn't been able to frighten off one lousy, already dead man.

She loved him. It was hard to fathom.

The fire suddenly sparked and flamed high. A wave of heat floated over his chest and arms. He prayed Harkins's remains didn't return at this inauspicious moment. He had no mind to battle a grouchy apparition who sported an ax in its head while he was naked as the day he'd been born.

An earth-shattering scream nearly sent him into the fire. He lunged to their bed and threw his arms around Libby. "What's wrong?"

She shook violently, tossing her head. Another scream sent a shiver down his spine. He ripped away the blankets, crawled beside her and then covered her body with his. Tousled hair covered most of her face. He brushed it aside.

Libby's eyes popped open. She looked ready to scream again but enlightenment dawned in her eyes. She threw her arms around his shoulders. She held him tightly; he clamped his arms around her.

"The dream," she muttered close to his ear. "It was awful."

"Of Trout?"

She nodded, a sob escaping her. "Of him and of you, too." When she pulled away, terror danced in her eyes. "We've come far enough. Let's not go on."

"Now, Libby," he said, his voice low and soothing, "we discussed this before."

"I know we did, but you don't understand."

"What don't I understand?"

"The part of the dream about you." She shook violently again. "I'm afraid."

"Tell me what you saw." Her breath came in pants, so he caressed her cheek with the back of his hand. "If you want me to understand, you have to tell me what you saw. Otherwise, I can't do anything."

"All right. The dream happened the same as before, you know, with Clarence leaving his cabin. He met a man, and they started to talk. Then the man had a dagger. But when he thrust it into Clarence's chest . . . Clarence became . . . you!"

"It was a dream. Nothing more. Even if we find the place, the man won't be there. And, anyway, we might find your fiancé alive."

How smoothly he'd just lied. He had no hopes of finding Clarence Trout alive. Seeing Harkins's ghost had made him realize there were things in the universe beyond his control. Libby's dream, which he'd dismissed, now seemed more plausible. Perhaps her lost intended *had* been sending her a message. He wouldn't have believed the notion a day ago.

"We have to see this through," he said gently. "We've come so far together. Besides, I suspect your Mr. Trout won't leave you alone until he's properly laid to rest and his murderer is caught."

"Do you really believe that?"

"I do now. From what you've told me, Trout's

too decent to haunt you for any other reason." He kissed her nose. "We've had a run-in with a ghost and survived. I'm confident you can hold on one more day."

"Then what?"

She *would* ask him straight out. He couldn't lie, not to Libby. "I've lived my life as it came. You don't expect me to change overnight, do you?"

She shook her head.

"We'll face tomorrow and the day after when they come. That all right with you?"

"Yes." She curled closer. She eased a leg over his and rubbed her soft, warm skin against him. "I've put my trust in you. I'll accept whatever you decide."

A ragged sigh tore from Reno's throat.

Libby fell strangely silent. He tensed when she dipped her head. Then he felt searing kisses which began below his collarbone and made a heady journey down the center of his chest.

"You're all hard and hot again," she said against his stomach. The kisses detoured upward, as did her teasing voice. "Can we make love one more time?"

A muttered oath slipped out before he caught himself. He gripped her waist and lifted her back in place. "Insatiable hussy," he taunted with a laugh. "As much as I want to do just that, you'll be sore as hell if I do."

"I won't. I feel fine. More than fine."

"I'll hold you, nothing more tonight."

"Am I, or am I not, your employer?" she asked as she tweaked a lock of hair on his chest. "Perhaps you'll reconsider for a raise?"

"Another warming fee? You refused my previous offer."

"That was then. Now, I know how very competent you are at warming."

Close to dawn Reno once again built up the fire. Libby sat huddled in the blankets, watching the only side of him visible as he squatted. Faint light lent him a ghostly appearance. She spared a smile. He made a magnificent apparition. A very naked, very virile spirit.

He turned his head and caught her scrutiny.

"Aren't you cold?" she asked.

"How can I be cold with your eyes searing me all over?"

"Not all over," she countered lazily. "There's much I can't see."

A wicked smile played on his mouth as he rose and strode toward her. "A situation easily remedied."

She swept her gaze from his shoulders to his toes and back again. She marveled that such a stunning man found her desirable. His entire body should be labeled a dangerous weapon, she thought. Dangerous to any woman daring enough to ogle him brazenly. She'd changed drastically in the short time she'd known him. Though he'd made love to her several times, she craved more.

He sat beside her and shoved both feet into his pants. "You've drained me, Libby."

Startled, she met his amused gaze. "Reno McCord, I don't recall asking you to move a muscle."

A booming laugh escaped him. "Maybe not in

so many words. The way you look at me gives away your torrid thoughts."

"So? Is it a sin to admire a very handsome, very naked man? Does it mean I want you to make love to me again?"

His laughter gave way to a knowing grin. "I like your phrasing, Libby. And, yes, I believe you want to make love with me again."

Libby lifted her chin. She glanced away, saying, "I suppose if you've grown tired, it's understandable. Apparently I was mistaken. I thought you possessed unlimited strength."

He jerked the pants over his hips before he lay back to fasten them. "It won't work."

She swiveled around. Her eyes drifted over his long legs and flat stomach, and lingered on his stomach. "What won't work?"

"Taunting me. You were very greedy last night. Whether you realize it or not, you'll feel it later."

"I suppose I was greedy." She slipped one arm out of the blanket to draw a finger up his arm. "But you were, too. I still tingle in indecent places."

He flashed her a broad smile, which showed his teeth to advantage. How she would miss him. If she couldn't bring him around to her way of thinking, memories of him would haunt her for the rest of her long, lonely life. No other man could possibly take Reno's place in her heart. But she'd already decided not to pressure him. She would take what he had to give and be satisfied. Well, maybe not satisfied. She'd simply cherish her memories.

"Have you seen my shirt?"

Libby pointed behind him. "You threw it there."

"Ah, yes, I remember now. I was in a hurry." He rolled over. On his knees, he inched far enough to reach a sleeve. Bringing the shirt with him, he swung around. Afterward, he flexed his shoulders. "You clawed my back."

"Did I?" When she saw humor glint in his remarkable eyes, she gave him an innocent look. "I don't recall doing any such thing."

"Liar."

Fiery heat flushed Libby's cheeks.

He captured her hand and brought it to his mouth. He kissed her fingers before he motioned toward her scattered clothing. "You better get dressed. I imagine Harkins might be near, since he seems to have staked a claim on this area. I don't know if I like the idea of any other man, alive or dead, seeing you naked."

Libby clutched the blanket under her eyes. She peered over the edge. Reno had made her forget about Harkins and the very real threat the apparition posed. She didn't want to think of what the day might bring.

"I'll stand guard, if you want."

"Be sure to reload your gun." Silence reigned. Daring a glimpse of him over her shoulder, she bit back a smile. Reno wore a scowl. "Forgive me," she added softly. "I didn't mean to remind you."

He seized a handful of her hair and leaned forward, his mouth hovering over hers. "Mocking your sole protector is risky, Libby."

Brilliant color streaked across the sky. The soft glow lent his mouth warmth. She stared at his lips, craving his kiss. Would she ever be able to be near Reno without hungering for his touch? A touch she now knew intimately. "How will you retaliate?"

He studied her mouth intently. "You could tempt a saint, Libby. And a saint I'm sure as hell not."

"Will you retaliate or not?"

"Your punishment is . . . I'm not eating my hat. Instead, I demand the right to claim the kiss you wagered."

"But you already have."

His mouth slanted over hers. He tasted her lips thoroughly before he drew away with a smile. "Get dressed or I might change my mind. We can't remain here all day."

She contemplated the folly of doing just that. She loved him too much now. Every time he made love to her, she felt closer to him. She despaired at the thought of his leaving her. His eyes suddenly narrowed into a thin slit of blue. Were her thoughts so obvious to him?

Seizing her arms, he brought her to her feet. "Put your clothes on, now, Libby. There's a private matter I must see to."

She watched him collect the rest of his belongings, and his coffeepot. He strode out of sight. Pain splintered Libby's heart. Reno had merely gone to tend nature's call, but even this short absence left her with a sinking feeling. Had she been naive to think she could live the remainder of her life sustained only by memories of him?

A chill crept through the blanket, reminding her of her unclothed state. She dressed quickly. Using water from Reno's canteen, she washed as best she could. With an eye tuned to her surroundings, she repacked Charity.

When she went back to their camp, she noted Reno had returned and the pot had been set on the fire. Apparently, he intended to remain long enough to drink his coffee. She watched him for several minutes. Warmth coiled around her heart. She'd grown fond of everything about him.

He needed a shave again, she thought. But the dark stubble on his lower face didn't detract from his potent appeal.

He glanced at her as he reached for the pot. He poured steaming liquid into one cup and held it out to her. Surprised by his gesture, Libby closed the distance between them. As she silently sipped, she shook her head. Again, warmth invaded her heart. "You've made me tea?"

A tinge of color crept up his neck. "I thought it might warm you up before we start out."

As if embarrassed by her open regard, he passed by her, heading for the animals.

Tears welled in Libby's eyes as she downed the tea. Reno had proven he wasn't the coarse barbarian she'd called him. Far from it. He'd turned out a gentle lover, a considerate companion, and a fierce protector. She wondered how many other women had discovered the same qualities in him and surrendered their hearts only to lose him in the end.

They traveled even more slowly that day. The mountain trail was oftentimes perilous, so Reno rode at her side. Though she wondered at his silence, Libby welcomed the quiet interlude. Her morose musings had left her feeling melancholy, consumed by an overwhelming sadness. She sensed their return trip would be much shorter.

Images of Clarence Trout also hovered in the back of her mind. She'd undertaken this journey on his behalf and hadn't spared him as much consideration as he deserved. The poor man had most likely come to a tragic demise, yet she had been so preoccupied with Reno, she'd relegated her intended to a meager portion of her attention.

He'd been such a nice man, a man who had loved her. She consoled herself with the thought that she'd loved him, though not with the intense emotion she felt for Reno. She would've married Clarence and made him a good wife.

Libby heard water gurgling nearby. The creaking of Reno's saddle drew her attention. She watched him change position and lead his horse closer to hers. When she caught his gaze, she warmed to his smile. Wondering if he had been trying to offer encouragement, she looked ahead.

Red rock littered the ground. Alarm channeled through her. She'd seen the same rock in her dreams countless times. When Reno gripped her arm, she knew her dismayed expression must've betrayed her.

"Is this the place?" he asked.

Unable to form words, she gave a curt nod.

Reno dismounted. Leading both horses, he slowly picked his way forward.

Dread filled Libby.

Her breath turned shallow. Ahead, past a bend, she saw a riderless horse. The horse she believed had belonged to Clarence. It was as transparent as it had been earlier. She darted a look at Reno. Her stomach dropped as a bolt of alarm struck her. He gave no indication that he saw the horse. In fact, he walked straight for the phantom!

"Don't you see it?"

He halted and shot her a glance. "See what, Libby?"

Libby closed her eyes briefly before she searched the area again. The horse still stood in the same spot. "The horse." She pointed with a finger. "There. Don't you see it?"

He turned back and stared for a long minute. "If you say a horse is there, I believe you." He came alongside of her, scooped her from her saddle.

She hadn't realized she'd been holding her breath and she expelled it in a rush as she squeezed past him. The phantom horse remained. "I think it wants me to follow."

"You're probably right. Let me secure the animals first." He gave her a crooked smile. "Just in case Harkins decides to visit. I'm not in the mood to scour the country for Charity."

"Okay. I won't move."

Minutes passed like hours. When Reno touched Libby's arm, she jumped with fright. Her heart began to thump heavily, refusing to return to normal.

"Why don't you wait here," Reno said. "I'll go ahead and check out the area."

She gripped his arm. "Don't leave me alone. Besides, I sense I must go. For some reason, the horse isn't visible to you."

"Not that I want to see another ghost, but—"

"I take your meaning," she countered, cutting off the rest of his statement. "I think I should go first. You *will* be right behind me?"

"Need you ask? I should be leading *you*."

Libby took a deep breath and started up the canyon. Rocks crumbled under her feet, the crunching noise sounding ominous. A slight breeze rustled leaves in an oak thicket. Shivers crawled along Libby's spine as she kept her eyes on the transparent horse.

But as she came closer to the apparition, it vanished, making Libby halt abruptly.

Reno grabbed her shoulders to keep from plowing into her. "Why did you stop?"

"The horse disappeared." She walked cautiously onward, until she spotted a dilapidated cabin. Recognition flashed in her mind. It was the structure she'd seen in her dreams, the cabin Clarence always walked out of before he got stabbed. "My God, it's really here."

Reno stepped beside her. "Is it the cabin you saw in your dream?"

"You see it?"

"Of course. Did you think it was transparent like your horse?"

"I wasn't sure. Do you think Clarence stayed there?"

"Yes, Libby, I do." He moved in front of her. "Wait here while I check it out."

Libby swallowed a protest. She didn't want to wait alone. Neither did she want to explore the place where her intended had spent his last days. Some of his belongings might still be inside. Memories of him weighed heavily on her heart. It wasn't fair that someone so good, so young, might have perished so violently.

She waited with bated breath as Reno headed for the cabin. He stepped carefully onto the leaning, unstable porch. One support beam listed dangerously. Boards groaned under his weight. A sharp snap preceded a gunshot.

Libby gasped and covered her mouth with a hand.

With a chagrined glance back at her, Reno waved his gun. He had drawn it. It must have accidentally fired when his foot had broken one of the wooden slats on the rickety porch.

Reno disappeared inside.

She moved another few steps forward. Not knowing what was happening inside the cabin was wreaking her nerves. When she saw a man leave the front door and walk a short distance away, a tremor shook through her.

The man holding a tattered hat in his hands was Clarence Trout!

Chapter 17

Clarence walked a few feet more before he stopped. He looked straight at Libby, aiming her a cheerless smile.

"You're alive," she whispered. "All along you've been alive."

He couldn't have heard her. She had spoken too low. Yet, very slowly he shook his head. An eerie premonition took root. She wanted to run to him, to question him, but her legs refused to obey her mental command.

Lines of fatigue radiated across Clarence's forehead, and his shoulders slumped in defeat. Breaking eye contact with her, he began to walk again.

Out of nowhere another man appeared. Libby couldn't see his features, merely that he was larger and broader than Clarence. They began talking.

Icy fingers of dread gripped Libby. This couldn't be happening, she thought. She blinked and noticed a cold, hard fact. Neither of the men had substance. Her knees buckled.

She had been watching a dream.

Or ghosts.

As she knew it would, a struggle began in

earnest. The larger man pulled out a dagger. Libby sucked in a breath, intending to scream. She froze instead.

Although she didn't dare take her eyes off the scene in front of her, Libby saw Reno leave the cabin out of the corner of one eye. He said nothing as he followed the line of her gaze.

She should have been prepared for the outcome. Being in the actual location, however, lent the dream more significance. She felt as if it were actually happening.

The dagger pierced Clarence's chest.

A cry of anguish escaped Libby.

Reno bolted to her side and wrapped a strong arm around her shoulders. Tears sprang to her eyes. Clarence had truly met a violent, untimely end.

"What did you see, Libby?"

"My dream. Only this time it wasn't a dream. It was really happening. I saw Clarence and his killer fighting. Then . . . Clarence was killed."

Using the back of his hand, Reno swiped a tear from her cheek. "Trout stayed here. I found some of his papers and things inside."

"I thought as much," she said. She sniffed and looked at the spot where she'd seen Clarence and his attacker. "The horse is here again."

Reno caught her arm. "Let's follow it."

"It disappeared before."

"I know. It's come back, though. I want to find out why."

She touched his cheek. "You're so good to me. I doubt any other man would take me after a phantom horse."

"We've come this far." He covered her hand

with his. "At first I didn't give a fig about Trout. Now, though, I feel as if I've known him a long time. He deserves to rest in peace, and I mean to see he does."

Despite her sadness, Libby gave him a smile.

Reno held her hand as they headed for the horse. The apparition didn't move for minutes, then it abruptly trotted up the canyon. "He's taking us to another place," Libby whispered.

Upon reaching another area of fallen red rock, the horse vanished.

"The horse is gone again," Libby announced.

"Mark that spot," Reno said, his voice urgent. "Don't leave, no matter what happens."

Not taking time to think, Libby did as he asked. When she stood where she'd last seen the horse, she realized Reno hadn't followed. The hairs on the back of her neck stood on end. "What are you doing?"

"Wait there," Reno yelled back from a distance. "I need something from the cabin."

Libby's heart skipped a beat. Tempted to protest, to voice her fear of remaining in the desolate spot alone, she swallowed the lump of fear which rose to her throat. Libby closed her eyes and prayed for courage. "Hurry, please."

When she opened her eyes, she found herself alone. She hadn't thought Reno would leave so quickly or so silently. Crossing her arms at her waist, she scanned the rocks and sparse foliage nearby. It had grown unusually quiet. *As quiet as a tomb,* she mused.

A glance at the ground beneath her feet unsettled her even more. A long, narrow portion appeared different from the rest, a bit higher with smaller-sized rocks scattered along its length. A shudder quaked through her. She knew what they'd find underneath.

A hard object touched her arm, making Libby leap into the air. But when she realized it was Reno, she willed her heart to beat at a normal rhythm. "You frightened me half to death!"

"Sorry. I thought you heard me."

Pick in one hand, shovel in the other, Reno gave her an apologetic look. He must have used the handle of the shovel to nudge her.

"If I find what I think I will, it's best if you wait back at the cabin," he said.

Libby inhaled a sharp breath. Her imagination worked frantically, conjuring up the most horrible images. Her intended had summoned her to his final resting place, but he hadn't known she'd turn out to be a coward. She couldn't watch Reno dig up Clarence's remains.

"Please, Libby. This is no place for you. Wait at the cabin but be careful on the porch." He spared her a rueful smile. "You can't miss the broken board where I put my big foot. The rest of the cabin seems sound enough."

"If you find . . . Clarence . . . there's a way to identify him." She shivered, then continued, "He always wore a gold chain around his neck. A small crucifix hung from it."

"Go on, Libby. I'll find him if he's here."

Needing no further encouragement, Libby retreated the way they'd come. She didn't dare dwell on the distasteful deed Reno tended. When she reached the cabin, however, she couldn't bring herself to enter. With a sigh of weariness, she perched on one corner of the porch to wait.

Reno used both shovel and pick to tediously remove layer after layer of dirt and loose rocks. Sweat beaded his brow, dripping into his eyes and hindering his progress. As he paused to drag his shirtsleeve over his face, he bowed his head. He wasn't overheated. A racking chill had seeped into his bones. No man should have to unearth another. The thought of what he might find held him immobile for a long moment.

But he mustn't tarry longer than necessary. He wouldn't put it past Libby to come after him. If he found Trout in the crude grave, the shock of seeing the man half decomposed would remain with her forever. Also, Harkins might decide to appear. The ill-tempered apparition was frightening enough with company present. He couldn't bear to think of Libby meeting the thing alone.

Nausea rose to his throat and left a foul taste. He cast the ghastly memory from his mind. He dipped the shovel into the earth more carefully. Trout's murderer wouldn't have spared time to dig a deep hole, especially in the wilderness where discovery would be unlikely.

The tip of the shovel struck an object that moved with slight pressure.

He knew instinctively he hadn't touched rock.

He dropped to his knees and tossed the shovel aside, using his hands to dig instead. Fifteen minutes later, he fell back on his heels to survey his handiwork, the outline of a body. A layer of dirt covered the remains. In the center of what appeared to be the chest, a sharp object pro-truded.

Reno hesitated to brush off his hands. Seconds passed while he stared at body. Finally, he held his breath and wrapped his fingers around the protru-sion. One quick tug and he held a dagger up to the light.

He fished in his pocket for his handkerchief and used it to brush the weapon clean, particularly the ornate handle. Engraved in the center were the initials JC. Reno shook his head at the incriminat-ing evidence carelessly left behind by Trout's ex-mining partner, John Cox.

"Dumb bastard," he said aloud.

After he'd stowed the weapon in his shirt, he eyed the grave with a grimace. If it weren't for Libby, he might call a halt to his digging now. He'd come this far and found enough proof to damn John Cox for his crime.

But *he* had to know for sure. He'd never met Clarence Trout. From Libby's descriptions of the man, Trout had been a good, decent man with a kind heart. He would've been the man she might have married if fate hadn't intervened.

If he accomplished nothing else, he intended to put Trout's soul to rest. He owed him that much because of the bond he felt with the man.

Libby.

Reno crawled closer. He loosened dirt over the deceased's neck, offering a prayer for any divine intervention the good Lord cared to offer. When, at last, his finger caught on what felt like a string, he gently raised it. Relief flooded him when he held up a gold chain.

His mood quickly lowered. How the devil was he to remove the chain? He sure as hell wasn't burrowing beneath a skull to find a clasp. Removing even one more layer of dirt would have him face-to-face with—He shook his head to dispel the thought.

Wanting to finish with the unpleasant chore, he searched until he found the small cross. He begged Trout's pardon, and that of any heavenly being who might've assisted him, and snapped the chain. He dropped it into his shirt pocket while he considered the dirt-laden form. Remorse washed over him. A decent burial was out of the question.

Reno swept off his hat and fitted it over Trout's face.

As carefully as he'd uncovered Libby's intended, he replaced the dirt. Afterward, he made the grave as presentable as possible. He built a marker from a variety of rocks.

On a ridge above him wildflowers grew in a crevice between two rocks. Though he wasted fifteen minutes climbing the jutting, precarious cliff face, he returned with a handful of flowers. He propped them against the crude marker.

Now, he had to tell Libby of his gruesome find.

Libby paced the dilapidated porch. Because of broken boards, pacing required concentration. She didn't want to think about what Reno was doing. He had been gone longer than she'd anticipated.

Cold air touched her neck.

Libby jumped in the wrong direction and heard an ominous crack. A board splintered and collapsed. Her foot went into the opening.

Demented laughter howled all around her. Her heart thumped against her ribs. Though reason told her Harkins thrived on his victim's fear, she couldn't calm herself. She was trapped in place with no means of escape. She tugged viciously on her boot to no avail.

She saw him then. Three feet in front of her Henry Harkins grinned evilly. Her eyes locked on the gruesome ax embedded in his skull. The image wavered, transparent and reeking of a foul odor. Libby felt close to swooning.

When the phantom drifted a foot closer, she squealed and jerked her foot again. Her foot popped free of the boot. She inched toward the door of the cabin.

Harkins threw back his head and laughed once more.

Sure she was about to lose control of her bodily functions, Libby burst into the cabin and kicked shut the door. Seeing a chair, she rushed across the room. Her hands shook as she rammed the top edge under the doorknob.

Discovering cobwebs clinging to her hands, Libby squealed again. Furiously, she wiped her fingers on her pants, shirt, even the wall until they were clean. Then, she dashed to the one smudged window and peeked out. She breathed a sigh of relief to find Harkins had gone.

"Libby."

Libby spun around. On the opposite side of the small room she saw Clarence Trout. Though transparent, she knew *this* vision differed from the others.

He held out a hand to her. "I've found peace at last," he said. "You've earned my eternal gratitude, Libby. I wish you love, happiness, and a long life."

When the image began to fade, she rushed forward. "Wait! Don't go!"

"I must go. Your man is coming."

Tears coursed over Libby's cheeks. A second later, when she found herself alone in the empty cabin, she fell to her knees, sobbing uncontrollably.

Reno returned to the cabin to find Libby gone. The faint order of rotting flesh lingered, and one of her boots was stuck in broken board. *Good God, Harkins has been here,* he thought. He tried the door. Though unlocked, it refused to budge. With a curse on his lips, he kicked the weathered wood and heard the hinges give way.

A scream came from inside.

"Libby!" he yelled. "Stand back. I'm coming in."

A savage kick broke the door in two, but an obstacle kept it from falling inward. Reno shoved his way past the two ruined sections and fell half over a chair. He sent it skittering across the room, where it hit the wall.

Then Libby flew at him. He caught her against him as her arms went around his neck.

"I shouldn't have left you alone," he said in an attempt to soothe her.

"Harkins . . . came . . . again," she stammered.

"He's not here now." He led her outside, onto the porch, and pulled her boot from the board. He waited until she'd put it on before he said, "It's done."

"I know you found Clarence."

"How do you know?"

She took a calming breath. "He came to me."

He held her away. "Libby, Trout couldn't have come. I just buried him."

"Clarence . . . his ghost . . . was . . . here. And my eyes were open the entire time." She trembled and moved against him again. "He told me he was finally at peace, thanks to me. Do you believe me?"

"After what I've seen, I'd be a fool to doubt you." He retrieved the chain and tucked it into her hand. "I tried to bury Trout properly. If you want to come now, we can say some words over him."

"Of course." Still clutching the chain, she walked off. "Clarence is grateful to you for all you've done. As am I."

He adjusted his stride to fit hers. "Don't thank me, Libby. I wanted to bury him right. In a way, I feel obligated to him." When she glanced at him, he explained, "If it weren't for Trout, I wouldn't have met you."

She gripped his hand before she continued on.

Upon reaching the grave, Reno stood back while Libby paid her last respects. He waited while she said her words silently.

"You made a marker. Where did you find flowers?" she asked.

Reno nodded at the jutting cliff.

"You climbed all the way up there?" Tears welled in her eyes. "I know you don't like me to thank you."

"Then don't."

Feeling her wilt against him, he pulled her against him for a long moment. Then he brought her back to the cabin, where she handed him Trout's crucifix.

"I imagine you'll need this as evidence."

"It proves Trout's identity, all right." He brought out the dagger but cursed his stupidity when he saw terror flicker in her eyes. "Sorry. I guess I should've kept this discovery to myself. I didn't mean to upset you more."

"It's all right. My dream was accurate, I suppose. Poor Clarence really was really stabbed to death with a dagger."

"More evidence. Enough to put the murderer behind bars, if he isn't hanged."

Her eyes widened. "But we don't know the man's name. I never even saw his face."

"We do now." After putting the weapon back in his shirt, he circled an arm around Libby's shoulder. Setting a path back to where he'd left the animals, he tried to put her mind at ease. "The dumb bastard had his initials carved into the handle. Guess he never thought anyone would find Trout's body, or suspect Trout had been killed by his own partner."

"John Cox? Mr. Byers mentioned him. He said Cox had last been seen in Canon City."

"What else did he say?"

"Only that Cox swore he hadn't seen Clarence for two months prior to his disappearance. Now we know Cox lied."

"If I'm not mistaken, and I know I'm not, we have our man. Or at least we will when I go to Canon City and confront him. I'm betting he'll be so surprised to find we're on to him, he'll either confess, or try to run. Either way, Cox is mine."

Libby halted abruptly. "You can't go after him!"

"Of course I can. I promised Trout I'd see his murder avenged. It was his reason for coming to you in dreams, you know. I'm sure of it. The man deserves to be avenged after what he suffered."

"But I'll not have you risk your life, too. Cox has killed once and has nothing to lose."

Forcing her to walk onward, he dropped his voice to a soothing tone. "Libby . . . we'll discuss this later. Right now, I want to get us out of here"—he raked the area with his gaze—"before old Harkins thinks to come back."

Despite her sad expression, Libby remarked, "My brave guardian, afraid of one measly ghost."

"You're damn right I am. He's out for my blood."

"He's had a chance to hurt us, yet he hasn't. I suspect he just enjoys terrifying people."

"Are you hinting we should bravely confront him?"

"Despite my intuition about him, he still frightened me out of my wits."

"I shouldn't have left you alone to face him."

"Don't blame yourself, Reno. You had a job to do."

Reno untied the animals before he lifted Libby to her horse. When he rested a hand on her thigh, he felt the muscles jump beneath her skin. He offered her the reins. "You're one brave lady. Most women would've turned back long ago."

"Not so brave. If you remember, I tried to persuade you to go back several times."

"But not because you were afraid. Because you

were worried for my safety. And because you cared deeply for Trout."

"I did love him," she said. Her lips rolled together briefly, her features clouding with pain. "Do you think he knows?"

He patted her leg. "He knows. I have an inkling he won't be bothering your sleep any longer."

"I'm glad. I would've hated to think of him wandering these mountains for eternity, like Harkins."

"You look tired, Libby."

She aimed him a poignant look, one which spoke volumes. "I guess I am, just a bit." She touched his cheek. "You're bristly again." Her gaze moved higher and lingered on his hair. "Where's your precious hat? You didn't leave it at the cabin, did you?"

Uncomfortable under her scrutiny, he capped his hand over hers. "I must have."

"Do you want to go after it?"

"Not *this* time." He pressed a kiss on her palm. "I think it's time to buy a new one."

When she lifted a finely arched brow, he knew she hadn't bought his lie.

Surprising him, she said, "Well, it's about time."

A twig snapped and startled him. Though he placed the noise as some small animal foraging for food or shelter, unease put him on alert. "Let's get the hell out of here. I want this canyon far behind us before nightfall."

Libby urged Sugar forward. "I hesitate to remind you, but Harkins appears during daylight as well."

"So long as he confines his attentions to me. If

he knows what's good for him, he'll leave you alone." He mounted and tugged Charity's rope to position her behind his horse. "I don't share my women, even with a ghost."

"The poor man went to his death by terrible means. It's no wonder he's remained angry. He's still wearing an ax in his forehead."

Branches of a patch of scrub oaks hung over part of the trail. Brushing them out of his way with his arm, he said, "Don't let it give you any ideas. I'm not about to search for *his* grave, too." When he felt Libby's gaze, he stared ahead. "I didn't mean that the way it sounded."

"I know you didn't."

"I have a feeling we won't see any more of Harkins." When Libby cast him a dubious glance, he clarified, "We met his test. He only wanted to frighten us, and he did a damn good job of it. But he didn't win. We did what we set out to do, despite his appearances. Now, we'll be doing what he wants—getting the hell out of *his* canyon."

She gave him a faint smile.

Libby was a problem he must deal with very soon, Reno mused. For the first time in his life, he regretted his loose ways. If he'd guarded the money he'd made in the past years, he might have had as much wealth as she. A man without money had no right to consider marriage. A woman like Libby needed a home, and a good provider to care for her.

He owned little, had no future, and no means to acquire one.

The only thing she craved which he *could* give her was babies. It was one area in which he might excel! Feeding, clothing, and raising them was another matter. Hell, he wouldn't even be a good disciplinarian. There was no way he'd take his belt to a child's behind.

She would be better off if he sent her back to Pennsylvania the instant they reached Denver. She'd find some one else before long, a man of Trout's caliber.

However, imaging Libby with another man's child in her arms left Reno wearing a dark scowl.

Chapter 18

⁓◦◦⁓

L ibby's somber mood eventually abated. She knew she owed Reno much more than she could ever repay. Together, they'd brought Clarence peace at last. When his ghost had appeared to her at the cabin, he hadn't seemed to mind that she'd come to love Reno. She always knew Clarence wouldn't have wanted her to spend the rest of her life mourning his demise.

She felt almost lighthearted, as if a great weight had been lifted from her shoulders.

Her heart swelled with love as she gazed at Reno's back. The last two hours he'd pushed them both hard. While she had expected him to travel faster on their return trip, mixed emotions churned through her. She wondered whether Reno's tendency to hurry generated from a desire to catch Clarence's killer.

Or from a desire to part from her.

Perhaps she'd been foolish to confess her love. Her admission might have frightened him. How different everything would be if he returned her feelings. Recalling her promise to herself not to pressure him, Libby dashed her hopes. He was hers only until they reached Denver. She would amass as many memories of Reno as possible in the time she had left.

The trail Reno followed led through thick foliage and wound downward. Travel became tedious, so he dismounted to lead the animals. Curious why he'd chosen this route when other, easier ways existed, Libby tuned her senses to the land around them. A familiar sound made her smile.

The waterfall.

Excitement coursed through her. There could be only one reason why he'd chosen to come this way. Did she dare believe that he intended to recapture the glorious passion they'd discovered behind the falls? If it turned out he'd stopped here simply because of the availability of water for the animals, her disappointment would be acutely painful.

They entered the small canyon from the opposite end, which directly faced the falls. Reno plodded through shallow water and rocks, thoroughly wetting his boots. The thought of him with soggy feet made Libby shake her head. The man needed someone to take care of him.

He needed . . . *her.*

She shoved the thought from her mind as soon as it came.

Without saying a word, Reno unsaddled his horse. Then he unpacked Charity and piled their equipment on the bank.

Libby silently watched from astride her horse. Suspense held her immobile. Or perhaps she longed to have him touch her, even if it was only to help her dismount.

Minutes passed before, leaving the two animals to drink their fill, he stood below her.

Libby opened her mouth to speak but caught the slight shake of Reno's head.

He came close. He draped his arms over her saddle, one in front of her, one behind. A strange expression flitted over his features. His eyes darkening to a shade of midnight blue, he said, "Lady, you have three choices."

He looked so handsome, she thought, his eyes so dark, his smile so enticing. Hair brushed his forehead in disarray, adding to his potent allure.

"I want to make you smile again, Libby. Which will it be? Rest . . . food . . . or me?"

"You," she said breathlessly.

His hands spanned her waist. "You never hesitated."

She leaned forward and held his head over her heart. "No."

As he lifted her from the saddle, he slid her slowly along his body. "I like a woman who knows her own mind. Especially if her thoughts mirror my own."

Several remarks came to mind. Libby ignored them all. When her feet met the ground, cold dampness penetrated her leather boots. She'd have soggy feet as well. However, she wouldn't break the spell Reno had cast over her by pointing out such a minor inconvenience.

He swept her into his arms so fast, she choked on a breath. A second later, she stood on a flat rock.

"Sorry," he said with a grimace. "I forgot about the water."

He left her long enough to unsaddle Sugar. After he'd hefted the saddle onto his shoulder, he carried it to the bank and dropped it unceremoniously on top of his own. Then, he hurried back to Libby. He swept her into his arms again and strode toward the falls, kicking rivers of water in every direction.

Libby ran her fingers through Reno's hair. As she kissed the small lump on his temple, she asked, "Are you kidnapping me, Mr. McCord?"

"I am."

"For what purpose?"

With a wicked gleam in his eyes, he shortened his stride. "You'll see."

She bit his earlobe. "Are you going to ravish me?"

He answered with a booming laugh. "Until you beg for clemency."

She nipped his ear again. "My pride won't allow me to beg."

"You've got me fired up too soon." He made a sound that sounded like a grunt. When he reached the bank opposite the falls, he set her down and clamped his arms around her. "Stop torturing my ear, Libby."

"I don't think so. I like torturing you."

Desire blazed in his eyes as he tossed her hat into a bush. He filled his hands with her hair. "I want to finish what we started here. I've thought of nothing else the past hours."

She met his fiery gaze. "Then I think you should finish what you started. I've been thinking of the waterfall, also."

He held strands of her hair, sifting them through his fingers.

"I should never have let you talk me into bringing you along."

With her arms around his neck, she pressed against him. "Why not?"

His mouth hovered over hers. "Because I'll never be the same again. Neither will you. Because you've made me—"

Libby's breath caught. Had he been about to say she'd made him love her?

"You've made me behave recklessly," he finished.

Though disappointed at his words, Libby hid her feelings behind a smile. "And you weren't reckless before you met me?"

He silenced her with a powerful, erotic kiss that pushed any remnants of melancholy from her mind. As his mouth slanted over hers, seeking entrance, his tongue grazed over her teeth.

Libby wilted and welcomed him with all the greed he'd accused her of earlier. Liquid fire sped through her veins and pooled between her legs. Remaining upright sapped her strength.

Reno cupped her backside. When he yanked her against him, the hot, hard proof of his desire jabbed her stomach. She slipped her arms free. She explored his chest, across his waist and sides. Then, she gripped his buttocks the same as he'd done to hers.

His tongue ceased its erotic ravishment of her mouth. But only for an instant. A groan came from deep back of his throat. His kiss adopted a sinuous rhythm which painted a titillating image of his lovemaking in Libby's mind. He kissed her until every nerve ending in her overheated body tingled.

Abruptly, Reno stopped to gasp a harsh breath. "Damn, Libby. You drive me crazy." As he worked feverishly at the buttons on his shirt, his eyes took on a glazed appearance. "Take off your clothes."

Breathless, dizzy with longing, Libby couldn't move a muscle. Instead, she watched him shed his shirt.

A captivating grin slid over his mouth. "Are you waiting until I'm naked before you undress?"

In response, she splayed her hands over the enticing maleness he'd bared. She pressed her lips to the center of his chest. Her arms crept around his waist.

He sucked in a ragged breath and expelled it slowly. "Are you trying to test my endurance?"

"Yes," she said as she unbuckled his gunbelt. She swung it clear and dropped it. "You're taking entirely too long."

"Two can play at this."

Libby intended to loosen the belt to his pants, but he deftly unfastened hers first. When he bent down to slip her pants over her hips, a tremble darted to her toes. He caught her waist and lifted her a foot off the ground, putting them at eye level. Sensing he meant her to shake free of the trousers, she kissed his nose. "They won't come off over my boots, you know."

He growled with impatience as he lowered her to her feet. "Sit and give me a foot."

Amused by his curt command, she did as he asked. Extending a foot, she smiled at his pained expression. One firm yank and he pitched a boot aside. Quickly, she held up the opposite foot. He tossed the boot over her head. With a grin, he hauled her up before she could think to rise on her own.

Reno bent over and took off his own boots then. When he straightened, he wiggled a dark eyebrow at her. "Have you any more impediments I should know about?"

"None."

"Good." He demonstrated his skill by whipping open her shirt and stripping it off. "I'm growing impatient."

"I wouldn't have guessed."

His gaze torrid, he released the buckle to his pants. "You could take over for me if you feel daring."

Glitters of gold in his eyes made the blood sing through Libby's veins. "Are you challenging me?"

He brought her hand to the sewn flap. "Sure enough. Are you up to it?"

"I do believe you've thoroughly corrupted me, because I am, indeed."

Libby swallowed around the lump in her throat. She moved close and brushed aside his hands. As she opened the buttons with painstaking care, she relished the tremble that rocked his large body. Growing bold from his enthusiastic reaction, she pressed her palm over the prominent distention in the front of his pants. Her brazen action brought a muttered oath from Reno.

"You feel so hot and hard, even under your clothes," she said, her tone betraying her amazement.

He moved so fast, she retreated a step to allow him enough room. His pants joined hers. Wearing nothing but a wolfish grin, he seized her hand again and pressed it over his arousal. "What do I feel like in the flesh?"

His husky, sensuous whisper played on her already simmering senses and robbed her of the ability to string her words together. She wrapped her fingers around the inflamed length of him. "You're . . . throbbing . . . and . . . burning . . . to the touch."

Reno muttered another oath. "God, it feels good when you hold me." He pulled her with him into the shallow pool of water. "Let's go behind the falls before I totally lose control and take you here in the open."

Giddy and flushed with excitement, Libby allowed him to lead her. Drenched from head to toe, shivering from the shock of plunging through the chilly water, her teeth chattered.

"Cold, Libby?"

Nodding, she hugged her waist.

He brought her hands to his shoulders. A wicked gleam in his eyes, he said, "I'll do my best to warm you up."

What began as a shiver swiftly turned into a quiver of anticipation. Water dripped from Reno's hair onto his brow, forming rivulets down his cheeks. Idly, she followed the flow as it meandered over his chin. "I suppose you're hinting at that warming fee, again?"

He grinned and ripped open the small buttons on her camisole. "The only compensation I want from you is to feel your nails dig into my back. A few moans and cries of ecstasy would also be appreciated."

Libby gasped as he swept open the undergarment. He covered her breasts with his hands. "Your fingers are like ice."

"Not for long." A determined look on his face, his blue eyes glimmering, he rubbed his callused fingertips over her nipples. "Still think they're cold?"

Heat swirled through her, and her knees were in danger of buckling. "Definitely . . . not."

His gaze locked with hers, and he untied the bow at her waist. He slid her drawers over her hips. "I hope you have other unmentionables."

"Fortunately . . . I . . . do."

"Are you stuttering from cold now, Libby?"

She adamantly shook her head.

"I thought you weren't. My hands feel blazing hot from touching you."

"They are," she gasped out. "It's amazing."

He caught her waist. He lifted her and set her on a nearby rock. Splaying his hands on her back, his lips nuzzled between her breasts. "What is?"

"How . . . hot . . . you're   able . . . to   make me."

"You do the same to me," he muttered against her skin. "I'm throbbing for you."

His lips suddenly slid around each breast in a sinuous dance that left her tense and aching all over. Inch by blazing inch, he narrowed the torturous path of his mouth, until he reached one swollen target. As he claimed his goal, she forced air into her tortured lungs. Fire radiated outward, and through her.

She felt so weak.

She pressed him closer, loving the exquisite

sensations he created. Minutes ago she'd shivered from cold. Now, she felt as if a torch flamed in her belly. When she thought the pleasure he brought could be no keener, he lavished the other nipple with the same adulation. Libby gripped Reno's shoulders to keep from falling into a heap of smoldering ash.

His mouth crept lower and detoured around her navel. As he licked a fiery trail across her stomach, his hands swooped to her backside.

Libby didn't recognize the incoherent cries she heard in the back of her mind, but she sensed they must've come from her. She felt as if Reno were using a red-hot brand on her skin instead of his tongue and mouth. Wildfire ignited everywhere he touched. Her knees chose that second to close under his burning caresses.

He straightened and crushed her against him. "I wasn't done yet, Libby. I was just getting to the fun part."

Recognition of his shameless intention sent fire to her cheeks as well. "Were you going to kiss me there, too?"

"Count on it," he mumbled against her hair. "And I will yet."

"Can you make love to me here?"

"I can now." Giving her no warning, he lifted her into his arms and strode the two steps to the glistening wet, smooth rock face behind the falls. "Now that you're an old hand at lovemaking, I know of a way."

He stood her between his body and the wall of rock and peeled the wet camisole from her arms. Libby's pulse pounded at the glinting light in his eyes. "How? There's no place to lie down."

"It'll take a bit of balance, but I'll manage."

As he captured her mouth in a possessive, sizzling kiss, he pressed her against the rock while he caressed her tender inner thighs. Only his arm around her waist kept her from crumpling to the shallow water lapping at her feet.

He kissed her for what seemed an eternity, until her blood turned hot, and until the moans he'd requested she give him sounded in her ears. She could kiss him forever. Her soul flourished on his sweet ravishment. Dizziness swirled around her and she felt as if they were merging into one.

Libby tensed as gratification came swift and mercifully. She returned Reno's kiss with savage abandon and noticed the change in him immediately. His mouth became even more demanding, razing her logic and charring her body.

How could she live without this? Without him?

She had been naive to think memories alone would sustain her through the lonely years ahead. Her love had advanced beyond reason. Beyond sanity.

But maybe tomorrow would never come. At the moment Reno belonged to her, every potent, powerful, throbbing inch of him.

He broke off his kiss slowly, as if it pained him to cease for even a second. Breathing heavily, his eyes narrow slits, he grabbed her waist. He hoisted her up and against the rock and wedged his hips between her thighs. "Wrap your legs around me," he grated out.

Libby stared at him in mute astonishment.

"Trust me. This can work."

When Libby had done as he'd asked, his hands cupped her backside to bear the brunt of her weight. She hugged her arms around his neck as an added precaution. "How did you think of—"

The remainder of her words were lost. Reno spread his feet apart and eased inside of her. Impaled, filled with his sweltering, rigid arousal, she bore down to take more of him. Her impulsive move caused him to stumble.

He chuckled as he recovered his footing. "Libby . . . you can't push down." He muttered an unintelligible remark which floated past her ear. "Let me . . . love *you*."

Libby swallowed a giggle. "You'll likely fall before you reach your objective."

"I've already . . . reached my objective." He adjusted his feet and tilted her against the rock face. "God, you're so hot and tight."

His last reposition angled her lower body against his, which proved easier to maneuver. Using his hands to support her, he thrust deep and buried himself to the hilt. He retreated very slowly, and then repeated the mind-boggling movement. It took extreme effort not to meet his thrusts. His tempo increased until a tempestuous friction drove all thoughts of their peculiar position from Libby's mind. She writhed and trembled.

The first wave of delirium came unexpectedly. Wave after wave followed, relieving Libby of control of her body. Her muscles spasmed around him each time he retreated. Forgetting he'd told her not to bear down, she met one of his thrusts forcefully. She undulated her hips, wanting him as far inside her as possible.

He stumbled. Libby's spine slid a foot down the cold, slick rock. Reno's recovery wasn't as smooth as before, but, expelling a guttural sound, he hoisted her back where he wanted her.

She was going to reach heaven again. The blinding spasms gripping her continued to build . . . and build. An earth-shattering climax left her dazed and weak-limbed.

Within minutes, Reno tensed and seemed to surge inside her. Warmth flooded to her core. He staggered before he bent slightly and slapped his hands flat on the rock on either side of her head.

"You make a very comfortable saddle, indeed, Mr. McCord," she mumbled.

Out of breath, veins in his neck prominent from the strain of maintaining his awkward position, he managed a laugh. "Is that so, Miss Chandler? I gather you've no complaint regarding the horn stabbing you?"

She brushed hair from his brow. "None whatsoever."

His laugh came again, low and sensuous. "You've become an excellent rider, Libby. Not many women could ride a man like you just did."

"You make a fine stallion." Seeing the broad grin he returned, she shook her head. "Though I suspect you're going to be smug the rest of the day."

"Probably so."

"I guess you have every right to gloat. You've just performed an impossible feat."

"What did you think of my feat?"

"Need you ask? But I think you should put me down. In case you hadn't noticed, we're slowly sinking." She kissed his cheek. "Have your legs grown weak?"

* * *

His entire body had grown weak, Reno thought. He allowed Libby to slip her legs from around him. She clung to him for a moment, the length of her soft curves pressed intimately against him. Inhaling her womanly scent, he closed his eyes to ward off the sultry images stirring his sated body to life.

He wanted her again . . . and again. Hell, their parting would be hard enough. He had accomplished much more than making love with her. He had shown her in his own way that, despite the startling revelations their journey had uncovered, she was still alive.

If he possessed a shred of decency, he wouldn't have stolen her innocence in the first place. But it was too late to lecture himself. He hadn't been strong, had surrendered to her sweet allure. And he would forever treasure the time he'd spent with her. When he put her on the train heading east, it would be the hardest thing he'd ever done. It would be his parting gift to her. He'd spare her a lifetime of misery at his hands.

Libby continued to cling to him in a fiercely protective manner. Love shone in her beautiful eyes as she gazed up at him. She shouldn't have fallen in love with him. It had been the worst mistake of her life.

He captured her hand and placed a kiss above her knuckles. Though he hadn't learned many social graces, he knew enough to get by. Perhaps it wasn't too late to treat her like a lady. "Wait here. I'll go find soap and return. This is your last chance for a bath."

"Don't dawdle, Mr. McCord," she said, in an amused voice. "I'll be cold without you."

He kissed her hand again. "Not nearly as cold as I'll be."

As he strode through the falls, he contemplated the time he'd spent with Libby. She'd hit him with all the force of the pounding falls and battered his defenses. He'd accidentally lowered his guard at some time or another, though try as he might he couldn't pinpoint the moment. He meant to bathe and leave the falls as quickly as possible. Libby too easily tempted him to forget his best intentions.

He found the soap and a towel. He left the towel near their clothes before he plunged through the water again. True to her word, Libby had begun to shiver during his brief absence. His intentions wavering, he rubbed his hands together on the bar until he'd worked up a lather. "Want to join me?"

Instantly, he chastised himself for his quick capitulation to his desire for her. Making love to Libby even one more time might bring about his complete downfall. He cared too much for her to ruin her life any more than he already had.

Libby, though, did the unexpected. She snatched the soap. Green flashes danced in her eyes.

His shoulders dropped with defeat when he met her gaze. "You're not intending what I think?"

"I'm sorry. It's a luxury I can't pass up." Her gaze slid to the thick pelt of hair on his chest, then lower. "It's another memory I'll cherish, one I'm powerless to resist." She smoothed soap over his shoulder. "You won't mind terribly, will you?"

"Mind?" Hell, her avid scrutiny had already sent a rush of heat through his veins, crumbling away his resolve once again. "I don't mind," he lied.

While she swirled the bar over his chest, her other hand followed in its wake. Reno went rigid under Libby's torrid assault. He cursed the weakness within him that had given way despite his warning to himself. The following minutes were sheer torment. Her slick hands glided over every inch of his fevered skin. He shut his eyes in self-defense, determined to hold his passion at bay.

He failed miserably. When her loving ministrations trespassed below his waist, he jerked in shock. Heat surged in his loins and left him pulsing with a primal need only Libby could ignite. He stole a glimpse at her face, and sighed. She wasn't merely bathing him, she was making love to him in her own manner. It was a searing possession which breached the tenuous grasp he'd hoped to exercise over his baser instincts.

"Libby."

She aimed an innocent smile at him. "Have I missed a spot?"

"Witch!" He skewered her with a knowing look. "Have you grown bold enough to wash even the part of me that hungers to fill you again?"

She swallowed hard as pink stained her cheeks. Darting her vision to his stiff sex, her voice faltered. "Why, Mr. McCord, it's you who are bold."

He laughed. "If it's your intention to kill me, go right ahead."

The first shock of her touch shot heat to every nerve of his body. Back and forth she slid her soap-slick hand before, robbing him of breath, her fingers cupped underneath his rock-hard member. "Christ!"

She immediately halted, her eyes wide with dismay. As she considered his pained features, her lips curved at the corners. "I thought I might've hurt you, but I see I haven't."

He gripped her shoulders and dragged her into his arms. "I've unleashed a temptress. All along it was your intention to arouse me."

She blinked in surprise. "Mr. McCord! Would I do such a thing?"

A smile hovering on his mouth, he confiscated the soap. "Not only would you purposely set out to inflame me, you've succeeded. My only recourse is to counter your assault with one of my own."

"Do it before the soap dries and you become crusty."

"Considering the fire blazing in my gut, and other more obvious places, exacting my revenge won't take long."

Her lips trembled as her passion-glazed eyes met his. The tide turned on a battle he'd strived hard to win. Despite the urgent drumming in his body, he soaped each of her luscious curves, but his pace slowed when he laved her breasts. Her nipples were hard buds when he finished. He felt an explosion near at hand. Gritting his teeth, he ruthlessly dampened his burning desire.

For the duration of his ministrations, Libby had held her eyes pinched closed. A blissful smile touched her mouth. He sent his fingers over her stomach and soft mound, into the heated cleft in which he longed to bury himself.

She choked and caught his hand. "You serve a scalding revenge."

"I haven't even begun yet."

A tremor rocked her slender frame. "I fear I can't stand much longer. You've turned my bones to water."

He held Libby under the falls for several minutes, rinsing them both. Then, he swept her into his arms, laid her down in a patch of grass on the bank, and lowered his body over hers.

Libby smiled and wrapped her legs tight around his hips.

"Damn, Libby, I want you so bad I hurt."

She caressed his cheek. "I want you, too. We're both doomed, aren't we?"

Chapter 19

‿‿‿◦OᄋO◦‿‿‿

Libby left the small railroad car with a heavy heart. They had returned to Denver too quickly to suit her, although she supposed it had been for the best. Prolonging the inevitable wouldn't change a thing.

Fluffing out her skirt had little effect against the wrinkles accumulated during their trip. Thank goodness she knew so few people in town. Reno had asked her to go directly to her hotel, but she'd lingered at the depot in the hopes of catching a glimpse of him.

She saw him hop from one of the end cars and drop a plank in place. One by one he led the animals from the car. With a smile she remembered their first day together and the trouble the animals had given him. There was no dissension within their ranks today.

As she continued to watch, she grew proud of the orderly procession. Reno had won Charity's heart, as well as her own. Proving her point, the mule playfully nipped Reno's ear and earned a soft pat on her head. Pain pinched Libby's heart.

Somehow, she had to acquire the strength to hide the devastation that pulled at her heart.

Reno had asked her to go to her hotel, yet here she stood, pining over him. She had many errands to see to before she met him for supper. And, since he intended to leave Denver tomorrow to capture Clarence's murderer, she wanted to look her best tonight.

Despite her mood, she found her room a welcome relief. It seemed an eternity since she'd soaked in a hot bath. But as she lingered in the warm water, her thoughts returned time and again to the invigorating cold baths she'd enjoyed with Reno.

Libby shook her head to dispel the memories. It would not do her any good to reminisce now when she would see him again so soon. She would have plenty of time later—the rest of her lonely life.

She dressed with care, wearing the gown she'd purchased the day of their first meal together.

A glance in the mirror above the bureau showed her a different woman from the one who had come to Colorado. It wasn't the looser roll she'd fastened at her nape, or the tendrils of hair she'd allowed to fall in front of her ears which accounted for the change.

Reno had made her a woman, stolen her heart, and ruined her for any other man. He had also cured dreams of Clarence, and seen her former intended laid to rest. A warm feeling swept over her.

She left the hotel to visit the bank so she could withdraw her money and close her account. With the large amount tucked safely in her reticule, she hired a carriage to take her to her friends' residence. Harry and Ema Taylor greeted her enthusiastically and assailed her with questions. She visited with them for two hours, filling them in on her trip and what she'd accomplished.

"So, you're going back to Pennsylvania?" Mr. Taylor asked as he walked Libby onto the small porch in front of the house.

"There's nothing to keep me here," Libby returned. Purposely, she hid the inner torment which brewed too close to the surface of her emotions. "Though I admit to having formed a fondness for the scenery and brisk weather." She glanced off in the distance. "And the mountains are especially splendid. I'll miss them."

Ema Taylor hugged Libby and then held her hand for a long minute. "You can change your mind at any time. We have an extra room. Really, Libby dear, you shouldn't live all alone. You're welcome to come back. At least you'd have someone to call your own."

Libby kissed the kind lady's cheek. If it weren't for Reno, she might consider the invitation. But being close to him when no hope existed that he returned her love would be impossible to bear. If she couldn't have him, it was best to put half the country between them.

"What of the nice young man you hired to find your intended?"

Surprised, Libby studied the woman briefly. "What do you know of Reno McCord?"

"Only what the sheriff told me," Ema said. "Forgive us, dear, but we had to make sure you were in good hands. We had hoped you might form an attachment."

"He was capable, trustworthy, and I owe him my gratitude," Libby said.

"Ema!" Mr. Taylor butted in. "You promised not to meddle."

Ema clicked her tongue as she patted Libby's hand. "Now there's the kettle calling the pot black. It was *his* idea to interrogate the sheriff about Mr. McCord's character."

"Don't worry about me," Libby said to both of them. "I'll be just fine. I'm used to fending for myself."

Ema shooed away her scowling husband and walked Libby to the waiting carriage. "I've always found life and love odd partners. Perhaps your young man will see the error of his ways and come after you."

Following a shocked pause, Libby recovered her poise. "I wasn't aware my feelings were so obvious."

Ema smiled sweetly and folded her hands over her round stomach. "Your eyes gave you away, child. Every time you spoke of him, they softened. I knew right off you'd fallen in love."

"Mr. McCord is not the marrying kind."

Ema waved a hand. "Why, they all say that! There's not a man who wants to surrender his precious freedom. I'll say special prayers for your young man to come to his senses like my Harry."

Mr. Taylor, having overheard, grunted.

Tears welled in Libby's eyes as she said good-bye. Once the carriage had turned onto another street, she whipped out her hanky and dabbed at the moisture streaming down her cheeks.

By the time she stopped at the jail, she'd gotten control of her emotions. The sheriff had already spoken with Reno, so she only needed to fill the lawman in on several small details. Considering her recent visit to the Taylors, she was happy she needn't carry on a long conversation.

As she stood to leave, Libby's vision lighted on the row of wanted posters behind the lawman's desk.

Sheriff Cook came to his feet also. "Reno said you're leaving us, heading back East."

Realizing her attention had drifted, Libby met the man's steady gaze. "I beg your pardon, but I'm afraid I had my mind elsewhere."

He glanced over his shoulder, to the posters, then back at her. "Reno said you're leaving town."

"I must return home. I have a house, and students I've neglected. I teach piano."

Still considering her, he nodded. He pointed at the posters. "You wouldn't know any of those outlaws, would you?"

His sheepish grin told her his remark had been offered as a jest. "I suppose you're wondering why I was looking at them overly long."

"Reckon so."

"The posters have given me an idea." She opened her reticule. "I want to offer a bounty for the capture of John Cox. However, I want my identity to remain anonymous."

"Uh-huh." The sheriff reclaimed his seat. He propped his elbows on the desk. Steepling his fingers together, he stared at her intently. "Would you care to explain?"

Libby sat also and returned his scrutiny. "Come, Sheriff, I have an inkling you'll figure out my motives soon enough."

"How much reward do you want to offer?"

"A thousand dollars."

The lawman's eyes bugged open before he caught himself. Quickly, he reached for paper and pen and began to write.

Libby counted out the money, but her mind had already moved on to a more pleasant topic—meeting Reno for supper. First, though, she must stop at the railroad office and purchase a ticket home.

Reno looked so striking as he waited for her in front of the restaurant where they'd first eaten, Libby's heart ached.

He wore a white shirt under a dark frock coat, a string tie at his neck, and new dark pants. Not a woman who passed by failed to notice. Even a stout, prune-faced matron turned her head and gave him a second glance.

His hair had been slicked back, and he was freshly shaved. She knew he probably smelled as sinful as he looked, and regretted he'd gone to such trouble for her. It would be even more difficult to get through the evening.

When he spotted her, he tipped his new black, wide-brimmed hat and flashed her a smile.

Libby's stomach tightened. She'd never be able to eat with tomorrow looming in her mind. This would be their last meal together. They hadn't made love since the waterfall—something she now regretted. He had held her in his arms but he hadn't made any move even to kiss her. She decided it had been Reno's way of letting her down gently. She wouldn't try to change his mind.

Gallantly, he offered an arm. "You're late," he

said, as he led her to the door of the restaurant. "I thought you might have stood me up."

Libby nearly laughed at the thought. Adopting a teasing manner to hide her distress, she countered, "Why, Mr. McCord, your ego must be simply languishing."

He chuckled and saw her inside. When he seated her at the same table as before, he whispered, "Too bad we're in public."

Heat washed over Libby's cheeks. She shouldn't have begun a teasing banter with him. He'd given her enough memories to cherish without adding more, or reminding her of their fiery lovemaking.

He came around the table and slid onto the bench, setting his new hat beside him. Libby spared a smile at his possessive action. "You never told me what happened to your old hat."

"Suffice it to say, it's gone to its final resting place."

Surmising he wouldn't elaborate, she pulled off her gloves and laid them aside. As she unpinned her own new hat and stowed it with her gloves, she warmed under Reno's avid interest. For a man who claimed he had no heart, he certainly acted peculiarly. He held his head slightly tilted. His captivating blue eyes roved her face in a loving manner.

In order to have their business out of the way as soon as possible, she fished money from her reticule. She pushed it to the middle of the table. "The remainder of what I owe you."

Though he stared overly long at the stack of crisp currency, he made no move to take it. After a moment, he pushed the currency back to her side of the table. "I don't want payment from you, Libby."

Too stunned to speak, she met his gaze.

Furrows crossed his brow before he smiled. "Are you confused?"

"I am. Did you, or did you not, haggle with me over the amount you wanted to work for me?"

He shrugged his shoulders. "I changed my mind. Even you have to admit that matters between us have changed somewhat."

"Changed somewhat?" Irritation coursed through her from his unemotional phrasing, lending her words a clipped edge. "My memory greatly differs from yours. The glorious moments we shared can hardly be regarded as merely a *change*." Seeing his expression cloud with guilt, she leaned forward and lowered her voice. "If reducing our . . . affair to such callous phasing—"

"Libby," he murmured softly. "Forgive me. It wasn't my intention to get you fired up. I was striving for discretion, in case someone overheard."

Libby sat back and inhaled a calming breath. Her cheeks felt as if they'd turned beet red from the sudden surge of anger which had arisen from his remark. "I'm sorry I overreacted."

"I can't take your money for the exact reason you just lost your temper." He glanced around before he whispered, "You gave me a precious gift. I won't tarnish it by accepting so much as a cent."

A ghost of a smile hovered on her mouth. "You told me your services came high."

He raised a brow. "You know I meant my professional services."

"You won't change your mind?"

"No. Besides, I'd never forgive myself if I accepted monetary gain for finding Trout."

Libby stuffed the money into her reticule, watching Reno at the same time. His barely perceptible sigh, the way he briefly closed his eyes, gave her cause to believe his noble gesture hadn't come easily. It was one more reason to love him.

"Miss Chandler, it's nice to see you again."

Libby glanced up. "Violet. We just returned to Denver today."

"Libby's heading back East tomorrow," Reno offered, avoiding Libby's gaze. "You make sure she gets the best meal possible to tide her over. But don't forget about me. I'll be leaving town again for a week or so. Make mine double portions."

Libby swallowed against the thickness which invaded her throat. He seemed to have accepted their parting so easily.

"You want the stew?" he asked.

Not trusting her voice, Libby gave him a curt nod.

When they were alone again, he folded his hands on the table and stared at her.

She loved him. Didn't he have the slightest regard for her?

"Will you say good-bye to me at the depot tomorrow?" she asked.

"Is that what you want?"

It wasn't what she wanted, not at all. She wanted him to tell her he loved her, that he could and would settle down. But she might as well wish for the moon. "Yes, Mr. McCord, it is."

He stretched out his arm, his hand palm up. "I

know what you want, Libby. But we've discussed this many times."

"Don't say more." She laid her palm on top of his and felt a shock when his fingers gripped hers. "You aren't the marrying kind. You've made your feelings abundantly clear. And I accept your need to live your life as you like."

"You look so down." He brushed the back of her hand with his thumb. "Damn, I didn't think it would be this hard. You have to trust me. I'm doing what's best for you."

"And for yourself?"

"What do you mean?"

"Nothing," she snapped as she drew back her hand. "Forget I said anything."

"Dammit, Libby, you mean to make me feel lower than a snake, don't you?"

She seized his hand and squeezed his fingers. "Truly, it's not my intention. You were honest with me. I knew all along loving you was a gamble."

He closed his eyes as he expelled a ragged breath.

Regretting her lapse, her weakness for him, she said, "Please be careful when you go after Cox. I don't suppose I can change your mind?"

"No, Libby, you can't. Someone has to see he pays for murdering Trout. It might as well be me. I, at least, have a personal involvement."

She offered him a smile. "Then I suppose Cox is as good as caught."

Their supper came. As they ate, Libby shoved all thoughts of tomorrow from her mind. Reno seemed content not to converse with her, and she found his silent company comforting. It was probably for the best, anyway. She didn't trust herself. If one day he decided he loved and needed her, she wanted him to realize it on his own.

When they left the restaurant, he offered his arm once more. Though Libby's heart ached for the duration of their walk to her hotel, she held a tight rein on her rash tongue. She chose only innocent topics.

"Did you sell Charity?"

"I didn't have the heart. Who else would want a contrary mule with an annoying tendency to bite?"

"She bites *you* because she likes you."

He cast her a glance, making her wonder at his thoughts. Did he remember *her* love bites when he'd made love to her? He had seemed unusually withdrawn since he'd met her in front of the restaurant.

"I boarded Charity at the livery. When I get back, I'll find some use for her."

He led her across a street, through the front entrance of the hotel. As he stepped behind her, allowing her to climb the stairs first, the temptation entered her mind. Did she dare lure him into her room?

When she handed him the key to her door, she noted the wrinkles that radiated from the corners of his eyes. He looked so uncomfortable as he unlocked her room, she decided not to pressure him in any way.

A woman had her pride. If he didn't want her, there was no way she would beg him.

Libby stiffened her spine. Holding her hand out

for the key, her voice dripped with formality. "I enjoyed your company, Mr. McCord. Thank you for having supper with me."

His mouth thinned into a tight line. His eyes closing to slits, he countered, "I'm not coming into your room, Libby. It's taken every ounce of willpower I have not to touch you these past days. I won't lose the battle now."

She lifted a brow at him. "I don't recall asking you into my room."

He blinked in surprise. Then he gave her a rueful smile. "You're right. You didn't."

"A good-night kiss is out of the question, also," she retorted. She prayed her weakening resolve wasn't obvious. If Reno guessed how desperately she craved one last kiss to see her through, he'd surely bolt.

Damn him. How could he act so civilized, so cool after the tempestuous way he'd made love to her at the waterfall?

He scowled. "You're not making this easy."

"Should I?"

"Hell, yes. It's just as hard for me."

"I don't think so." Her control fled under his piercing gaze. "I think you can hardly wait to be rid of me. Then you can go back to being the rascal you've been for most of your life. Why, you probably have a woman picked out to offer you comfort tonight."

Anger flashed in Reno's eyes.

She relished any emotion from him, even wrath. Perhaps she'd taken the wrong course with him all along.

"You're afraid of me, afraid I'll make you feel. Afraid of having a family, of committing your heart to one woman. I want a man who will love me for the rest of my life. A family and lots of children." She strode through the open door and whirled around. "But I knew you weren't the man I wanted from the first. I was a fool. But you surpass me. You'll live your life in search of a good time, and you'll never even know what you missed."

Libby wavered. She reviled herself for speaking rashly, when she longed to throw her arms around him instead. He looked like a thundercloud.

"Good-night, Mr. McCord. Have a good life." She stepped back and soundly shut the door.

Her shoulders slumped with defeat the instant his grim visage disappeared from her sight. She tossed her reticule onto a small nearby table. Infuriating man. Would nothing penetrate the hard shell he'd erected around his heart?

Despair sapped her strength. She sank on the chair beside her bureau to curse her own stupidity. A wise woman would've behaved in a dignified manner, allowed him to say his farewell without acting like a shrew. Or a desperate old maid.

Suddenly, the door burst open, banging against the wall. A small mirror crashed to the floor.

Libby shot to her feet. Her heart lurched at the sight Reno made as his large body filled the narrow space. His furious gaze raked the room before it collided with hers. Two long strides put him a hairbreadth from her.

Libby opened her mouth to utter some word of apology, but he moved too fast. He dragged the pins from her hat and flung it on the floor. Her pulse pounded faster than her heart, leaving her blood pumping at an accelerated speed.

Minutes passed as he stared her down.

"Everything you said was true," he finally said. "And there's not a damn thing I can do about it. Except this."

Reno dragged her into his arms and seized her mouth in a demanding kiss. He devoured her, as if his passion had suddenly breached a wall he'd erected.

Curling her fingers into his lapels, she clung to him as desperately as she had when they'd dangled over a sheer cliff, supported by a single rope.

Reno might not have the ability to return her love, but he wanted her physically. She'd thought desire alone would be enough. But she'd learned she craved much more. She tried to put all her love into the kiss she returned. His heat enveloped her.

His arm clamped around her waist, binding her to him. A raw, pained sound rumbled in his chest. Then, much to her surprise, his mouth gentled on hers.

Fearing he meant to stop kissing her, she stood on her toes and pressed her mouth tighter against his. Her action made no difference. His lips still brushed softly over hers. He caressed her cheeks before his fingers tangled in her hair.

She realized a fact she wouldn't have believed. It wasn't passion that inspired him now. It was a much deeper emotion.

Dear God, if she didn't know better, she would think he loved her.

He broke off his kiss and held her at arm's length. Her startling realization had caused her to freeze.

"I shouldn't have kissed you again," he said,

disgust lacing his tone. "I should've put you on the train as soon as we hit town. Now, I have another day to repent my sins."

He hadn't changed his mind, she thought with a sinking heart. He would never say the words she longed to hear. She had nothing left to say, no means with which to persuade him.

"But it's just as well I kissed you good-bye tonight. I couldn't have done as good a job tomorrow with half the town present."

In vain, she searched for an appropriate response.

"I'm not sorry I ruined you, Libby. I suppose it sounds selfish."

"No, not selfish. I'm not sorry, either." She fingered his tie, repairing the damage incurred during their kiss. "Will you write to me?"

"I'll let you know when I capture Cox."

She resisted the overwhelming urge to pound her fists on his chest. But even a sound battering of Reno's heart wouldn't change a thing. Her only recourse was to retire with dignity, to let fate have its way.

She went to the door. Her hand strangled the knob as she allowed enough space for him to exit. "Until tomorrow then. I look forward to seeing you at the train depot."

Reno left as abruptly as he'd burst into her room. It took every ounce of strength she possessed not to call him back or run after him.

Chapter 20

∿∿

Reno mouthed a vile curse.

It had been damn hard to survive the past hours, harder yet not to take Libby to bed one last time. But he'd managed to pull it off.

He strode with purpose down the street. His boots punished the wood walk as he neared his destination. He needed a strong drink, something to dull the pain in his heart and the passion in his veins.

The last few days flashed through his mind. He'd won a similar battle then, though it had been hell. He dare not hold Libby in his arms again, or experience her sweet responses and soft, warm body. He meant to succeed this time.

He had nearly failed tonight. If he had confessed his love for her, he would've done the inexcusable and claimed her forever. Hell, he couldn't even be sure what he felt was love.

The swinging doors of the Crooked Creek Saloon loomed before him. How easily he'd sought out the one place where he could drown his pain. He entered without hesitation, confirming he'd made the best choice for Libby. A card game went

on in the corner, while men clamored for a spot at
the long bar. Music blared from the piano in the
center of the back wall. The money Libby had
paid him at the beginning of their travel burned a
hole in his pocket.

Stopping at the bar first, he ordered a bottle of
whiskey. A man at the table spotted him and
waved him over. Damn his hide, he couldn't wait
to join the game. He might get lucky, win enough
to set him up for life. It was a high stakes game,
and he had just enough to buy in.

A vision of Libby floated across his mind. Her
hazel eyes glittered green, and the sun bathed her
hair with warmth, betraying its auburn color.
Before another image came to torment him, he
opened the bottle and took a swallow. The liquid
fire tore past his throat, searing a path to his gut. It
wasn't the same as kissing Libby, but it was sure
as hell safer.

The man beckoned again, pounding his hand on
the open spot at the table. Reno hesitated only a
second before he accepted the invitation.

When he left the saloon in the morning, Reno
knew he must look like hell. He'd been lucky, had
doubled his money during the course of a long
night.

Wishing he'd thought ahead and quit the gambling hall early enough to clean up, he set out for
the depot. Libby would see him for what he was
now—a man who lived for a good time. A man
who had spent freely of his money with no
thought to tomorrow.

A man who had no right to love her.

She made a lovely sight with her reticule clutched to her bosom as she glanced up and down the platform. A wave of acute longing kept him from approaching her. He watched her from a distance for several minutes, until the locomotive belched smoke and gave a shrill, warning whistle.

Reno broke into a long-legged stride and reached Libby within seconds. When she turned and saw him, her features flooded with relief. He doffed his hat. "Good morning, Miss Chandler."

"I thought you weren't coming," she urgently whispered.

Reno wove his fingers through his tousled hair. "I was almost too late."

If he hadn't been so intent upon observing her reaction to his pitiful state, he would've missed the slight shake of her head. The least he deserved was criticism for his night of debauchery. Libby, though, silently scrutinized his face. To his consternation, he saw no hint of reproach in her eyes.

"The train will be leaving in a minute," she said.

Guilt stabbed him. She deserved a man like Trout. The sooner she came to her senses the better. He aimed her a shameless grin. "My evening of fun sped by faster than I intended."

Dismay registered in her eyes. He could tell she was reading many possibilities into his statement. Though he'd meant to show her his true self, he relented. "I was playing cards at the Crooked Creek Saloon with three other men."

Her brief sigh confirmed he'd been right to offer an explanation. But he wondered how she could think he'd been with a woman. He doubted he would desire other women for a very long time. They wouldn't compare to Libby.

The whistle shrieked once more, startling her. She threw a frantic glance at the locomotive. The conductor stepped from a car and waved at Libby. "Get aboard now, miss."

"Is your baggage on the train?" Reno asked.

Her gaze left the conductor and settled on him. "I took care of it earlier."

He steered her toward the closest car. "You'll miss your train, Libby, and there isn't another today. I want to know you're safely on your way before I leave."

"You're still going after Cox today? When will you sleep?"

He stopped at the door to the car. "I'll be dead tired by tonight." So tired that maybe he wouldn't miss having her huddled close against him. "Don't worry about me. I've gone without sleep more times than I can remember."

She touched his face. Even through her glove, he felt her warmth.

"Take care of yourself," she whispered. "I'll always remember . . . and love you."

He opened his mouth, prepared to lecture her about the pitfalls of wasting her life on his account, but she swept up the hem of her skirt and climbed aboard the car without a look back at him.

The temptation arose to run after her. Clamping a tight rein on himself, he stood where she'd left him. He knew he'd done her a favor. The train squealed and lurched forward, and his heart turned over. The cars began to move.

Minutes later a window slammed open. Libby's head popped out. "You're a stubborn jackass, Mr. McCord. But if you ever change your mind and want to make an honest woman out of me, the sheriff knows where I live." Then she waved and disappeared back inside.

Reno spared a mirthless laugh at Libby's audacity. Several people on the platform cast him reproving looks. Heat crawled up his neck. Leave it to Libby to have the last word and make him the center of attention.

He touched the brim of his hat and hurried out of sight.

Three weeks later, on the outskirts of Denver, Reno urged his horse into a run. Bone-tired, dusty, hungry, and ill-tempered, he craved a taste of the amenities the town offered. He hadn't planned to be gone for so long, but he hadn't expected Cox to evade him so easily. His experience with the army had served him well. He had finally tracked the man to a mining camp.

Cox, who had not taken the precaution of changing his name, had been easy to find amid the assortment of ragtag men seeking their fortunes. But the man had no idea his crime had been uncovered, and therefore had taken no measures to hide his identity.

Instead of going to the hotel, Reno went to the jail. He wanted the matter over and done with as soon as possible. Then, perhaps, he could banish the memories of Libby from his mind. She'd tormented him enough during the past weeks. If he tried hard enough—

His shoulders slumped. He would never forget

her. In his heart of hearts he knew she would always possess a part of him.

He found Sheriff Cook lounging behind his desk with a cup of steaming coffee in his hands. "Got some to spare?" Reno greeted the man. "You're working hard, I see. What, nobody bustin' up a saloon so you can arrest him?"

"Help yourself, McCord," the lawman said over the rim of the cup. "For your information, I was taking a break after a very hectic morning."

Reno dropped his dusty hat on the lawman's desk. Coffee in hand, he dragged a chair close and propped his feet on the scarred corner.

"You look like the devil, McCord. Forget to take a razor along?"

Reno scrubbed a hand over his jaw. "Guess I resemble a grizzly. Didn't have time to bother cleaning up."

The sheriff wrinkled his nose. "You might've done me the courtesy. My office is gonna stink for a week. Did you find Cox?"

Reno fished in his shirt pocket, then shook out a crumpled document. "Here's proof. Ten witnesses who will swear the man was Cox."

"Did you bring him in?"

"He's dead." Seeing the supposition in the man's eyes, Reno continued, "Cox heard I was asking around about him. When I finally cornered him and showed him his own dagger, which he'd left in Trout's chest, he made a play for it."

"He didn't succeed?"

After he'd fortified himself with a swallow of coffee, Reno shook his head. "Actually, he almost did me in. But because of a dream Miss Chandler had, I was ready when Cox went for the dagger.

His strength surprised me. The bastard tried to stab me, too."

"Obviously, you bested him."

"I got the dagger back, if that's what you mean. Cox took the cowardly way out. He shot himself in the head."

The sheriff grimaced. "He saved the town the trouble of a trial." He dipped into his desk drawer and brought out a paper, which he handed to Reno. "You've got a reward coming. Take this to the bank and they'll give it to you. Should make you a very happy man, indeed."

Reno snatched the paper. Seeing the amount of the reward, his eyes widened. "Who knew Trout well enough here to put up such an amount?"

Over the rim of his tin cup, Sheriff Cook lifted his shaggy dark brows at Reno. "I'm not at liberty to divulge the person's name."

Reno slammed his feet to the floor. He leaned forward and pierced the lawman with a pointed look. "A secret, huh? Do I have to guess?"

"Nope. Can't tell you. I promised."

As Reno rose, he thought of only one candidate. He paced the room.

Only Libby knew Trout.

Only Libby had reason to put up such a large amount.

An instant rise of anger made the veins in his neck pound. She had known he would catch Cox and claim the reward. It had been her way of forcing him to accept the money he'd refused.

He spun around. "When did Miss Chandler come to see you?"

"The afternoon before—Goddammit, McCord! You tricked me."

Reno muttered beneath his breath as he sank to the chair. Libby had put up a thousand dollars to assure he had enough money to last for years, enough money to see to the future she'd seemed so concerned he wouldn't have. In one fell swoop she'd vanquished one of the reasons he couldn't be the man for her.

"You could do far worse, you know," Cook said with a definite hint in his voice. "A woman like Miss Chandler would overlook a man's failings. And she's got enough sand to even put up with *you*."

"You don't know what you're talking about!"

"You're no prize, McCord, but she's loco over you. If I'm not wrong, you feel the same." From the middle drawer in his desk, he brought out an envelope. "She wrote me. Got her address right here. Now, if you want a word of advice—"

"I don't. I haven't anything to offer her. A woman like Libby needs a home."

"Funny thing you mentioning a home."

Reno scowled.

Cook reached into his drawer again. "I know of the perfect homestead. Remember old man Felp?"

"Yeah, I remember. What has Felp to do with me?"

"His wife died several years back. That ranch of his needs a bit of work, but his stock has always been the best in these parts."

"Don't tell me he wants to sell?"

"Not exactly. Felp passed on. The place is up for grabs. I happen to know a man could pick it up for next to nothing. All he'd need is a strong back, grit, and a good woman at his side."

Reno shot to his feet. He scowled at the lawman

again. "I'm not the marrying kind. Hell, I'd squander away every cent within a month."

Cook hooted. "Why, you just let *her* keep your money, and you'd have no trouble at all. Miss Chandler has a head on her pretty shoulders."

Reno grabbed his hat and turned toward the door. "You're right about something at least. Libby is sharp as a tack."

"You want to make an offer on the place? It won't last long."

"No! I'm heading for a bath and a decent meal. Then, I'm going to bed. You know what's good for you, you'll stay the hell out of my business."

"Now, wait just a galdarn minute. There's another thing I've been meaning to ask you."

"Ask me quick," Reno said over his shoulder.

"I wanted to ask the lady, but I figured I'd ask you instead." The sheriff fell silent for seconds. "About that nonsense of a ghost. Did you see it when you were up there?"

Reno tensed. "What do you think?"

"Dammit, McCord. That wasn't an answer. Now, I'm going to ask you again. If you don't give me a straight answer, I'm locking you in jail!"

Reno laughed and spun around. "All right, since you've put it nicely. Henry Harkins does, in fact, call Dead Man's Canyon his own. Anyone who trespasses risks his sanity. Not only *is* there a ghost, he still has an ax in his head. You can shut your mouth, now, Sheriff."

Cook grumbled as he came around his desk. He handed Reno a small object wrapped in newspaper. "She said to give this to you when you got back."

Reno closed his fingers around the gift.

"You're as crazy as Potts," Cook said.

"If you don't believe there's a ghost, take a ride up the canyon and see for yourself."

Sensing the lawman meant to lock him up anyhow, Reno abruptly exited the jail. He tore at the simple string bow. Then, air rushed from his lungs. The piece of tree bark lay in his hand. Damn.

Maryville, Pennsylvania

Seated in her customary chair in the kitchen of Clara Peabody's Boardinghouse, Libby held a hand over her mouth. She had thought the queasiness which had plagued her every morning for the past week would eventually pass.

A gentle hand on her shoulder brought her to attention. Gazing up at Mrs. Peabody's kind but frowning face, Libby knew her secret suspicion was no longer her own.

"You haven't told me the whole story, dear," Clara remarked.

Libby's shoulders drooped under the weight of her burden. "I purposely omitted the best parts."

As Clara squeezed Libby's shoulder, she commiserated with a sigh. "I thought as much. Naturally, you love him."

Libby nodded.

"The man's a fool. Where, pray tell, can he hope to find another woman like you?" She stooped beside Libby and took her hand. "You don't have to tell me the rest, dear. I've been around long enough to have heard it all. From what you told me of Mr. McCord, he isn't ready to settle down.

I'm tempted to write that young fellow and give him a piece of my mind."

"But you'll do no such thing." Libby gave her friend a pleading look. "I haven't given up hope. One day I might see him striding down the street. But if he doesn't . . . I'll manage."

"You brave dear. How will you manage alone with a child?"

"I'll sell my house and move to another town where no one knows I'm unmarried." Libby glanced past Clara, past the ruffled curtain at the window, and smiled. "If I can't have *him,* at least I'll have a part of him. He's given me my heart's desire. A child of my own."

"I'd still rather write to Mr. McCord. Surely if he knew of your trouble, he would want to do the honorable thing."

Libby searched the woman's eyes. "Promise me you won't interfere. It must be Reno's decision; otherwise, he'd never be happy. And neither would I."

"It's *your* happiness I'm worried about, dear."

Libby rose, bringing Clara with her. "I'll be fine. Now, I want your promise."

Clara's mouth slanted into a grim line. Several minutes passed before she said, "I'll promise not to write him, but only if you agree to go to the fall celebration the town's holding Friday night."

"What reason do I have to go, Clara? I will have no escort, and everyone will whisper about how another man who had been in love with me met a tragic end. Word of Clarence's unfortunate demise has given them even more reason to believe I'm ill-fated."

Clara shook her head as she picked up a small

kitchen towel. She opened the heavy door to her stove to peek at the cake inside. Although the aroma smelled wonderful at first, a second later a wave of nausea assailed Libby. Without thinking, she groaned.

Immediately, Clara shut the stove and poured a cup of tea. Handing it to Libby with one hand, she led her back to the table. "Drink this. It'll make you feel better."

Reno McCord was the only one who could make her feel better, Libby mused. However, he hadn't so much as written a word to her in the five weeks since she'd left Colorado. Yet, she would never regret the lovely moments they'd shared. If the townspeople did regard her as ill-fated, she didn't care. *She* knew the truth.

Reno McCord had loved her and nothing awful had happened to him. Sheriff Cook had sent her a telegram telling her about Cox.

But he hadn't truly *loved* her, her conscience reminded.

"Now, you're not leaving my kitchen until you agree to go to the dance," Clara said in a firm voice. "If you're so worried about not having an escort, I'll see what I can do."

"You'll do no such thing!" Libby sipped her tea, searching for an excuse not to attend the social. "I feel too poorly to go."

"Nonsense." Clara shook a finger at Libby. "The sickness will pass soon. It will do you good to forget your troubles for a few hours. I'll be there, and I haven't an escort, either."

Libby lowered her head in defeat. She had yet to win an argument with Clara Peabody.

"We'll go together," Clara continued. "You wouldn't want me to have to stay home, too. Why,

Mr. Culpepper has smiled at me every day for two weeks. How will I know if he's interested or not?"

Libby looked up. "Mr. Culpepper? I wasn't aware you were *interested* in him?"

A faint flush tinged the older woman's cheeks. "He's been most attentive when I've been in his store."

"But it isn't what I asked you, Clara."

Clara inclined her head and whispered, "Imagine a woman of my advanced years falling in love again. I believe he intended to ask me to the dance, but I had already told him I would be going with you. He's quite fond of you, dear."

Libby held up a hand. "All right. I surrender."

"I have the perfect ribbon to go with your yellow dress."

"I doubt a yellow ribbon will help my appearance." Seeing lines gather on the older woman's brow, Libby laughed. "Clara Peabody, you're as stubborn as a mule I once knew."

"You'll be grateful to me, you'll see. You'll have a nice time for a change, instead of fretting over your young man."

On Friday night, Libby stood alone on the sidelines, watching couples dance. Some things never changed, she realized. Despite all that had happened to her, she was still Maryville's resident old maid. Not that she wanted to dance. There wasn't a man in town, or the world in fact, who would interest her.

Except Reno McCord.

When a couple passed by, the woman's dress captured Libby's interest. Neither the style, nor the woman's shape, were spectacular. The color, however, held Libby spellbound. The deep, riveting shade of blue reminded her of Reno's eyes.

Her fingers tangled in a fold of her own yellow dress. She closed her eyes as a moment of pain tugged at her heart. She missed him.

She missed everything about him . . . his teasing banter . . . the cups of tea he had made her . . . the magic of his kisses . . . his lovemaking.

Not a night had passed that she hadn't lain awake for hours, missing his hard length stretched beside her. How many times had she turned over in her sleep and reached for him?

Libby smoothed the wrinkles she'd made in her dress. She wouldn't remember. She wouldn't dwell on things best forgotten. She would make a new life for herself, without him. She would give all of her love to the child they'd created— hopefully a boy with dark hair and blue eyes.

He would be a constant reminder of his father, she thought. Libby wrinkled her dress again.

"You look lovely tonight."

Libby started at the familiar voice. Smiling up at Mr. Culpepper, she gave thanks for the interruption to her sad reflection. "Why, thank you, kind sir."

"I haven't seen you wear your hair in so lovely a style before."

Libby touched the yellow ribbon tied at her nape. She remembered the time she'd longed to buy ribbons in his store. But she had felt they would do nothing to help her plain appearance. She no longer felt plain. Reno had thought her pretty, had found her so appealing he'd made wild, passionate love to her. Libby smiled.

"The hair style is quite becoming," Mr. Culpepper said. "I don't understand why every eligible man here isn't asking you to dance. I'd ask you, myself, but I suspect Clara would skin me if I hobbled about with the prettiest woman in town."

Libby felt a laugh bubbling in her throat and quickly subdued it. She'd seen the storekeeper and Clara on the dance floor, and he did, indeed, hobble about.

"Thank you again, for your compliment. I'd rather not make a spectacle of myself, anyhow."

Clasping his hands behind his back, he rocked on his heels as he surveyed the room. "Oh, I almost forgot to tell you."

Her attention drawn by the sight of Mrs. Peabody dancing with the local shoemaker, Mr. Culpepper's remark nearly escaped Libby. "Did you say something?"

"You should've been in my store today. You missed all the excitement."

"What excitement could there have been in Maryville?"

"A man came in. Don't know where he hailed from. He was a different sort, that's for sure. Wore his gun like he knew how to use it. Darn good-looking fellow, or at least several of my lady customers seemed to think. Harriet Hopper drooled all over my best dresses."

Clara's toes suffered more abuse, and she glanced at Libby. Seeing the shoemaker's red face, Libby struggled not to laugh. Mr. Culpepper's last remarks floated in the back of her mind.

Darn good-looking fellow. Wore his gun like he knew how to use it.

"This man didn't give his name, did he?" she asked.

Culpepper scratched his chin. "Come to think of it, he didn't. I should've asked, I see that now, in view of his inquiries."

A shiver darted down Libby's spine. "Inquiries?"

"It's odd I didn't think of it as strange."

"Think of what?"

"The man expressed an interest in anyone in town who taught piano. Curious, don't you think?"

"I most certainly do." Libby twisted her hands together in front of her. "What did he look like?"

Culpepper wrinkled his forehead. "Wide shoulders, dark hair. Tall fellow."

Libby swallowed and asked nonchalantly, "What color were his eyes?"

"Don't rightly recall. You might ask Harriet. I'm positive she knows every detail of his appearance."

Libby scolded herself. Many men wore guns and were considered good-looking. She mustn't allow her imagination to run wild.

"Clara has promised me the next dance." Mr. Culpepper swept Libby a bow. "I intend to keep her busy the rest of the evening, if she'll have me."

Libby smiled at the storekeeper. "Good luck."

No matter how hard she tried, she couldn't dismiss the man's words from her mind. When she spotted the woman he'd mentioned, Libby wandered to the corner in which Mrs. Hopper sat alone.

"It is very hot in here tonight," the woman said by way of greeting.

"Yes, it is. I hope you don't mind my company."

"Oh, no. I simply grew weary of chatting and thought to rest my jaws for a few minutes."

Libby passed the next few minutes in idle talk before she broached the subject she wanted. "Mr. Culpepper mentioned that a peculiar man came into his store today."

"I'm surprised he called him peculiar. Men hardly notice such things." She leaned close, whispering, "That man was something to look at." Her cheeks grew pink. "Goodness, I shouldn't be carrying on so. A body'd think I've never seen a winsome man before. Why, Mr. Hopper would stew for a month if he found out."

"Did you notice the color of the man's eyes?"

"Do you think you know him?"

"The description Mr. Culpepper gave me sounded similar to the man I hired to find Mr. Trout."

"I never saw eyes as deep a shade as his. They were most definitely blue."

Chapter 21

B^{lue.} Libby laid a hand over her mouth. Was she crazy to think the man who had visited Mr. Culpepper's store might have been Reno?

"Libby, Clara is waving at you."

She followed Mrs. Hopper's gaze and saw Clara beckon her.

"Go on," Harriet said. "I've rested long enough. There's something going on across the way." She stretched her neck, trying to see past a group of people. "I don't want to miss out on it."

The minute Libby joined Mrs. Peabody, the woman pressed Libby's arm. "Close your eyes, dear, and make a wish."

Speechless from the odd request, Libby stared dumbly. "Clara? Are you playing a game?"

"No, dear. Close your eyes and don't move. Count to thirty before you open them."

A reckless suspicion took root in Libby's mind. Clara's flushed cheeks and the urgency with which she'd spoken caused Libby's pulse to pound with excitement. Only a fool would jump to such a preposterous conclusion.

Reno wouldn't have come after her.

Clara had merely planned some sort of surprise to lighten her mood. Schooling her features in a mask of calm, Libby did as her friend had asked. As she counted off numbers, she made a mental note to remember to hide her disappointment when she discovered the reason behind Clara's request.

Sounds became clearer. Normal conversation ceased altogether, then an occasional whisper carried to her. The music, which had been a rousing tune, stopped. Then, it began again as a romantic waltz. Realizing she'd lost count, Libby opened her eyes.

A path stood open through the throng of people on the dance floor. Clara had moved to the other side of the room and she saw only her back.

Everyone was looking at *her*.

Tense from confusion, Libby twisted her fingers in the folds of her dress again.

Clara moved aside and quickly faded in with a group of people. Then her vision fell on a man at the end of the cleared path. Tall, dressed in a dignified suit of black, his crisp white shirt had been starched so stiff the collar jabbed his neck.

He wore a smart hat, so unlike the wide-brimmed ones Reno preferred. Seconds slipped by before his identity registered in Libby's mind.

Reno!

A soft cry of astonishment escaped her lips. She blinked to make sure she hadn't imagined him. Her first instinct was to run to him, but she couldn't bring her body to move. Sure he would disappear if she so much as looked away, she bit her bottom lip and waited.

His stride confident, he started across the room. When he reached the halfway mark, he removed his hat and handed it to a gentleman for safekeeping.

Libby's heart beat an erratic rhythm.

And then Reno stood in front of her.

She felt faint. He looked handsomer than she remembered. Good Lord, even his hair had been slicked back so neatly he resembled a polished gentleman.

"This is a dream," she mumbled.

Aiming her a devastating smile, he brought her hand to his mouth and pressed his lips above her knuckles. Amusement glittered in his spellbinding eyes. "If this were a dream, Libby, my collar wouldn't be stabbing the hell out of my neck."

She laughed. "You're not very romantic, are you, Mr. McCord? You were much more eloquent in my dream."

"Mrs. Peabody told me what I was supposed to say. Damn, I wasn't supposed to tell you."

"I should've known Clara had a hand in this."

He pulled her roughly against him and clamped an arm around her waist.

Libby smiled as she settled a hand on his shoulder. "You're supposed to ask me first and then *gently* take me into your arms."

He rolled his eyes heavenward. "There's a waste of time. You're dying to dance with me, Libby. And I couldn't wait to have my arms around you."

"Reno McCord, you are incorrigible."

His warm breath played havoc with her neck, stealing her own breath.

"But you're happy to see me," he said with confidence.

Libby sighed. Over his shoulder she saw that, though many couples had begun to move about the floor, dozens of eyes still remained on her. Having so handsome a man claim her for a dance must've shocked them. She didn't care. She was with Reno again. But he was holding her much too closely.

"Propriety demands a discreet distance be left between the man and the woman."

He chuckled at her remark and yanked her closer. "I wonder what they'd say if they knew exactly how close our naked bodies have been."

"You skunk." Libby attempted to put a space between them. Reno, though, held her too tightly. "I'll be the talk of the town."

"At least they won't call you an old maid anymore. I bet every female here envies you right about now."

Stepping on his foot, she countered, "Conceited rogue. But you're right. No woman in town has such a handsome partner."

"I've brought your money, Libby." He allowed enough space between them to narrow his eyes at her. "You were very clever to see I collected a reward for capturing Cox. But you were wrong."

"I won't take it back. You earned every penny."

"You will take back the money, Libby."

He spun her around so quickly, she gasped. As soon as his steps resumed a slower pace, she said, "You're very sure of yourself, Mr. McCord. What makes you think you can make me do anything?"

His fingers tightened on hers. "In some areas I haven't changed, Libby. The money is better off in your safekeeping."

"But you won't have—"

"I will," he cut her off. "But only if you'll have *me*."

Libby froze. Reno stopped moving also. Before she could collect her dizzy thoughts, he'd dropped to one knee. His gaze warm on her, he held her hand between them.

Loud gasps and hushed whispers abounded.

"Miss Libby Chandler, will you marry me?"

Libby's mouth fell open.

Amusement flickered in his eyes as he gave her a broad grin. "I've left you speechless."

"You most certainly have," she said. "Did I hear right? Did you just propose?"

"He did!" a female voice yelled. "Grab that handsome devil quick. If you don't want him, I do!"

Her cheeks hot, Libby muttered, "Yes."

"We can't hear you," bellowed a male voice across the room.

Reno stood so fast Libby nearly lost her balance. "She said *yes!*" he announced.

He swept her into his arms and navigated a wide circle around the floor. People clapped and offered their congratulations. Some of men even hooted. Libby never took her eyes from Reno's face.

"Lucky for you, you said yes," he whispered. "I was prepared to toss you over my shoulder and carry you off if you refused."

Mindless of the spectators, she hugged her arms around his neck. "Rightfully, I should've withheld my answer."

"Why?" he asked against her ear. "Sheriff Cook said you were loco about me."

Angling her head, she nipped his ear. "There's a

small matter you neglected to add. Surely Mrs. Peabody told you what else you were to say."

"That I love you?"

She pulled back to see his eyes. Amusement and love glowed in the magnificent blue depths. "Do you?"

"Yes, Libby, I do. I knew how I felt about you before we reached Denver."

He spun her in a wide circle, nearly plowing down a slow-moving couple.

"Why didn't you tell me how you felt?"

"Because I hadn't come to my senses then. I didn't know that living without you would be so hard. It was hell, in fact. I wasn't sure what I felt was love."

She touched his cheek. "You missed me?"

"Something awful. I want you enough to gamble on the future . . . enough to try to be the man you deserve. But it's only fair to warn you. I haven't made a miraculous reformation."

"I never expected you to be perfect." She wove her fingers through his hair. "I love you as you are, and I always will. I suppose you'll want to slip into the Crooked Creek Saloon to have fun now and again."

"You won't mind?"

"I won't mind as long as you come home to me."

"Would you mind living in Colorado?"

"I won't care where I am so long as I'm with you."

"Lady, you're going to keep me busy running a ranch and keeping you supplied with babies at the same time."

"Ranch?"

Reno slowed his pace, barely moving on the floor. "The ranch I bought. I got lucky after you left. The place went for next to nothing. Sheriff Cook enlightened me to the deal." He grinned. "I still think he was playing matchmaker."

Libby grinned back. "I'll have to remember to thank him."

"He also said you'd be good for me. He said you have a head on your pretty shoulders." He paused long enough to allow another couple to move past. "You'll have to mind the finances, Libby."

"I think I could do that." He spun her around again, stealing her breath. When he'd slowed to a respectable pace, she asked, "Where did you learn to dance so beautifully?"

"From my commanding officer's wife." He gave her a wry grin. "She wanted a partner who wouldn't crush her toes. Since her husband was a natural-born ox, as she phrased it, the chore fell to me."

"Such accomplishment is out of character for you, though I'm pleased you were such an excellent student."

"Say, let's get out of here. Everyone keeps watching me." He gave her a coaxing look. "Besides, I want to kiss you. And there's another matter I want to ask you about."

Not waiting for an answer, he seized her wrist. He unceremoniously hauled her with him as he cut a zigzag course across the dance floor. When they passed the man who still had Reno's hat, the fellow grinned and plopped it on Reno's head. They reached outside, where he glanced up and down the street. "Which one is it?"

"My house?"

"When I asked around town about you, I forgot to ask where you lived."

Locking her arm through his, she led him down the street. "It's not far."

"Good. I can't wait much longer."

Libby's heart swelled. She still couldn't believe everything that had happened during the past hour. At Reno's urging, she quickened her pace. When they reached her house, she dug the key out of her pocket and handed it to him. Reno swung open the front door and they walked in. Reno studied her silently.

Libby was growing impatient, but she took her time lighting the lamp and contemplating what he wanted to ask her.

A devilish grin played over his mouth as he turned her to face him. "Are you anxious for me to kiss you?"

She leaned against him. "Yes," she said breathlessly.

He ran his thumb over her mouth. "You lied to me, Libby. You let me believe you were wealthy, when all along you only had what your father left you, and what you make teaching piano."

"I'm sorry. You wouldn't have agreed to work for me if I hadn't lured you with money."

"Probably not."

She stood on her toes and draped her arms over his shoulders, placing her mouth so close she felt his warm breath against her lips. "Will you forgive me?"

"I don't have any choice. You won't tell me any more fibs, will you?"

"No more fibs." She traced a nail over the

pinched skin above his tight collar, and then she kissed his chin. "When are you planning to make an honest woman of me, Mr. McCord?"

"In a hurry, Libby?"

"I want every woman in town to know you're mine as soon as possible."

He bound her in his embrace. "About all those babies you want."

"What about them?" she asked as she loosened his collar.

"I think we should wait a little while, until I have the ranch in better shape. The house needs a lot of work. It won't be an easy life, Libby, but I'm willing to try if you are. There won't be much money at first. I know cattle and horses, so I think I can make a go of ranching."

Libby giggled and yanked the collar free. She noticed the red crease around his neck. "We'll be busy, indeed, to have everything ready in time."

Reno froze. "Are we in a hurry?"

Libby worked several of his shirt buttons free. When he loosened his hold on her, she captured his hand and held it over her stomach. "Indeed, we are. Looks like it won't be any trouble at all to have a dozen babies. You're a potent lover, Mr. McCord."

As the truth of her words registered, a broad grin stole across his mouth. "Libby!" He ran his fingers through his hair. "When had you planned to tell me?"

"I don't know. I thought I'd never tell you if you didn't come after me. Although, I probably would have changed my mind and come after *you* before too much longer."

He gave her another broad grin. "I hope you have a boy. Looks like I'll be needing help to feed all the mouths you're planning to give me."

"Hush and kiss me."

"Libby," he said as he cupped her face. "I love you. If it takes a dozen babies to make you happy, it's one job I'm going to enjoy."

"Kiss me senseless like you did at the waterfall."

Gripping her chin, he tilted her head and did just that.

Epilogue

Colorado, 1878

A sudden bump in the road jarred the seat in the buckboard and bounced Libby inches closer to her husband. Finding the jostling had dislodged her bonnet, she lifted her head to retie a neat bow beneath her chin. Aware he had followed her movement, she flashed Reno a sweet smile.

"Sorry. I didn't see the rut."

She touched his arm gently. "If you kept your eyes on where we're going, instead of on me, your driving might improve."

"It's more fun to watch you." His gaze swept from her face, over the tight-fitting bodice of her green dress, and lingered on her bosom. "You sure don't look like an old married woman, Libby. Every day stretches forever until I have you alone and I can—"

"Hush!" Libby threw a worried glance to the rear of the buckboard. "Little ears have no business hearing what's on *your* lusty mind."

Reno grinned shamelessly as he turned his attention to handling the two horses.

A piercing squeal came from behind. When Libby wiggled around on her seat, three sets of innocent blue eyes fastened on her. Her three rambunctious boys, ages five, four, and three sat huddled together. Forcing steel into her voice, she reprimanded, "Chad, Seth, and Joey! Which of you pulled Millie's hair?"

When no admission of guilt came forth, Libby groaned in exasperation. Her gaze warmed on her two-year-old daughter, who was wedged along the side of the buckboard, next to Chad. With a chubby thumb stuck in her mouth, the little girl turned large, tear-filled hazel eyes to her mother.

"Maybe a bee bit her," Chad offered.

Libby pierced her two remaining sons with a stern look. "All right, I know one of you pulled Millie's hair."

A soft nudge to her side drew her attention to her husband.

"Let them alone, Libby. Millie will learn to defend herself before long. I'm betting she's inherited her mother's fierce temper."

Libby pinned him with a reproachful glance. "You're entirely too lenient, Joseph Reno McCord. If you'd take your sons in hand more often, we'd have less chaos."

He aimed her a wicked grin. "Dissension within your ranks, Mrs. McCord?"

Libby gritted her teeth to ward off a smile. Reno had turned out a good father, loving and gentle with his children. He was also a good provider, with the best producing ranch in the area. Although he worked endless hours, he had never once complained. She loved him more today than she had six years ago.

"Remember what you once told me about Charity?" he said.

"I was referring to your treatment of women. The boys don't fall into the same category. They're wild animals when you're not around, and I have the worst time with them."

"I'll have a talk with them tonight."

Another squeal came from the rear. Libby pinched Reno's arm and swung around. "Gentleman always treat ladies with respect."

As she expected, her youngest laughed. Immediately, he slapped a hand over his mouth.

"Joey McCord," Libby chastised her three-year-old, "boys do not pull a lady's hair!"

Libby held out her arms and Millie climbed up. Scooping the little girl onto her lap, she met Reno's amused blue eyes.

He halted the buckboard and twisted around.

"Sorry, Pa," three voices chimed together.

Then, Reno whipped the reins and had them on their way again as if nothing had happened.

Libby shook her head. She wondered how he always managed to restore order with such minimal effort. But however he achieved peace, she was grateful. Having four children was tedious at times, a blessing at others, especially when three of them were perfect replicas of their father. It took effort to discipline them when it would be so much nicer to hug them.

Reno ruffled Millie's hair. Leaning down and kissing her cheek, he asked, "What's wrong, dumpling? The three bad wolves after you again?"

As usual, the little girl wiggled from Libby's lap onto Reno's.

Balancing Millie on one knee, Reno handed her the reins.

For safety, he anchored his fingers farther along the reins, keeping the tension tight. He winked at Libby. "If I'd known what fun little girls were, I wouldn't have skipped two years."

She aimed him a smug smile. "You haven't skipped two years, exactly."

His eyes widened briefly before he aimed her a very wicked grin. "Is number five started, Libby?"

"Two months ago, if my guess is right."

"I thought you felt a bit more womanly lately. Do you think it'll be another girl?"

She shrugged her shoulders and leaned against him. "Does it matter?"

"Not a bit. I'll love them all almost as much as I love you." He laid an arm around her shoulders to give her a tight squeeze. "You'll have help soon to keep your ranks in line."

"Help?"

"I've hired Mrs. Johnson to cook and wash, and do whatever you need to free some of your time. Her husband died last month. I heard she's having a hard time without him."

Libby's heart swelled with love and pride. "It was decent of you." She drew her fingers along one side of his face. "Did you also hire another man to help with the cattle?"

"Mrs. Johnson has a fifteen-year-old son. A double income will have them on their feet soon."

"You'll be a cattle baron before long."

Reno threw back his head and laughed. The man who had once had no future had become highly respected in Denver for his business acumen.

They came in view of the town. Reno handed his daughter back to Libby. "I wonder what everyone would say if they knew you were the actual brains behind our outfit."

Libby smiled as she checked for any tendrils of hair which might have worked free of the loose coil at her nape. "They won't find out if you don't tell them. Besides, you run the ranch." She fetched her reticule from the floorboard and dipped her fingers inside.

"You've let moths loose again, Libby."

Libby ignored Reno's amused remark. She tucked a twenty-dollar gold piece into his pocket.

He reciprocated by pressing a kiss under her ear, dislodging her bonnet.

Libby straightened Millie's pink dress before she tugged at the bow beneath her chin. At Reno's insistence, she had always kept control of their money. It had been an arrangement which suited him. She always allowed him enough to have a good time in the Crooked Creek Saloon, provided he didn't break mirrors or furniture.

"What are you doing today while I'm having fun?" he asked.

"I thought I'd drop by the bank, pick out some new material for kitchen curtains, load up on supplies, and then take the children to see Violet."

He placed a kiss beneath Libby's ear again. When she turned her head to chasten him for knocking her bonnet askew, he captured her mouth in a leisurely, heated kiss. Against her lips, he whispered, "Think I'll pass on the saloon today. If I help you with your chores, maybe we can get back earlier." He waggled a dark brow at her. "While the children nap—"

Giggles came from the back of the buckboard, cutting off Reno's words.

"Aw, Pa, only a sissy kisses girls."

"Yeah, Pa."

Reno grinned at Libby. He turned around to shake a finger at his sons. "I'm going to remind you what you said in about ten or fifteen years. Why, your ma tastes better than apple pie."

To a chorus of objections, Reno kissed Libby again. He wore a broad grin the rest of the way into town.

Libby's heart felt close to overflowing. Not only had she found a husband, she'd found a man worthy of a woman's love, a man she'd love beyond eternity. How could she have been so lucky?

And just yesterday she'd received a long letter from his mother. They were coming to visit next month, but she hadn't told Reno yet. Happiness swelled within her. He'd given her all the family a woman could want.

Laying her head on his shoulder, she sighed with pleasure. "Don't dawdle," she whispered. "Nap time is in four hours."